A Maid's Life

Unexpected Love in Gilded Age New York

Joseph P. Garland

DermodyHouse.com

ISBNs: 978-1-7355923-9-8 (ebook)
979-8-9868992-0-6 (paperback)
979-8-9868992-1-3 (hardcover)

The Cover: *Young Woman Braiding Her Hair* (1876) by Auguste Renoir (1841-1919). It is kindly made available by the Open Access policy of the National Gallery of Art.

https://www.nga.gov/collection/art-object-page.52207.html

Introduction

This is one of a series of stories about life chiefly in New York City in the 1870s. I earlier wrote the novels *Róisín Campbell* and *A Studio on Bleecker Street* as well as several shorter pieces. Although one character, Inspector Washington, from *Studio*, appears here, there is no other overlap.

1.

I arrived in New York in early June of 1872 on a warm day, the likes of which I never before knew. I was barely able to walk down the gangway after ten days mostly belowdecks on a steamship called *Nevada* with so many others who like me had seen the sea but never spent a moment on it till the lot of us were all crowded on board in Queenstown, County Cork, Ireland. There were times when I hated being there, whatever my prospects, the puke and the smell and the crying. Those first days with food that couldn't be kept down even were it actually food. Listening to men beat their women for something or other like my papa sometimes did to my mama when the portions were too small or whatever meat we had too tough or for no reason at all.

Unlike many who started the journey before me, though, I made it across. My older brothers couldn't stay home in County Mayo either. They found work in Liverpool. I was sent to America, far away with no hope of going back. Maybe I would get a position as a maid in one of the mansions that lined the great avenues we all heard about.

We all were hoping, those of us on board who were still in our teens. We didn't have much beyond hope, though I was blessed to have an eye and an ear for reading and writing, unlike most of the others. I knew parts of the Bible by heart, it being one of the few books in our cottage. Sometimes I read parts of it to my mama and the others. From someone else in Backfox—my little village—we heard of a place some

Irish nuns had set up in New York for those of us from the country, to learn to become servants in the great city with those grand avenues. I was told that somehow there was a place for me there, and I got the address of where I could sleep when I arrived so I wouldn't be wandering the streets.

It was still dark on the tenth morning on board the *Nevada* when a crewmember, an Englishman, came into steerage and began banging on a bucket. "Get up you. We be in New York in two hours and yer need to be gone as soon as we do." A second crewmember (he wasn't as mean to us as the first one though he was also English) carried a torch and began lighting the candles in lanterns that lined the wall as he followed his mate. They did a circle, clockwise, with their banging and their message and then went back to the deck. After some trouble getting awake and up, we all were able to do what needed to be done for our toilets.

I pulled together my belongings—a pair of everyday frocks and one for Sunday, undergarments, and shoes, all well-worn, and the small Bible given to me by our priest before I left Backfox. In it were letters from my family and friends and some documents that were protected in its pages. As I was finishing, someone shouted that he could see land. We wouldn't be allowed on deck just yet, but lines formed at the portholes on the right side, and I almost thought the rush of people might capsize the boat.

But people were kind, and few overstayed their time looking out. I had my first view of America, which I now understand was the southern coast of Long Island, the great approach to New York City itself.

Things seemed to move very quickly then, in contrast to the slow pace since we'd last seen land, the coast of County Cork. In no time, they let us on deck, kept well away from those who were of the more important (and far more expensive) classes who we had seen only in the brief time allotted to us to walk on part of the deck each day.

The hands kept order, preventing too many from flooding the right side as we saw the beaches and the houses built on them and the greenery a little in from the water.

Suddenly someone shouted, "This side!" and those not leaning to the right hurried to the left. There were more beaches and more houses. A tug came out to us, and two men from it climbed up a rope ladder dropped to them, and we watched as they shook the captain's hand and one went to the front of the boat. We could hear the other calling out orders to the crew and the ship slowed and it felt like we were walking, delaying our arrival in the New World, delaying the moment when the horrors of the journey would be over.

The *Nevada* moved carefully through the traffic. So many boats of all sizes, coming and going. I found myself on the rail on the right side, and word spread that it was Brooklyn we were looking at and there was dock after dock and men waving to us and blowing their boats' horns as we passed. It was still early in the morning and the sun was low and very bright and the air was hot and sticky.

The rest was a blur as we came to a stop at a dock, and all we could see in front of us were buildings in size and number I couldn't have imagined at home. So many and so wide and so high. What I think were doctors came on board to examine us, pulling several of us to the side for what I expect were more complete examinations. But I was handed a blue card and was told not to lose it.

I was confused and more than a little frightened as I held my satchel and followed the others through some kind of official building with my information taken down by a man in a uniform sitting at one of the many tables set in a long line:

Name: Margaret Treacy.
Home: Backfox, County Mayo, Eire.
Age: Eighteen, born on 18 March 1854.

I was told to show where I intended to stay and pulled out a piece of paper from my Bible on which was written: *Mrs. Caitlan Bulger. 47 Henry Street. NYC.* It had been sent to me by a distant cousin of someone my papa knew in Backfox.

"'Tis not too far, lass. Someone'll tell you. How do you intend to make a living?" the man asked.

"I hope to become a maid."

He looked at me as he lifted a stamp.

He smiled. "Good luck to you then. Welcome to America." He stamped my blue paper and as I began to walk, he called out "Next" and I was in America.

When I reached the street, seeing more people in a moment than I saw my entire life before I left Backfox, my first task was finding 47 Henry Street. I tried to ask several people, but they raced by until a nice, older man with a grey mustache was kind enough to send me towards it.

"I'm not sure about number 47, but it'll be easy enough to find when you get there."

I thanked him and he tipped his hat and resumed his going wherever he was going.

I wasn't used to seeing buildings next to buildings, the closest being when my papa took me to little Castlebar to the north and Tuam to the south at home and they had at most five or six buildings connected and no one needed a number to find where they wanted to go.

It was all almost more than I could take, far more than I expected. Dust rose from the street that ran up along the docks, and wagons were going this way and wagons were going that way and their drivers were shouting at their horses and at the other drivers and at pedestrians threatening to get in their way. How I was to cross I couldn't imagine but I joined a small crowd. I heard a whistle, and a police constable stopped the wagons on the street and the crowd hurried across, all the time while being shouted at by drivers telling us "to get a move on now."

Once I was across and heading away from the river, things began to quiet. There were many people who all seemed to be ignoring each other as they were going where it was they were going. Fast as they went, they somehow seemed able not to run into each other and some said very unpolite things to me when I was not going fast enough to suit them. There were, though, fewer wagons than by the docks. When I came to the first street, I turned right like the old man told me. "The street's name'll change," he said, "but stay on it till you get to Henry Street."

I wanted to stop I was so tired and amazed but I didn't think I could start again and was ever more curious about this Caitlin Bulger woman and what she would be like and what my room would be like and whether I could ever be happy in America. Girls on the boat said they had sisters and brothers who'd come before them and in some cases helped pay for their own passage and who wrote home and said how very different it was from Ireland. Nervous as that made me, I could never have prepared myself for what I was seeing and hearing and smelling.

Of course I had no choice but to make myself happy as there was no going back and with each step I got closer to where it was I would finally begin this new life of mine. I became more and more frightened because I couldn't imagine how this could ever become my home.

But that stranger was right and as I was a literate girl, I found number 47 with no trouble, though I was sweating greatly by the time I did. I couldn't ignore the smells of the manure and the garbage waiting to be collected in large piles here and there. There was even a dead horse pushed off to the side of one street waiting, I hoped, to be collected by someone, though no one seemed to pay it any mind except for the flies circling it. Everything was so different from the boat and far different from my farm and seemed like a blanket in the heat. Indeed, it must've warmed up several degrees since I left the water and the sun beat down on my back as I walked north. I was wet and I stank.

Forty-Seven Henry Street had four stone steps that led to a black door with a brass knocker. With my satchel over my left shoulder, I used the knocker and stepped back to the sidewalk. I looked up at the five stories and on the third floor a head popped through.

"The door is open. You must be new?"

I could only make out a round head of an old woman with a scarf. She—it was Caitlan Bulger herself—was coming down the stairs as I entered. It was by far the biggest house I was ever in, for sure, and I was amazed by the wide staircase she hurried down. It was black and it creaked here and there as she came to me.

"And who might you be, love?"

And there she was, my first acquaintance in America, a short, skinny woman in a black frock and red scarf, with a white apron tied around her waist. Her hair was white and she flashed quite the smile, and it calmed me down right off.

2.

I was only to stay at Mrs. Bulger's for a few days. Irish girls just off the boat like me kept coming and going, and I used the opportunity to explore the area with some of them. So many people and (living) horses and muck. If we went far enough to what we were told was the west, we could watch fancy carriages pass with coachmen and footmen and people whose faces we could barely see. If they were stopped in traffic, we could peek in, but they would ignore us, and someone said they were the types we would serve if we got a job as a maid, which we all wanted.

We saw boys run out and bang on the sides of carriages asking for coins, but the coachman or the footman, dressed finely, each time pulled out a whip and shooed them away and the boys would laugh and say rude things to them and all the time those in the carriage paid it no mind and the carriage would follow the others to a dance or a party or we knew not what.

We thought that is what they must do, these rich people. Dances and parties and teas. There were rich people in Backfox but not enough to have a ball except once a year when similar people from nearby towns would come. We'd watch their carriages pass by the farm, going to and fro one of the big houses of the Protestants who lorded themselves over us.

We girls from Mrs. Bulger's were all waiting for our first Monday in New York. We went to Mass together on the Sunday, and on the Monday I went to the House of Mercy with two others.

It was a large building on East Houston Street, with four stories covered in a yellowish stone. The entrance was up several steps to a pair of doors with windows, and above the entrance, which was curved, was a large crucifix. We entered and the ceiling was very high, higher than I ever saw, except of course, in a church. Its walls were very dark wood but there was a hallway to the right side. The room didn't smell. It seemed that everything in New York smelled, mostly of manure and at times garbage and things that I realize great cities create. Perhaps that was the thing I most remember about this room and that first time I was in it. It didn't smell.

There was a row of wooden chairs along the left wall and a large desk along the right, but no one was there, and we didn't dare go down the hallway. One of the others noticed a bell on the desk. She lifted its hammer and banged it two or three times.

"Coming, coming" we heard from the hall, and soon a nun appeared in full habit. She seemed about my mama's age, in black and, around her face, white.

"You be a little early," she said. "We are waiting for several more so please sit, sit." We each found a chair along the left wall, as she sat at the desk. I think the others were like me. My stomach was sick and none of us ate much before we left or said much once we got there. I just wanted it to start. After we sat, a second nun, much younger, joined her and the two were going through papers. More girls came through the door and sat with us. It felt like church, so we all kept our voices down. The others were western Irish too and none of us had any idea of what was to happen to us.

Soon, though, we found out. We were marched inside to a large room on the second floor. I was told that for some reason the first floor at home was called the second floor in America. No one knew why as far as I could tell. A large room facing the back of the house on the "second" floor was lined with cots and thin mattresses. We were each given a small box, a cube of maybe three feet on each side, where we were told to store what we could with a closet over by the door for us to hang our other things on assigned hooks.

By noon, we'd been provided with maids' frocks and aprons and hats and stockings and shoes, and by one and after a cold meal in the small room where we would eat three times a day, excepting when we ate with the sisters, where we would eat three times a day, we began our training to become servants in the houses of wealthy New Yorkers. We had no idea what wealthy people did, let alone how to care for them, but we learned. The arts of cleaning silver and sewing fine fabric. Carrying and curtseying. We were given uniforms to care for and each morning at seven we went to Mass in the House's chapel with the Sisters of Mercy.

Once a week, after Sunday Mass, we were allowed out. Everything was wonderful and scary to us foreign country girls. All the buildings and people. Horses pulling wagons and carriages this way and that, all in a hurry. We wandered about as I had in those first days when I was at Mrs. Bulger's. Things weren't quite so sad and dirty where the House of Mercy was and the accents of the people we passed weren't all so Irish and some were speaking languages that were so difficult I couldn't see how anyone would understand them.

Some of the girls were lucky. They would get jobs in a kitchen. This was good, solid if often very hot work more regular and not dependent on the mood of a member of the family on a particular day. Some of us weren't lucky at all and after several weeks some girls were forced to leave, likely to work as seamstresses for little pay or in some factory or other.

I was neither and was getting used to the weather. There were some very hot days, as bad as when I arrived, but as autumn got close, there were more cool nights and fewer of the bugs that plagued us all.

3.

I t was early autumn and after we'd been at the House for over a month of classes and exercises when Sister Reilly came to us one night to prepare us for the next day, which was a Monday.

After our daily Mass and breakfast, we each put on our best frock. Sister Reilly inspected us. After a smile and a nod, she led us to the ground floor. There was a large room just off the one we sat in on our first day. This room was used mostly for the dinners held twice a week with all of us and all of the nuns. We ate, just us students, in a smaller one off the kitchen the other days. We took turns helping with the cooking and the cleaning up.

On the day I'm talking about, though, the dining tables were off to one side. Instead, small tables were set in two rows of six. At each, there was a single chair on one side and two or three on the other. With their backs against the wall there were twelve chairs, and Sister Reilly had us sit. I was the fifth girl. I wasn't sure, but I think it was shortly after ten and we were sitting for ten minutes afraid to speak and my stomach was increasingly off just like that first morning there. Then the door to the foyer opened and a flood of women's voices entered, followed by Sister Olson—the mother superior of the House—and the women themselves.

These women were all dressed in a way I only saw when we girls wandered about on the streets on Sunday afternoons. All sorts of colors, and their hats matched their dresses, and their dresses and their hair were very complicated. They came in in twos and threes. Most were about my mama's age but there were several younger women, who couldn't be more than a few years older than me, and even a few girls, too. Each was next to an older servant, as was clear from her simple dress.

Sister Olson directed them to the chairs at the tables. The ladies were looking at us. Some were pointing. We were called in order. I walked to the proper seat at the proper table. A mother, daughter (about my age), and older servant. The daughter was quite plain looking and fat, and her mother introduced her as Elinor Palmer. Mrs. Palmer and the servant, Mrs. Burnley, asked me questions about my background and experience

I was as honest as I could be because I didn't want to mislead them about something, which could get me dismissed if they discovered it. It wasn't as if I had anything to lie about. They knew my general history as someone forced to leave the west of Ireland, like most of the other girls meeting potential employers. I was a little different from most of the others, though, because I could read and write.

When she and the housekeeper were done, Mrs. Palmer asked her daughter if she wanted to ask me anything. I realized that while I was paying attention to the other two, she kept her eyes locked on me. It suddenly made me nervous and uncomfortable, her seeming to study me like a cat getting ready to pounce on a trapped mouse in the barn at home.

She didn't pounce, though. She smiled and shook her head.

"No, mother," she said. "I think I've heard quite enough," and she again smiled, at me I thought. I got up to return to my original chair by the wall, and when I sat, she was still looking my way, though she turned to her mother when I caught her.

I was soon called to meet with another family, though I can't (and don't want to) recall their name. A mother with two daughters, one several years younger than me. I don't recall the name because this younger girl took a disliking of me from the start, which I know because within a minute or so she said, "I don't like her" to her mother and the interview didn't last much longer. I can't say why she didn't like me, but she didn't, and I was glad to be back in my seat, waiting for the other interviews to be done with.

As I sat, I watched the Palmers. The daughter kept looking over at me. She seemed to be paying little attention to Rowan, who sat where I had, and when Rowan got up, Miss Palmer leaned over to her mother, and her mother then signaled to Sister Reilly who, after she got there, looked at me and nodded and I watched the three leave. One other lady and her maid followed the Palmers out and the next round of interviews began except Sister Reilly took me and Aine (who thought it best to call herself Annie since she arrived) to the back when the other ten were settled.

We—Aine and me—were told we didn't have to meet with anyone else because we were selected, and it was only a few days later that I was saying goodbye to the others and stepping into a fine carriage for the first time in my life. We headed to the north. I didn't have much, so it was all in the carriage with me. It wasn't long before the streets were smoother and numbered, and I swear the smell was nicer.

4.

We—the fancy dark green with a dark maroon trim brougham and a coachman who introduced himself as Henry Covings, a footman called Patrick Norman, and a pair of chestnut horses plus me—turned onto Twenty-Eighth Street. We stopped in front of a house with the number 45 in gold paint above a wood door shining in black. I heard the coachman put the brake on. As we stopped I opened the door and, forgetting that steps needed to be pulled down for me—I should've known though it was my first time in a fine carriage—I dropped straight onto the sidewalk, my satchel flying somewhere, and I was lucky I extended my hands to break the fall.

The footman, Patrick, was on me in a flash and helped me to my feet and seeing that I was no worse for my adventure except for scrapes on my left knee and my left hand, he put his hands on my upper arms. "You'll be fine," he said and he smiled and he helped me with my shaking.

With that bit, I brushed the front of my frock as best I could and got my first good look at the house. It was on the north side of the street not far from Madison Avenue.

The house wasn't large and the others on the block pretty much looked the same. The only difference I noticed was the colors of the front doors and the variety in the flowers popping out from the boxes that hung beneath nearly every window (except those small ones on the top floors). There was some type of fancy carvings above the entrance with columns on either side. Above the ground level were four floors, with three windows on each and very small ones, like eyebrows, on the top one.

It was, all in all, a handsome house with several small bushes to the left of the steps. A black wrought-iron fence with very sharp points was on either side of the stairs and it connected with its neighbors. There was a gate to the right, which led to several steps down and then to a simple door directly beneath the top of the stoop.

"That's where you go, Miss," the footman pointed out before wishing me good luck. "Mrs. Burnley will see to you. We must put the carriage and the horses away. I expect I'll be seeing you often enough here. 'Tis a happy house."

He had a soft brogue, and I was very glad for what he said, tipping his hat sharply as he did. I opened the gate, with one last look at Henry Covings, Patrick Norman, and their carriage with those two horses, and waited until they were gone down the street before I went down the steps. After a final, deep breath, I pulled the cord by the door and another footman in an apron opened it.

"What you want?" he said, in yet another brogue.

"I'm to work here." It wasn't the kind of welcome I at least hoped for.

He looked me up and down, me with my satchel held in front of me. "Mrs. Burnley didn't say nothin' 'bout you. Come in and I'll see if I can find 'er."

I followed, and he shouted for Mrs. Burnley. He was told she was with the mistress, and I was told to wait. There was much running around in the kitchen of the sort I'd never seen, and I was forever being yelled at to get out of the way till the cook pulled out a chair to the side and told me to sit there and stay there. Which is what I did, my satchel in my lap, being afraid to move a muscle as I watched the hurried goings on.

The housekeeper finally appeared. I stood and recognized her right off. "'Tis very nice to see you again, Margaret Treacy," she greeted me and then grabbed my hand to get me out of the way of the cook and the others working to make lunch and led me into a small windowless office down the hall. It was painted in some kind of old yellow that was stained and faded in spots, and the only thing on its walls was a calendar on which I could see but not read notes, which was on the wall behind her desk.

Mrs. Burnley closed the door so we wouldn't hear the noise and smell the smells from the kitchen and pointed to a rickety wooden chair. The room was small, as I said, and the desk was too large for it, but as she was a small woman herself, she could squeeze by it and when she did, she dropped onto her own larger wooden chair. She didn't seem quite so proper now that she was in her own place and not with Mrs. Palmer at the House of Mercy. She was still very severe.

"We've had success with girls from the House of Mercy and I hope you prove up to the task. Mrs. Palmer and Miss Palmer liked you. That's good enough for me. But it won't be good enough no matter who likes you if you cannot do your job. Is that understood?"

I nodded.

As the housekeeper, Mrs. Burnley was in charge of us maids. She explained my role: *do whatever either she or a member of the family told me to do. Do not speak unless spoken to. Smile and be glad and thankful for the opportunity to serve a family as fine as the Palmers.* (I had no idea the degree of fineness of the Palmers, but I accepted that if Mrs. Burnley said they were fine they must be so.)

I followed her to my tiny room on the top floor, and there on the small bed were several maid's uniforms—black frocks that more or less fit based upon, I guessed, rough measurements someone had got from the House of Mercy—as well as white aprons and small white caps. She told me to get dressed in my uniform and be quick about it and then to return to the kitchen to begin work. There were two pairs of black shoes that fit as well as stockings and undergarments given to me at the House of Mercy in the satchel I carried, and the latter I put in a small bureau. My photographs of my parents and members of my family that were taken in a studio during an outing to Castlebar I put on top of it, beside a small mirror, and I placed the brushes and combs I was also given at the House of Mercy next to them. I'd written home since I arrived, and I put the two letters from my mama in a drawer.

There was a small toilet at the end of the hall on the floor below mine for the servants and after I changed, I took care of myself. I hoped I did a good enough job to make myself presentable when I appeared again before Mrs. Burnley in that office off the kitchen.

Another Irish girl, only two or three years older than me herself and also from County Mayo, though I didn't know the town, was assigned to see to the education of me. That girl, Bridget Fallon, was relieved to have me take the place at the bottom she held for over two years.

"You get used to it," she said about midway through her tour of the house. We went from floor to floor and from room to room (except for the two that had one of the Palmer women still inside). She explained that the family consisted of Mr. and Mrs. Palmer and the three children.

Bridget pointed to several photographs on a round table in the drawing room on the second floor. The biggest was of Caroline Palmer—now Caroline Evans—in her wedding gown and with her groom and members of the two families.

"Mr. David ain't our concern since he's married and living elsewhere. He be nice enough for a man of his sort but you won't have many dealings with him. If he sees you, he'll try to flirt with you. Don't pay it no mind. He and his wife come regular for Sunday dinner.

"Miss Caroline is married and away, too. She's Mrs. Evans now. She be expecting her first child in a few months. I was here when she was married. It was quite the thing, watching her leave the house for the last time as Miss Palmer. She comes back more than Mr. David. She's very nice, all smiles and even 'how do you do?'"

After telling me about those two, Bridget pointed to a shorter woman on the right.

"And that is Miss Elinor Palmer. 'Miss Palmer' since her sister got married. She's my responsibility though you'll see her."

"She was with her mother," I said as I looked at the image, "when they came to the House of Mercy."

"She's the one I'm responsible for. I was like you, doing the worst jobs, before I got me promotion. I'll try to teach you what I can. Miss Palmer is nice enough. Nothing like I hear others have to deal with in other houses."

Bridget lowered her voice. "There was a maid who cared for Miss Elinor. The fool left for a boy she took a fancy to. We liked her well enough, and me and the others sometimes think of doing the same but what would become of us if we did? Our life in service ain't great but we be in a good house and 'tis safe and secure and for girls like us that's what matters, ain't it?

"Her leaving though was a blessing to me and maybe to you since it's why they hired you and why I got promoted to care for Miss Eli...I mean, Miss Palmer.

"You have to understand that what you call someone is important, so be careful about it. Don't ever call anyone in the family by their first names as I'm sure they beat into you. *Always* curtsey when you see them and when you leave them, even if they ignore you. It ain't such a bad place from what I've heard from others."

We had this talk while we were finishing the second floor and going up the back steps to the third. She reached the hall there and stepped ahead before I could say anything, and I hurried to catch up with her as she went on with her tour and gossip till we were back down in the kitchen. It took me time to get over everything, it all being so new to me. Bridget and I sat together, at the table where we had our meals and where chores of all sorts were done at other times of the day.

5.

At about four o'clock on that first day, Mrs. Burnley came up to me at the kitchen table and told me to follow her. We climbed the servants' stairway to the third floor and down the hall to Miss Palmer's room. Mrs. Burnley knocked, and she and I entered without waiting.

"Yes," Miss Palmer said. "I was expecting you. Of course I remember you. I hope you are settling in."

"Yes, Miss. 'Tis me first day."

"Be a while," Mrs. Burnley interrupted, "until she is passable, but Bridget will be helping her."

"Very good. Thank you." She turned to me. "Can you—Margaret, is it?—can you and Bridget come up at six to help me prepare for dinner?"

With a curtsey, I said I would.

"Good," she said as I turned to leave.

At six, Bridget and I were at Miss Palmer's door. Just as the clock in the foyer struck the hour, Bridget knocked, and Miss Palmer told us to enter. She was, I'm afraid to say, not a very attractive girl, especially for someone so rich. Rich girls, I thought, must be pretty and she wasn't. She was short and dumpy and had a round face below very black hair and long eyebrows. Were I asked to describe her, that would be what I would have said, though no one ever asked. (I should say now that time and familiarity, though, would greatly soften her looks in my eyes.)

For months, I had little to do with her or any other member of the family directly. When I did see her, though, it lifted my mood and I did not know why and

I was disappointed if I missed her coming or going. This was true even though she usually called me "girl" if she saw me. *"Pick that up, girl." "Why are you always in the way, girl."* Like that, and I fell over myself apologizing. It seemed I was always apologizing to her.

Her mother then heard her call me "girl" and got very cross and said Miss Palmer had better call me by my true, Christian name. Then I was afraid that Miss Palmer would be mean to me for having gotten her in trouble with her mother. From then, she made a point to almost always call me "Margaret" in a nasty way— Mar-Ga-Ret—(except when her mother was near her and she was all sweetness) and strangely I missed her simply pointing and saying "girl" to me.

If I did see her, it was by luck. My job was harder and more tiring than I expected, at least at first. I opened the draperies in the main rooms in the morning and cleaned and washed the furniture and the rugs. Once it turned cold, I'd be going from room to room to set and check the fires, but it wasn't yet cold. The others warned me that winters in New York were something I'd never experienced in Ireland.

I spent hours at the table in the kitchen to either polish silverware or sew some tear in a garment. On Mondays and Thursdays, I had to gather all the dirty linen and clothing and such and do its cleaning for both the family and the servants.

I hated those days. The work was backbreaking and as I wasn't myself responsible for any member of the family, like Bridget now was with Miss Palmer, I didn't get a break from after breakfast until we had dinner. Sometimes, I got some help from one of the footmen.

Some of the sheets and such were too large and heavy for me to handle on my own, so he helped with the scrubbing and the hanging—so they would dry—and the folding.

How I cleaned the dresses depended on the material and whether there were stains. Even those gowns that would be worn only once or twice had to be cleaned after wearing to preserve them so they could be put into storage. The room for doing this off the kitchen was large because of all the various vats and powders that were needed, not to mention the ironing, which required an open board. Thank goodness the family had one of the new Mrs. Potts' Irons, which allowed it to warm in a fire without the handle attached. That way I wouldn't burn my hand too often on it, as I did back at home.

This made the work easier. It didn't make it easy, I promise you. And the room had no window, only some sort of ventilation grill that led to a pipe that went up to the roof and if the door was closed one might quickly suffocate, it was so harsh.

Certain ladies' garments were exclusively my responsibility. Early on when I was still learning, I might have torn one of Miss Palmer's dresses. I didn't notice it and hung it where her dresses were kept. It was a few days after that when I was sitting at the table in the kitchen doing polishing and I heard an angry voice calling, "Where is that girl?" several times and when I looked up Miss Palmer, with Bridget close behind her, was coming at me very fast.

She wore a dress she said I'd torn. It was a green but not particularly fancy thing, with some yellow and red striping and a low collar. Its bottom hem dragged along the floor because she was in bare feet, or at least she wasn't wearing shoes. She was staring at me. I jumped up so fast that the chair I was in crashed loudly to the tile floor behind me. Everyone in the kitchen stopped whatever they were doing to see what was happening.

Miss Palmer stopped perhaps a yard in front of me. I saw Bridget was over her left shoulder, shaking her head with very big eyes.

"You. Girl." Everything was quiet before Miss Palmer spoke and stayed that way while she did. "You have ruined my dress. I should have Mrs. Burnley take it from your salary."

Now, this would've been difficult since I was paid so little. My room and board were taken care of. It was thought I had no reason to have any money, but as we had to be paid something, and several of us, myself included, sent money home when we could, we got a meager salary. In those days, there was little for me to use it on. At most I might buy candies at a shop after Mass or save up to buy a book. I was also saving to buy a proper dress to wear when I wasn't at the house, like for strolls after Sunday Mass. But that would take some time and I was left with a simple frock that was the nicest that I brought with me from home.

Miss Palmer's threat was therefore real to me. I could never pay for the dress. It was, as were all the family's clothing, made by a dressmaker and I couldn't imagine how much it cost and how many years of working it would take for me to afford such a thing.

Everyone in the kitchen moved so they could watch, and Mrs. Burnley hurried down the hall to reach us. With a "may I, Miss?" she bent down, and Miss Palmer lifted the skirt so the damage I caused could be examined.

"Miss Palmer. 'Tis not so bad. I think we can fix this right off. I'm sure it was an accident." She looked at me and so did everyone else. I, though, could only really see Miss Palmer.

"If I did it, Miss, I didn't mean to. You must know that."

"Are you calling me a liar?"

I couldn't mumble a response, and Mrs. Burnley later told me she feared I would shake myself dead.

"It is torn. Why did you allow it to be sent up when you did it?"

"Miss, I didn't know. I swear I didn't know."

Miss Palmer glared. She, too, seemed not to care about the others.

"Come," she said.

I turned to Mrs. Burnley, who asked Miss Palmer, "What are you going to do with her?"

"Oh Mrs. B," she said in a completely different tone, "We are only going to my room. I promise you I shall not murder her."

Mrs. Burnley directed me to "do as the lady says," and I handed my apron to her and followed Miss Palmer. It was like the parting of the Red Sea as everyone in the hall squeezed to the sides as well as they could.

Miss Palmer called over her shoulder to the housekeeper. "And if I do murder her, I'll try not to make too much of a mess," and she laughed and I heard a "thank you, Miss," from Mrs. Burnley as we started up the servants' stairs.

6.

We climbed, me behind her of course, and as we did, Miss Palmer calmed herself. She opened her room's door wide and turned to me with…a smile. She pointed to one of the small chairs in a corner, separated by a small, dark table, and reached her right hand to my waist to direct me to it.

"Come now," she said. "I just wish to speak to you for a moment."

I was still confused and getting nervous but she smiled again and, of course, I could not refuse. I had never sat in any chair in the house other than those in the kitchen and servants' quarters. "It's quite alright, you know," she added as she took my chair's twin. I was afraid I might be dismissed, out on the street with nothing.

The room itself was large, though not as large as the two her parents had. Her bed was grand with four posters. Our chairs were near the corner closest to the foot of the bed, and in the other corner by us was a vanity and a small bench. A large oval mirror was attached to the vanity, and the mirror was surrounded by a frame that was painted in a very light blue and had speckles of red and yellow throughout. There was a group of cosmetics and lotions and such on the table. As with most of the other rooms, fresh flowers were placed in vases throughout. One of my responsibilities was changing them each day (but Sunday).

It was a pleasant blue room with lighter blue bed coverings and two floral pillows next to one another leaning against the headboard. The windows faced the back and across to the line of houses on Twenty-Ninth Street and they all seemed to match the Palmers' like the front doors did.

There was no closet—her clothing was on the fourth floor—but there was a wide dresser. On top of it was an oval tray, with a mirrored base, and a collection of rings and bracelets were strewn about it. There was a single photograph in an intricate silver frame. It was of the family—the two parents seated in formal patterned chairs with wooden legs and bare arms, and the three children standing behind them—formally posed in a studio.

Miss Palmer wasn't the tidiest of people, and when she left in the morning to go visiting or shopping or whatever, I often helped Bridget to tend to what was strewn here and there, bringing her undergarments downstairs to be cleaned, and remake the bed, so those pillows were properly displayed. Now her tone was infinitely softer than it had been even with Mrs. Burnley, and I was, well, shocked but I did as I was instructed to and sat on the chair at the side of that small table opposite her. She got up in a moment, though, still in the torn dress.

"Help me off with this rag," she said. I think she saw my expression because she added, "I'm only teasing. The dress is fine and the tear is slight. I wanted an excuse to see you."

"Me Miss?" I was disturbed by this.

She flung her arms above her head. "Come, come. Help me out of this."

I stood and undid and loosened the laces that crisscrossed up the dress's back and undid the snap at the top so the dress opened, and she helped me push it down over her hips and it dropped to the floor. She placed her hands on my shoulders as she stepped out of the dress. I lifted it and folded and laid it on the bed. I ran my hand to the tear and saw that it was easily mended.

I turned, and she had her back to me.

"The corset too, girl," but her voice remained light-hearted, and I was still very confused about why she'd had me come up to her room. I undid the laces for that and opened it up and she pulled it off and flung it onto the bed.

She was in her chemise, corset cover, and bustle, but I could see far more of her than I ever did. She was, as I said, a broad woman, but not nearly so unattractive as I first thought. Her skin was very pale, and it was dappled with freckles and her hair draped well down her back. I thought it was too bad that few saw how beautiful her hair was when it was allowed to flow freely.

She turned to me. Her breasts were large so far as I could make them out, no longer pushed up by the corset, and they fit perfectly to her body. I think I stared at them seeing as she made no effort to shield them and didn't move until she pointed to the dresser. I looked up at her and think I blushed for what I'd done and hoped she hadn't noticed though I think she had. I think she blushed slightly herself.

"I don't intend to go out today. You can get me that dress," she said when we'd both recovered from whatever we were feeling, pointing to a pink artistic dress that was on a hook beside an oriental screen that was over to one side. I got it, and she put it on with slight help from me. She didn't put her corset or her shoes on and plopped back on the seat by the table. She told me to sit again and asked me my story and how I came to be at the House of Mercy. I told her as best I could until there was a knock on the door.

"Come in," she said. It was Bridget. She seemed very upset by the liberties I seemed to be taking with her mistress. Mrs. Burnley sent her, she said. Miss Palmer, though, paid her look no mind and turned to me. She thanked me for helping her and said I needed to get back. She told Bridget we'd resolved whatever trouble I caused and that she should make sure to tell Mrs. Burnley that. She dismissed me and I went back down to the kitchen, with Bridget right behind me demanding I tell her what happened. I said I was only being polite and Miss Palmer was saying she regretted being so abrupt with me since the tear wasn't very large, which she realized when she examined it more closely.

"I think she might have felt a bit guilty," I said, "when she started asking me about myself and I was glad you came to rescue me from her."

* * * *

I DIDN'T UNDERSTAND what happened with Miss Palmer that morning and resumed my duties. Bridget remained her maid. I didn't know why, but I started to resent Bridget, if just a little, and spent more time where I thought Miss Palmer might appear. When she did, she ignored me except to give me, I thought, a wee smile as I stood off to the side. Perhaps she'd say "Margaret" as she passed, though not in the mocking way she used before, and I curtsied, and she continued on to wherever she was going.

And though I tried not to be obvious or to get in trouble for it, whenever I had the chance, I did my work where I might just see her, be it dusting in the foyer or cleaning windows that looked out onto Twenty-Eighth Street when I expected she'd be going out or coming in.

7.

I was at the house for nearly half a year, polishing in the kitchen, as usual in my "free" time, when one of the older maids who cared mostly for Mrs. Palmer went into the housekeeper's little office. I didn't mean to stick my nose in what wasn't my business, but I couldn't help seeing the maid—Deirdre Sullivan she was—run from that office almost right after she went in and hurry towards and going up the servants' stairs crying. Mrs. Burnley came out and waved for me. I was scared that the same would be happening to me, but she called to me that it was alright, and those in the kitchen returned to whatever they were doing before this interruption.

Mrs. Burnley was in the hall outside her office. She said, "Margaret. Can you get Bridget for me? I must speak to the pair of you."

I found Bridget tidying Miss Palmer's room—Miss Palmer was out making calls with her mother—and we went to Mrs. Burnley's office. Mrs. Burnley told Bridget to close the door.

"I'm afraid Deirdre has gotten herself in a bit of bother. She is leaving the house. I won't say why. 'Tis enough that she is leaving. So, Bridget, you need to take her job with Mrs. Palmer and that means, Margaret, that you'll be Miss Palmer's lady's maid."

Bridget and I looked at one another and I think she was a bit scared too, suddenly having to care for *Mrs. Palmer* and I was a bit scared 'cause suddenly I'd be at Miss Palmer's beck and call. While by that time I saw her often and she always smiled and sometimes asked me how I was and even once or twice ran a hand across my arm when she passed closely by me, I don't know that I was truly *afraid*, but I was sure things would be much different for me. My life would be all about pleasing a conceited fat rich girl who was sometimes nice and sometimes very mean to me but who for some reason I liked to be near as often as I could.

Mrs. Burnley asked if I was up to it but I couldn't say I wasn't up to it so of course I nodded. She said, "good" and got up. As she slipped her way between the desk and the wall, she told us to follow her, and up we went to Mrs. Palmer's study on the second floor.

Mrs. Burnley knocked lightly on the door and after a moment we heard a "come in." The three of us stood, with Bridget and me closest to the desk. Mrs. Palmer wore a pink morning robe.

It was a woman's room, with light blue striped wallpaper, the up-and-down stripes being of the slightest yellow. A loveseat was against one wall beneath what looked like an expensive landscape painting of a rolling field in the countryside. A largely maroon Persian rug with cream trim was in the middle.

But more than anything was the desk, its top far too small to be a man's, painted very fancily in a cream color with lines of blue and green paint and small red flowers along its top, sides, and legs. I dusted nearly everything in the room most every day.

"Bridget. Margaret," she said. "As I believe Mrs. Burnley has told you, something has come up with Deirdre. She may not be returning to us. She may, but now I do not know.

"This means you, Bridget, will be doing Deirdre's work. Miss Palmer, therefore, will need someone to take care of her in Bridget's place." She looked at me very hard. "Mrs. Burnley says that she believes you are up to the task, Margaret. I know you haven't had extensive dealings with my daughter or any member of the family for that matter, but I would like you to see if you can handle it. I've spoken to my daughter about it. She says she does not object. Do you think you can do the job?"

I nodded again, and Mrs. Palmer smiled.

"Good," she said. She tapped her fingers on the desktop and got up.

"Let's go see her, then."

We climbed to Miss Palmer's room. Her mother knocked, and Miss Palmer told us to enter. She too was in a morning robe, though it was light blue, and she didn't wear it nearly as well as her mother wore hers. She was at her vanity, glancing in its mirror as she brushed her hair when the four of us entered. The room suddenly seemed very crowded. Her hair, as I said, was long and very dark brown and fell well below her shoulders. Whenever she went out in the world, though, she wore it in a tight chignon that left her neck open. Which, as I also said, was a bit of a shame, seeing how fine her hair was. She jumped up when she saw her mother.

Mrs. Palmer said I was taking Bridget's place, and Miss Palmer looked from her mother to me and back to her mother.

"As I said, we will see if it works out, mother."

Mrs. Palmer didn't seem happy with this answer and how it was said and paused a moment and after a slight but clear huff said, "Yes, we *shall* see." I can't say how grateful I was for Bridget's presence beside me, though we were both standing with our hands appropriately behind our backs and our spines still and straight.

Mrs. Palmer turned to Mrs. Burnley—and when she did, her daughter looked very cross at me, and I'm sure I blushed at the attention—and she said to her housekeeper that she would "leave matters to you," and she was gone.

"I believe she is capable, Miss Palmer," Mrs. Burnley said, twisting her hands in front of her.

She turned to me and lowered her voice, with her back to Miss Palmer and a hand on my wrist. "Margaret. I believe in you but remember it's not me you must satisfy. 'Tis Miss Palmer."

She turned back to my new mistress, and with a nod said, "Good day, Miss" with a "come with me, Bridget," she and my friend were soon out the door too and I was alone with Miss Elinor Palmer for I think the first time since that incident with the torn dress some months back.

Miss Palmer resumed her seat at the vanity with her back to me. She positioned herself so that as she brushed her hair, she could watch me in the mirror, though there wasn't much to see since I was afraid to move an inch. She didn't offer to have me sit.

"Bridget has been promoted because one of the servants found herself with child. It is a very bad thing, and we had to be rid of her." She didn't try to shelter her voice for the scandalous things she was saying. "What will become of her I cannot say. She may have family. I don't know. She will likely give the child up, if it is alive, to the asylum to take care of and what becomes of her, I cannot say."

She turned on the small bench and looked straight at me. She was very hard and cold, and I was even more afraid of her like this.

"I tell you this so you know that you mustn't do something so foolish. You may be tempted, an innocent, pretty-enough girl like you, but you must resist. I won't preach to you that it is a sin. That is for your priest. I only tell you that the reality is that should you become with child, you will be ruined. If you should survive. You don't look to be one of those stupid girls, and I hope that you aren't."

She paused. "You do know how a woman becomes with child, do you not?"

I said that of course I did though in truth I wasn't sure. But I did know enough to keep away from a man until I knew him quite well and not to go farther till we were married.

"Good," she said. "You must never allow a man to…penetrate you before you are married to him," and that I think I understood. She said, "That's all I will say on the matter."

She turned back to her vanity and mirror and resumed her brushing but again stared at me and I felt like I did that time she seemed angry at me about the tear in her dress. Now, I thought she was very much and truly angry. "I don't mean to be unkind. But that girl made a mistake, and she must pay for it. I know you say, 'what of the father?'"

She saw my nod, and turned again towards me, this time putting the brush down.

"Of course, you do. I'm not so heartless not to ask the same question. But this is the way of the world, our world and your world. It must be tolerated. Yes, yes, a woman of means could take care of such an eventuality, and perhaps our former servant will seek to do the same, with all its risks. I cannot say. But that is what I wanted to tell you if no one else has. Do you understand?"

"Yes, Miss."

Her tone softened like she'd freed herself of whatever possessed her. And she smiled at me.

"Good. Bridget will explain to you what my needs are. I cannot say they are extensive, but she may differ. For today, I wish you to come here at six-thirty to prepare me for dinner. We are eating in tonight. Then I require that you be with me when I'm preparing to retire."

I said, "Yes, Miss Palmer. I'll be here then."

"Good."

With that, she turned back to her table and lifted her brush and resumed brushing her hair. Her eyes were no longer on me, and I left her room.

Bridget was waiting near the door. She put her finger across her lips so I wouldn't call out. We began to head down to the kitchen. I told her what was said about Deirdre. "She be harsh in her words sometimes. But she is right and means well. You must resist temptation 'cause if you don't you may well end up a beggarwoman in the street. Or worse."

Deirdre Sullivan never did return to the Palmers'. I heard, though I can't recall how and I can't say whether it was the truth, that she'd had a baby boy who was sickly but who survived and she found herself with the baby living in a tenement without a window and with another mother and child and that she scraped together some type of survival but, as I say, I cannot swear to the truth of it.

I can swear that she was gone, and I was now made to take care of Miss Palmer. In the first days, Bridget helped me as much as she could but after a week or so Miss Palmer told Bridget that she was no longer needed, and it was only she and me. It was some time before I felt even a little bit comfortable with her or, I think, that she felt comfortable with me. Little by little she confided in me and even sought my advice about some things, even to what I thought of this or that man she met at a dinner or ball based upon her description of him.

You must understand that at that point Miss Elinor Palmer's life was about one thing only. Finding a husband I was told at many of our late servants' sessions sitting in the kitchen waiting for the family to return for the night. I was also told that though the Palmers were rich, they weren't among the truly wealthy. They were in society, but not too high in it and were invited to some balls and dinners and parties but never to the more significant ones. And Elinor Palmer was a plain-looking woman. At best.

She was, according to Bridget and what Bridget heard, smart and able to talk when she had the chance to, though Bridget heard that being able to talk wasn't so attractive to most men, before or after getting married.

As far as I was concerned, though, what mattered was that she softened more and more towards me after I became her maid. She'd come out to society some months before I got to the house, and she and her mother were trying to find her a husband. She admitted this, and at times as she was preparing for bed she told me that it wasn't as simple as it sounded since there were many girls and many boys and many mothers and it could be hard to find a match.

Miss Palmer was always going to balls or dinners or parties and though I knew nothing about it in New York, I thought it must be in some ways like Backfox, where I did know that the higher, mostly Protestant rich there and nearby had such fancy events. It happened also with some of the richer Catholic families. They were always on the lookout for good stock for their offspring to breed with (which as I was a farmgirl it sometimes seemed exactly to be what was going on).

My own former duties were taken up by Mary Kavanagh, a girl even younger than me, who'd not gone through the House of Mercy but who came to the house on the recommendation of a friend of Mrs. Palmer, who employed this new girl's older sister as a maid. The new girl was American but nice enough and we chatted now and then in the kitchen at meals and when I was doing polishing or sewing while Miss Palmer was out. I helped Mary when I could, as I guess older maids had done with younger ones forever.

8.

Most days I helped Miss Palmer get dressed after lunch so she and her mother could do their visiting or be prepared to wait in the sitting room for the visitors that would be coming to the house.

In the evening when she was out, I'd hurry to the foyer when I heard she was home with her parents. She never went out at night without at least her mother. If she had a coat, I helped her out of it and then she'd hand me her hat and her gloves in the foyer. Mary would take them to a closet at the end.

Miss Palmer's parents would be gone to their room by the time she finished, and I'd walk behind her up to hers. There, she usually fell on her bed and would kick out her legs so I could remove her shoes. She'd be on her back and staring at the ceiling and telling me of what the ball or dinner or dance or opera was about and how much she enjoyed it. She'd tell me of the young men she saw and the young woman she wished she hadn't seen. Eventually she'd raise herself so I could undress her and, as I say, she'd ask what my opinion was of some boy she described and since I knew she needed me to sing his praises, I always did.

I could never admit it, but this was the best thing about being her servant. Listening to her go on and on with me nodding and saying, "Yes, Miss Palmer" and "He"—no matter who it was on that night—"sounds like a true gentleman" when I thought I was supposed to and then when she ran out of steam she would stand and let me finish taking care of her.

Sometimes it was very early when she came home from an evening and sometimes it was very late.

It was one of the early ones—they were always bad—that changed both of us. The three Palmers were gone for under two hours and I'd just placed some of my mistress's undergarments on the table in a small room off the kitchen for scrubbing when Patrick, that first footman I met on my first day, came down and said they were home.

"My, they are back early," one of the other servants said. "You had best get up there."

And I did—so did Bridget and Mr. Palmer's valet—scrunching the undergarments and putting them in a straw basket until I could return to them. By the time I got to the foyer, Miss Palmer had already gone up to her room. I knocked on her door. I heard nothing but dared open it.

She sat on her little bench, staring in the mirror, brutally brushing her hair. Her mother was behind her, her hands on her daughter's shoulders. She whispered that "Everything will work out," and pushed away and turned to leave, wishing me a "good evening" as she passed. Mrs. Palmer closed the door behind her.

Miss Palmer still wore her elaborate dark purple gown with bits of sparkle—she'd attended a ball—and she barely could sit on the bench let alone run the brush through her hair. She didn't look at me in the mirror at first, perhaps not realizing she wasn't alone. She started when I touched her left shoulder and then she turned in a rage.

"How dare you touch me? How dare you not be ready when I came home? Is that too hard for you?"

She spit it out, directing it to the innocent table and then flinging the equally innocent brush across the room and into the wall with such rage that it shattered into (I later counted) six pieces.

"Get out! How dare you?"

I never saw her like this. She hadn't told me how her heart was set on Charles Nelson, who I learned was the source of her anger.

I decided I'd wait till she told me to leave a second time. But she didn't. Instead, Miss Palmer, Elinor, broke down. Still not looking at me in the mirror or in life, she said, getting louder with each word, "Ugly, stupid Shirley Johnson. He wouldn't look at me for her. She is rich, of course, and in fairness she is neither ugly nor stupid but beautiful and quick and so I cannot blame him so much for showering her with attention. But he told me we would dance when we last met and he never came to me. He danced with Shirley enough times for it to be noticed but not once with me. I'm sure everyone saw that. Mother is surely furious. She is furious with me for rushing off as I did but I think she will be more furious with that rake for leading me on as he did, only I think to cause Miss Johnson to be jealous and to humiliate me. He is a horrid man and I never wish to set eyes on him again."

I wasn't clear whether Miss Palmer took a breath during this excepting to blow her nose in a handkerchief she grabbed from her sleeve and to clear her tears with the back of her hand. It had the effect, though, of calming her and, in some way, calming me. For the first time since she cursed me, she looked at me. First in the mirror and then after turning to look at me directly.

"You must think me very silly."

I did think this but also felt so very sad for her. She held her hands out. I stepped closer and when I was close enough she took my hands and I didn't want her to let go.

"I'm sorry, Margaret. I had such expectations of Charles Nelson, and they were foolish expectations I know. You must allow me to degrade him at least for a little time. In truth I cannot help but think of how handsome he was and how polite he was to me and mama when he was, as is now clear, seeking to attract another. She is a friend, though not a particularly good one, and she may have him, I say. Lock, stock, and barrel. She may have him and that is the end of it."

I wasn't so naïve to believe this for a moment, but I'd do what I could to make it so because Charles Nelson had broken her heart. She turned back to her little mirror, and I moved behind her. Her hands were crossed on the vanity, her fingers moving a wee bit, and she was looking down at them. I'd never seen her so hurt and vulnerable and while I felt a jolt or something when I looked at her sad face, I didn't dare do anything but look.

After a long pause, she got up and allowed me to remove her dress, rotating for me to unlace her and bending towards me so I could pull it up over her head. She had her favorite corset on. The burgundy one with four clasps in front and bits of intricate lace detail seeming to caress the underside of her bosom. A wonderful cream-colored lace trimming at its top, grazing across it.

Before she let me help her unclasp and remove it, she sat back down in a sulk, and I stared at her, though

I hope she didn't notice. I don't know if I'd ever seen her this, well, nervous.

"Margaret. Do you think me pretty?"

I'd thought of her often since that day with the torn dress and the corset she had me remove from her with little beneath it. From that day, she did seem to get prettier to me, even—though no one would believe me—beautiful in her way. But I was a girl and a servant and not a man and not in society.

I was very uncomfortable. I noticed her eyes for the first time that night. They were brown, so brown and obvious with her formal hair as usual in a chignon style, baring her shoulders, and with her round face and slight neck. It made her more elegant than she was when she allowed her hair to drape down, as she normally did at home, which I'd become very fond of. I was looking down at her shoulders to avoid her eyes in the mirror.

"Yes, Miss. I think you very pretty."

She turned. "That is what you are expected to say."

I wasn't lying. She wasn't as pretty as I'm sure Miss Johnson was. Even when she was well painted, Miss Palmer didn't compare favorably with those of her friends that I'd seen with her. I still thought, though, that she was pretty in her own way, very pretty at least to me, and this thought flustered me.

She stood and, facing me, spread her arms to either side and nodded, and I stepped forward to unclasp the corset. Top to bottom, and then I released her from its restraint and before I could pull it away she grabbed my left hand with her right and I thought she would pull it to her and she might have started to when she stopped and quickly let go of it and stood and stepped around me for the final stages of preparing her for her toilet. She placed a robe that was hanging on the side of the tall screen in the corner across herself before she turned back to me.

"We shall not speak of him again. Is that understood?"

It was like some fever broke, and I said I understood and I never did speak of him again. I don't know how or why, but from that brief period where she wanted to know my opinion of her, I looked at her differently and from that moment I couldn't look at her without pleasure. It was very wrong of me in many ways, but I confess that I began to see her as a *woman*. I confess, too, that I couldn't help myself from running my fingers across her with every opportunity. She didn't feel it, I don't think, but *I* did. And I didn't understand.

But on that night, when I was done with my duties, I was back in the kitchen, finishing what I had to do with her undergarments.

"My, they be home early," Bridget said. She'd done whatever she had to do with Mrs. Palmer and came down to the kitchen. It was where we servants congregated after the day, some of us doing the slight things that we were responsible for. Cook usually set aside something for us, and that night she had simple milk and cookies, the cookies in a large plate in the middle of the table.

Bridget said, "'It went very poorly,' the mistress said. 'Very poorly.'"

While we sat, one of the footmen who'd gone with them to the ball said Miss Palmer came out of the house in a huff and it took time for the carriage to be brought around—it would have been faster if they'd hailed a brown coupe—and by the time it had, the Palmer women were very angry standing on the sidewalk. It was a ball at one of the newer, bigger houses on Fifth Avenue, and the footman said Miss Palmer couldn't keep herself quiet the whole trip back.

"I'm tired of hearing her cry as we come home," he said. "I just wish Mr. Palmer would arrange something so we can get the thing over with and she can get married like Miss Caroline did. I mean, some of the footmen be betting she'll be an old maid if Mr. Palmer don't make an arrangement soon."

I wanted to say something to this. That any man with any sense would be lucky to get her. But I couldn't dare say that, even if it was just us servants.

* * * *

AS WE WAITED FOR her engagement to finally happen, Miss Palmer and I again did what we'd been doing. She'd come home, early or late, and I'd help her undress and get ready for bed. Usually, she said little about what happened. I felt I was a piece of furniture to her, silently doing what I was paid to do. And there was never a repeat of the episode regarding Charles Nelson.

The family had installed a copper tub in the bathroom on the floor where their bedrooms were and it was quite the something to see. We servants had a bathroom on the floor above. It had a toilet but also a spout we could stand under to clean ourselves at the end of the day.

The family's tub, though, was a marvel, having both cold and hot water so footmen didn't have to carry water boiled in the kitchen up the back stairs as my mama and I had to do again and again in Backfox. And thank goodness the pipes extended to our shower.

As Miss Palmer's maid, I was with her when she bathed, sitting on a small wooden chair in the tiled room while she cared for herself. When she said she was done, I handed her towels so she could dry herself and then held a robe for her to put on. All the while I half-listened to whatever she was going on about. Back in her room, I half-listened to her as she got herself ready to retire, standing and fetching whatever she wanted as demanded, until she was in bed. She sometimes took out a book but usually read a magazine after dismissing me.

While I was with her in her room, Mary Kavanagh cleaned up the mess of the water and the damp towels in the bathroom, and when I was dismissed for the night, I went to my own room and prepared myself for my own bed, sometimes reading some light thing that we maids shared among ourselves. More and more I found myself thinking of my mistress as I drifted off and more and more they were pleasant thoughts.

Then, some weeks after her disappointment with Charles Nelson, she was in the tub. This time, though, she asked me to pull my chair close to it so I could rub her back and shoulders. At first it was just another of my chores, but more and more I could feel her relax at my touch, as I dabbled my fingertips down the nape of her neck and along her arms and back. She reached up with a hand to hold one of mine to her and I felt my breath catch. Perhaps hers did as well. But she immediately released it and neither of us seemed to pay it any mind though I felt it long after we'd left the room.

It was something that she didn't do again. Still, from then on she insisted that I be near her throughout her bath and she allowed my hands to run against her neck and upper back. I thought of asking her if they could roam freer but I never did and she never offered to hold my hand against her, much as I wished she did.

9.

Whatever feelings Miss Palmer had towards me seemed to fade not long after the unpleasantness about Charles Nelson when her mother resumed the search for an eligible man who would be true to her daughter. It was not long after *that* that Miss Palmer returned from a party describing how she was smitten with someone else and within a fortnight she said she was deeply and totally happy with a man—she didn't say "love"—who wasn't shallow like the idiot Charles Nelson.

The fortunate gentleman's name was Francis Ballard. He became the topic of conversation for us when we sat in the kitchen doing whatever needed doing. Mostly it was from the footmen who waited with the Ballards' footmen during parties and balls and dinners.

Francis Ballard was the second son of a well-off family that occupied the same rung of society as the Palmers did. I didn't know there were "rungs" when I arrived. I thought there was rich and there was not rich till Bridget and the rest educated me on how society in New York worked. The Ballards' money came from a successful railway investment that multiplied its profits from the war, made in a series of supply contracts with the United States Army that had been negotiated with the help of bribes paid at the going rate. I was told it wasn't "old money."

Only later did I learn that the Ballards' fortune was drained by several bad investments that made it harder for Francis to find a match. Someone in the kitchen who knew about such things said he might have to settle for someone whose most attractive quality was her father's money and not her looks. Someone like Miss Palmer.

"The way of the world," a footman said. This world had a lot of ways, though I guess we had our share in County Mayo.

Francis Ballard, they said, worked in his father's investment firm doing little beyond arriving late and leaving early, interrupted by an extended lunch at his club, and spending much of the summer in the family's house in Saratoga.

"The staff don't think much of this Francis fellow," the footman who was the source of this knowledge said, "but they say he ain't the worst they ever seen."

I learned far more interesting things about Francis Ballard from Miss Palmer in dreamy words she sometimes used before or after some event or other, almost always then an event where her Mr. Ballard would be or was. Sometimes when she was lying on her back after I'd taken her shoes off and before she allowed me to undress her.

His character, she said, was neither much better than nor much worse than most of the others. I think she thought he was rather bland at first but began to like him, or at least the *idea* of him, each time she returned from seeing him as a way to do what everyone expected her to do. He was two or three years older than her. He was also, she told me, a little short and somewhat stout himself and wore a thick beard and large sideburns and his ears were somewhat too large for his round face.

"All in all," she said, "he isn't at all unpleasant to look at and to dance with and to talk to," and more than once she insisted that I tell her that I was truly and honestly happy for her and I did as I was told, though I was not as happy as I probably should have been about the chance of losing her to him.

That hardly mattered though. It wasn't long after I said I was happy that the house was all excitement about the events surrounding the youngest Palmer girl.

Everything between Miss Elinor Palmer and Mr. Francis Ballard was racing ahead, and it was less than a month after Miss Palmer confessed to me how "smitten" she was with the man that the engagement was announced at a party at the Palmer house.

Given how important the party was, after I prepared Miss Palmer, I was told to remain in the kitchen to assist with the preparation of the dishes before they were brought up and in clearing them when they returned. As the evening wound down, Mrs. Burnley took me into her small office off the kitchen. She closed the door to remove the hubbub.

"You must understand, Margaret, that Miss Palmer is now embarked on her great journey. She'll be better served, both now and perhaps after she is married, by one with more experience than you have. 'Tis not you. 'Tis your youth is all. Bridget will return to caring for her personal needs. You continue doing the other things that you have done."

Since we'd hired someone, Mary Kavanagh, to do most of those things, this didn't make much sense to me but what was I to say?

"Now, the family has all gone up and Bridget is with Miss Palmer so you may go up and help tidy the drawing and sitting rooms."

I asked who would take care of Mrs. Palmer and she said that she would. With that, Mrs. Burnley rose and more from rote than anything I stood too and walked in a daze upstairs to help with what I was told to do. I was to have nothing more to do, though, with Miss Palmer that special night.

I didn't see Miss Palmer on the next days and then I was back in Mrs. Burnley's office. It was late May of 1873, and it would be a lavish June wedding at the Church of the Incarnation on Madison and Thirty-Fifth Street.

"The family is preparing for the season in Lenox." To my stare, she said it was a resort in Western Massachusetts where the family kept a house.

"Mrs. Palmer has in particular asked that you accompany Patrick Norman"—the footman who rescued me from the sidewalk on my first day—"there to assist with the preparation."

"But what about the wedding?" After what I'd been through and what I thought I was to Miss Palmer I hoped to participate even if I wasn't to go with her on her wedding trip.

"My dear, all of that is well in hand. After all, Miss Palmer's sister married only three years ago, and we haven't forgotten how to do it."

"When must I go?"

"You go tomorrow."

10.

Once up, and after I helped Mary with the opening of windows and drapes and such and had morning breakfast with the others, and before Miss Palmer rang for her breakfast to be brought up, Patrick and I took a carriage to the Grand Central Depot. Trunks had been sent the day before and they were in the baggage car of the train he and I were taking to Lenox.

Miss Palmer's window faced the back but I still looked up. Perhaps she'd gone to a room overlooking the street to watch me leave. But she wasn't in any of those windows. She hadn't rung for her breakfast, and I was surprised and a little sad that Bridget didn't go to wake her. She *knew* I was being sent away yet didn't come down the night before either or have someone bring me up to her, the last time I would see her as the unmarried Miss Palmer.

I liked Patrick, the footman I was going to Lenox with. He was born in America, but his parents fled the Hunger from County Galway. He was a quiet sort, like me, and didn't say much while we all ate together or did chores or relaxed as well as we could in the Palmers' kitchen. He turned out to be grand company on the long ride north, though, and said a local boy'd be joining us when we got there to help. "And keep us honest," he said with a smile and a wink.

The train clanked and was noisy with lots of stations we quickly passed by in the hundred or so miles to Massachusetts. Patrick said he was there the summer before and that some of the others said it had a bit of Ireland in its hills and green (though he admitted he didn't actually *know*, never having himself been there).

"The family is always coming and going. Things much more relaxed than in town. But we see the same people again and again, and there are large parties on the lawn every few weeks. But 'tis so much cleaner and they let us all go to a big lake once a week and we get to meet others like us there."

As we rode north on the train, I began to forget at least a little about Miss Palmer and that I'd be missing her fine wedding. My mood was much helped by the passing countryside. It was early spring yet there were so many more trees than in County Mayo, which was mostly farms and fields with trees doing nothing but separating parcels. These trees were beginning to blossom. We passed little towns and one or two larger ones every few miles in the long valley.

For the first time since I came to America, I felt I could breathe. I didn't realize how much I missed blue skies and clear air, even with the soot flowing back from the locomotive.

After about an hour with the stations more spread out, the train began to stop at each. People in our train carriage would get up and take their small cases and satchels from the rack that ran the length of the car. Big trunks were taken from another car and placed on the platform by railway workers. The maids and footmen who'd left the carriage would point and a lad or two loaded their family's things onto the back of a wagon and they'd head where they were headed just as the train began to move again.

By the time we got to Lenox, there were only a few groups still in the car. Another maid and footman got out at the station. Patrick waved for a wagon that was waiting. It had one horse, and the Palmers' trunks were loaded on it. It was just the one lad, and Patrick helped him. The three of us sat in the seat. I was in the middle and Patrick was to my right and the boy held the reins to my left. Off we went just as we heard the train whistle and it started to go after an "All Aboard."

I don't know how far we went in the wagon, but the ride was rough at times. Now that too reminded me of home as we were in the fresh air under a blue sky. We finally got to the Palmers'. It was a grand house on a street with other grand houses. I think it might have been even bigger than the Thomas's mansion west of Backfox. That was the biggest house I ever saw in Ireland.

Unlike Twenty-Eighth Street, each house was different from the ones near it. The Palmers' was set back though not too far. You could see the mansion from the road up a slight hill. It had a straight driveway to a large circle where carriages could discharge and collect their occupants.

While the house next to it was white with columns, the Palmers' was brick, like the house on Twenty-Eighth Street but much wider. There were stables off to the right, and that's where Patrick directed the boy. There were no horses there, but Patrick said there would be soon enough.

"We'll be needing to come and go, so Mister Palmer has arranged for a pair to be brought over in the morning."

A plain wagon, a fancy brougham carriage, and a trap were in the garage area to the right of the stables.

Patrick gave me a set of keys. After trying many, and I found the one to open the door at the side of the house while he and the boy unloaded the trunks. The door led to a large storage area. It had windows on either side, and I opened them to try to get rid of the closeness. I didn't know how long it was since any fresh air was in the place, and there was dust pretty much over everything and a lot of it ended up all over me.

As I got back to the yard, Patrick told me to open the door to the kitchen, which he pointed to. It was towards the back of the house, and I found the right key. The door was sticky, but I managed it after a few shoves from my right shoulder. It also was very stuffy and dank. I could smell the remains of some critter coming from a floorboard in a corner. It was just a kitchen, but far different and bigger than the one in the house in town.

It was in the corner of the house, and there were many windows, which I set about opening to get the air in and the smell out. It took no time to realize that the conveniences used in the kitchen in town weren't there. But I wouldn't have to cook anything until the next day since Cook included plenty for our dinner in a small hamper we carried with us.

I was still looking around when Patrick came in with the hamper. He put it on the large table in the center. I heard the boy roll away in the wagon.

"Let's have ourselves a look around," Patrick said. He smiled and bowed and held his arm out, so I knew to put mine through it, but not before an appropriate curtsy to my "gentleman." We went from the kitchen through the butler's pantry to the dining room and foyer and sitting room on the ground floor. I was amazed. Each was far bigger than in the house in town, and in each, we opened the windows. The stink of rotting creatures was in several and getting rid of them would be one of the first things we would take care of. It was beginning to get late, though it was still light, with the wind picking up and the curtains moving slightly in the breeze.

There was a mighty staircase in the foyer. A tall clock was there, but it was stopped at 6:23 and it didn't tick or tock. Patrick grabbed my hand, and we flew up the front staircase laughing like children at the liberties we took. At the landing, he turned to the right, still clasping my hand at first, and began opening each door, and he and I took turns opening the draperies and opening the windows wide as we raced from room to room till we were done and back at the landing and breathing hard and laughing harder. My God how I felt like a child dancing in the halls of the mansion or like I'd been invited to a ball at the Thomas's estate and was in my glorious burgundy gown and sparkling tiara with guests looking up and waiting for me to come down to greet them.

Patrick wouldn't know about the Thomas's, but he must have been thinking something similar about being, for just a moment, the lord of this domain next to his lady and I felt his arm around me and for a moment I thought he might turn me to kiss me and I didn't know what I would do if he did and I didn't know if I wanted him to. But he merely pulled me close and said, looking out over and throwing his free arm across the banister, "You ever wonder, Meg, what it'd be like to have a house like this be yours?"

I put my arm around his waist and felt how strong he was, but it was a purely physical sense of two souls acting well above their station sharing the brief fantasy that they were better than they were. I put my head on his shoulder.

"Aye, Patrick," I said, "we all have our dreams." I released him. "But they just be dreams, you know? We both are here because they're nothing but dreams and soon enough we'll wake up."

I don't know that I'd even been so deep in anything I thought or said before, but it came to me as I was there. It was gone nearly as it began, though, and I moved from him and went into rooms on the other floors. We repeated the opening of the doors and the windows and then went down more slowly than we went up till we sat in the kitchen and unloaded our dinner from Cook's hamper.

* * * *

REALITY CAME IN THE morning. I'd had a very good sleep even if it was quieter than I had known since I left Backfox nearly a year earlier. The night birds and the frogs were somehow a comfort to me, and I had drifted off easily.

Cook had packed food for breakfast, but I had to light the fire in the kitchen for us to eat it. It was simple: eggs, bacon, and bread. I, being a farmgirl at heart, was up soon after dawn and went into the yard, which was quite overgrown. The chicken coop and hatching barn were empty and weeds were climbing up their fence. That hardly mattered, though, as I breathed it all in. With the morning dew wetting the bottom of my dress and the birds making a fuss, for the first time since I'd left Backfox I felt young and free like I did as a girl.

As with our standing overlooking the foyer in our brief time pretending to be the master and mistress, these thoughts couldn't last long. I still enjoyed them, though, as the sun rose above the tops of the trees, full of their green and in one case red leaves.

There was work to be done and it was up to me to start by making breakfast for Patrick and me. I was soon at it, including making a pot of coffee. It was just about the end of what we brought so we'd have to go into town. I hoped the horses would appear for the wagon. The family would arrive in three weeks, though Elinor, who'd of course be Mrs. Ballard by then, wouldn't be with them.

As for breakfast, though it was quite a while since I'd cooked, Patrick said he enjoyed it. While we ate, we agreed that I would start with the house and he with the stables and yards. Some of that'd have to wait till he got horses so he could mow the lawn, but he started on getting the stables ready.

And there I was, up on the top floor, below an attic. It was where we servants would sleep—I'd slept in Mrs. Burnley's room and Patrick in Williams's, which we planned on enjoying till they arrived—and I opened the windows, removed the sheets that covered the furniture, dusted, and started to scrub the floors using a bucket of water Patrick carried from the pump off the kitchen once he got it primed to work.

I heard horses coming up the drive. I looked through the small window in the room I was cleaning and saw an older rider on one, a boy of maybe fifteen or sixteen on another, and a third connected by a rein to the older man's horse.

Patrick hurried to meet them. He and the riders' voices carried up to me. By the time I got to the drive, the boy had jumped off his horse and held the reins for it and other one without the rider as the older rider was trotting away.

The boy introduced himself as James. He was from a nearby farm and said he'd been hired to help with getting the house ready for the family and to stay with Patrick and me until the family arrived.

Patrick said, "People have to be careful about a pair of young folks being together out in the country," and he smiled and laughed.

As to the horses, a pair of chestnuts, they were far better than the one we had on our farm in Backfox and even the equal of the best ones in the county, not accounting for the Thomas's pair that pulled their carriages and the group that didn't pull at all but rode to the hounds.

"Flicker and Casey," Patrick said, pointing to the horses in turn. They were handsome and I ran my hand across each of their snouts and whispered into their ears how pleased I was to meet them. The Palmers kept some horses at a stable on Twenty-Fifth Street, but I only saw them harnessed to a carriage and never dared to approach one.

Patrick seemed happy that I was happy to see Flicker and Casey. They shook their heads and snorted when I ran my hand along their snouts, and I again felt more at home than I had since coming to America. More and more I was excited about being in the country, and I got Patrick to promise that he would take me in the wagon for a tour of nearby farms at the earliest opportunity.

"I wonder what it'd be like to live here," I told him.

"Maybe someday you'll find out, but I think it'd be a hard life was you to work on one of the farms nearby."

I thought it might be, but not so hard as on the farm back home.

"And I think you'd be lonely up here, being a stranger and all. I don't know that they take much to foreigners but maybe they'll take to you and maybe you'll be a farmgirl again."

"You're probably right, Patrick," I said. "I may be too used to being near people now that I've done it for so long. You may be right."

"No need to decide yet. Just enjoy being up here for now, aye?"

I agreed and there was no more time to dawdle. Once Flicker and Casey were settled, Patrick had me show James to his room on the servants' floor. That done, I returned to what I'd been doing and James went to join Patrick in the yard.

I finished cleaning out the servants' rooms some hours later and went down to the kitchen. The other two weren't far out in the yard, and I called to them, saying it was time to eat. There was just enough left over from breakfast that we could have that, but when we were done, we'd have to go into town for provisions. Patrick quickly had the horses attached to the wagon and he and I left James and were heading down the drive to the road into town.

Lenox, the town, wasn't very large. It was bigger than Backfox but that wasn't saying much. There were two roads north-south and three east-west and various stores lined the sidewalks. Both the sidewalks and the roads were paved in stone, but the road was dirt until we were right at the outskirts and it rose as we reached Lenox itself.

As we rode in, Patrick told me what we'd be getting and where we'd be getting it. He'd handle the heavier things and I was to go to the general store for food and other provisions to keep our bodies and souls together. He pointed to the fine, stone church—St. Ann's it was—on the main street where he said "our souls" would be taken care of.

There were only a few fancy carriages in town. Mostly there were wagons like ours. In the general store, the customers were all maids or cook's assistants who lived there or came up from town doing pretty much what I was doing. We all were carrying our leather bags. A big man with a red beard was in charge of things that we couldn't get ourselves. When it was a person's turn, he'd call out from the other side of a tall counter, "What'll it be?" and before you knew it, he'd gotten whatever it be that the customer wanted and when I got to him he made short work of my little list of basics.

He smiled at me, though he smiled at everyone, at least the "ladies," and he said he liked my Irish accent and that he threw in a bit of extra bacon for "my sweet lass," as he called me. There was a woman in front at a cash box and when I got there, she told me to pay her husband no mind.

"He's far too old and fat to do anything with young 'uns like you but talk." She laughed as she toted up what I owed and smiled as she put everything in my bag. I said I was with the Palmers.

"I'm Mrs. Patterson," she said, "and I'm glad to make your acquaintance." She said she'd put everything on the Palmers' account. As I started to go, I heard her Mr. Patterson telling some other girl how she too was his "sweet lass," and Mrs. Patterson rolled her eyes as she wished me a good day and turned to take care of yet another sweet lass who was behind me.

Patrick wasn't back when I got to the wagon, and I walked a bit up the street to look into the shops. Again, the windows were far better than what was in Backfox but far below what was in the windows in town. Still, I didn't dare go into any of the little shops, and after looking back at the wagon several times, I saw Patrick walking to it. He carried a few things. I hurried to him, and he said he needed to bring the wagon around to get some of the heavier goods and hay. When that was done the two of us headed back to the house, sitting together on the wagon's bench, and I told him that I was far more tired than I expected.

"That's just the fresh air, you know," he said. "We can just relax when we get back. No one'll know. We've plenty of time to get the place ready for the family."

Back at the house, the three of us sat on chairs Patrick and James brought from the garage where the carriage and other outdoors things were kept. They set them up on a patio that was on the eastern side of the house; there was a far more formal patio for the family on the opposite side, looking west. Our rough patio was a simple spot off the kitchen where some slate was placed, and it was surrounded by a low stone wall.

I dropped into a chair and suddenly I was even more tired than I thought. Patrick and James seemed the same and it was all that we could do to simply look out at the slight hills that flowed away with the treetops moving in the wind that had come up and talk and speak with James. But needs must and with it starting to get dark I forced myself up to get our simple dinner ready, and the others followed me into the kitchen.

This is how we spent the time preparing the house for the family. In the morning, I went from room to room as Patrick and James did whatever they were doing in the yard. We sat on the eastern patio for sandwiches I made—excepting the days when it was raining, when we sat at a small table in the kitchen, sometimes with a small fire going in the hearth off to the side. I did have time to write home, which I hadn't done as often as I should have when we were in town.

Every few days, Patrick'd harness Flicker and Casey to the wagon and roll into Lenox with me or James. Sometimes we'd drop James off so he could walk to his family's farm for a few hours before walking back to the Palmers'. If I went into town, I'd drop off my letters and the report I helped Patrick write to Williams, the Palmers' butler. Mr. Patterson would give me extra bacon and call me his sweet lass and Mrs. Patterson would make me promise that I was paying her husband no never mind as she put what I bought on the Palmers' account. We collected a small flock of chickens and a rooster which we'd put in the coop after we'd cleaned it up, though the rooster'd be allowed to roam free.

The three of us had to make the house presentable. We quickly got the coverings off the furniture, where they'd been since Christmas time (when I stayed in town), and then set about going room by room scrubbing away at the floors. I did most of the scrubbing after Patrick and James moved the furniture and carried up the bucket for me.

We had three weeks to complete the job and, as I said, I started on the top floor where the servants' quarters were. These, of course, needed little seeing to beyond a hard floor scrub and the airing out of the mattresses and draperies. The paint was adequate and these rooms were quickly done with.

At one end of this floor was a large room where the family's clothing was kept. In all likelihood, much of it would be transported to some charity in Pittsfield (the mill town a few miles to the north) to be distributed and would be replaced by more recent summer things brought from town.

All the material in the room had to be aired out. If we expected the day would be sunny without rain, we—Patrick and James mostly—carried what wouldn't be given away out to the back. We hung each item on one of the lines Patrick ran between two trees.

On some nicer days and well after I'd come to look at him like a kind of brother to me, Patrick escorted me around the village, letting me stop at the windows I fancied. I began to recognize other servants from town and sometimes Patrick would chat over with another footman while I strolled a bit with one or two other maids and that is how I learned about how the little society of Lenox, Massachusetts worked.

Most importantly, I was told that most servants had off from noon on Mondays and that wagons would be loaded with staff who'd meet in town or at the bowl—the lake southwest of town—and cooks at each of the houses would prepare hampers and we'd have grand swims and picnics. Patrick laughed when I said I didn't know how to swim and said I'd learn right fast if he just tossed me in, though he never did that to me.

He, I learned on our train ride north, was born in New York. His folks fled County Galway in the early days of the Hunger, way back in '48. They survived the crossing, and his dad got a job on the docks and his mother as a seamstress. He was the oldest of four children, two of each. His father was big and muscular, Patrick said with a bit of pride, and he had taken after him.

"Like now, ya know. Who'd want to be sitting on Twenty-Eighth Street in the muck and soot when they could be up here?"

One afternoon at the house when James was still at his folks' place, I can't say why I did it, but I asked Patrick if he'd ever been in love. It just came to me and was something I was suddenly curious about as we were lying on the grass looking through the tree leaves to a sky rarely seen in the city's darkness.

"Are you tellin' me you are in love with me?"

I raised up to look over at him.

"Don't be daft, Patrick. I don't think I've been in love with anyone, least of all you. But have you loved a woman?"

I flopped back down, and he continued where he was.

"'Tis not so easy now, is it? I mostly only see you girls and them that pass by when I happen to be on the street and the ones who'll go to the types of taverns where I like to go with my mates. But they ain't the type of woman you fall in love with, if you know what I mean."

I was used to such brave talk in the Palmers' kitchen and paid it no mind.

"Yes, but," I said, "have you have ever had your heart skip a beat at the sight of someone?"

"Ya been reading too many silly books, you have."

"No, I mean it. You know exactly what I mean. Have you ever...dreamed of a woman. Being with a woman?"

"You mean—"

"Be serious. I don't mean like that. You men are dogs if you ask me. I mean something sweet."

I didn't know what I was going on about and knew almost nothing about men and women but enough to know that men could be dogs.

"Okay, then," he said. "There was a girl I knew before I came to the Palmers. Her ma and my ma were friends. Still are. She was the prettiest thing. I even thought of marrying her. We were just children. Had I gotten a job on the docks, perhaps I would have. But my papa wouldn't allow it. 'Too dangerous,' he said, though I think my ma put him up to it. She didn't want to have me end up like some others, dead or crippled. She'd say she didn't come all this way to America to have her oldest boy taken from her.

"No. She was the one who insisted on service as the life fer me. Course it creates its problem about love and marriage and all. But I'm happy enough, I suppose. Maybe I'll find someone."

"Won't that mean," I interrupted, "leaving service."

"Perhaps it would. I know it usually does at least for the wife, but I hear of husbands and wives who are allowed to work in the same house. Don't happen often, but I've heard it.

"So other than that girl, I ain't been in love. I haven't found it."

"What happened to her?"

"Her? Of all things, she went to a convent. Sisters of Mercy. It was something I think she and her mama thought would be good for her." He lifted himself to look at me again. "You might have met her. You went to the House of Mercy, aye?"

"I did. But most of the nuns were old and feeble. I don't think you would have fallen in love with any of them."

I laughed and he did too. Though I did think fondly of one or two who weren't old or feeble.

"Yeah. I suppose not. I think of her now and then, you know. Maybe if my horse comes in, I'll go and knock on the door of that convent and take her away."

I laughed again as our conversation was becoming more and more relaxed, like we were old friends sitting by the stream back home. "Do you have a horse that might come in?"

"Nah. Just me. But if I can dream of her, I can dream of having such a horse, now, can't I?"

And I admitted he could and wondered whether I would ever have my own such dream and remembered that there was still work that needed to be done to get the house ready for the Palmers.

11.

The last room I got around to was Miss Palmer's. Or at least it had been Miss Palmer's before she became Mrs. Ballard. Mrs. Burnley told me to see if Patrick and I could make into a room suitable for the married Mr. and Mrs. Ballard when they came to Lenox. The same had been done to Caroline Palmer's room.

Elinor's hadn't been painted or papered for two or three years. It looked like a young lady's special place. It had light green wainscoting and yellow wallpaper in a floral pattern, with red and blue flowers connected by streams of green stems. The ceiling was an ivory color with a sculpted dental molding, but it didn't have a chandelier. Instead, pairs of candle sconces-+-the house had no gas lamps—were on each of its four walls, including on either side of a large window that faced the rear of the house.

The room, looking to the north like it did, wouldn't be nearly as hot as those that faced west or especially south. Those rooms, Patrick said, would broil in the August heat even with the green-striped awnings. While they would surely be more tolerable than the rooms in the house on Twenty-Eighth Street, they would be uncomfortable for sleep, even with the windows open wide thanks to the installation of screens to keep the mosquitos out.

A large, four-poster bed was centered against the wall to the right of the door and left of the window.

"We'll need to redo the decorations and linens," I told Patrick, who was blessed with neither an interest nor any knowledge about that. He said he'd go with me to Lenox the next day to get what we needed to transform the room into a marriage bedchamber.

* * * *

IN THE END, I THINK we did a very good job with the house. It took the three of us nearly the entire exhausting three weeks to be done with all the rooms.

The family arrived by train a few days later. It was only Mr. and Mrs. Palmer, Sr. and Mr. and Mrs. Palmer, Jr., the latter with their son. Patrick and I rode with Flicker and Casey and the wagon to fetch them and the members of the household who came. Because Patrick said it would be a day or so before the family's own horses arrived in a special train car made for horses to be brought from town, we hired two carriages with horses to collect everyone and attached Flicker and Casey to the wagon. After the family was in the carriages, the men loaded the trunks and other luggage onto the wagon, and the members of staff piled where they could for the ride to the house.

12.

The grand success of Miss Palmer's—now Mrs. Ballard's—wedding was the constant topic among the Palmers—when I was in earshot of them—and of the staff virtually every waking hour.

The dress. The veil. The flowers. The music and the so many guests. On and on through the description of the happy couple riding away to catch a ship for their extended trip to London and Paris and Berlin and maybe even Venice. Accompanied by Ballard's man and by Bridget.

July and August passed slowly for me in Western Massachusetts except on the days of and after one of the parties held on the house's lawn, when I barely had time enough to breathe, and we had our afternoons with the other servants at the Stockbridge Bowl, as the nearby lake was known. After three weeks at the house, the two Mr. Palmers took the train back to town regularly for the week before retuning in the early evening of Friday. Things moved even more slowly when they weren't there but livened up a bit when Caroline and her baby arrived with her Mr. Evans.

Nice as that was, I really only cared about when Mrs. Ballard would be there. Then I was told that she and Mr. Ballard were extending their trip in England for several more weeks than was planned— apparently thanks to an invitation to an estate in Derbyshire or some other northern English place— and wouldn't be joining the family until it was back in town.

I went to her—*their*—room after I found this out and slowly looked at it and what we'd done to it. It was quite sad, really, that they'd never be there, at least that season.

13.

In mid-September and after a horribly warm August in which our only refuge was the weekly trip to the bowl, everyone reversed what they'd done in coming up to the Berkshires. The house would stay open and family members would still be coming to it once in a while, but as with the other families, they were moving back to town.

It was just Patrick, James, and me in the end, though this time it was days after the family left as we handled the simpler task of closing things up and covering the furniture before a final look around—with a final, slow walk around the Ballards' room—and returning to the village in a hired wagon carrying the last things that the Palmers wanted brought back. We said a fond goodbye to Flicker and Casey, who snorted, I think, their own regret in our leaving. And goodbye to James, too, who'd become like a little brother both to me and to Patrick, and we expected he'd be quite taller the next time we saw him.

I enjoyed the train ride down more than I expected. Patrick and I didn't talk much. We were both exhausted. I soon got tired of looking at each little village that we passed and took to reading one of the detective stories I found in a storage room in the house and that Mrs. Burnley said I could take with me. I only revived and put down my book when I knew we were nearing town.

More than anything, after the time away I was excited that I would *finally* see Mrs. Ballard. She'd have so much to tell me of the places she visited. I'd missed Bridget very much, and she would tell me even more. Far better than the nothingness of months in Lenox in which you saw everyone you were going to see within a few weeks of getting there.

I'd be living at the Palmers' until the Ballards got back from Europe. They'd be moving into a house that was a gift of Mr. Palmer, the Ballards having become (the kitchen gossip had it) a bit short of money.

Although the Palmers were English and Episcopalian, virtually the entire staff was Irish and Catholic and the servants (not always including the men) went to Mass together. We'd be back for a break-fasting meal and then would prepare the Palmers' post-services dinner like we always did.

On the second Sunday that I was back from Lenox, Mrs. Burnley stepped beside me as we walked home from church. It was a bright day. Not a cloud in the sky.

"I must speak to you when we are at the house."

This was unusual, being a Sunday. Even without getting changed from her Mass clothes, Mrs. Burnley brought me to Mrs. Palmer's study. I followed the housekeeper in, wearing my own Mass dress, after we heard Mrs. Palmer instruct us to enter. The room had a perfect aroma from the flowers spread around, and the window was open so it wasn't stuffy. Mrs. Palmer was in the dress she wore to Sunday services a few blocks away, at the church where the Ballards got married. She was there in her chair at her desk, her back stiff. There was a single piece of stationary centered on her side, and she held a pen in her hand, the top of which she drummed on her left, non-writing hand.

I stood, with my back as straight as I could make it. Mrs. Burnley stood behind me.

"I'm afraid, Margaret, that we are forced to dispense with your services. You have performed well since you arrived, but...circumstances dictate that a change be made. I hope you will understand."

I didn't but didn't dare say so. I stared like a fool down at the desk in my Sunday best.

"With Elinor—Mrs. Ballard—gone, there is simply no more need for you."

"But...but I thought I'd be back with her. Or if Bridget went with her, I would take Bridget's place here."

All my composure disappeared.

"Margaret, we believe we can make do. Bridget will be staying with my daughter. It is simply that with the change and her moving out and it now only being Mr. Palmer and myself living here, we don't need the staff we have accumulated over these years."

I still didn't understand. There was more than enough work to be done in the house and from all indications, there was no suggestion that the Palmers might be strapped for funds. I was kept busy enough in Lenox. Why would things be different in town?

And what was to become of me? Being dismissed from a society house. *Who would even think of retaining me?* But Mrs. Palmer addressed that.

"I have arranged for you to take a position at another house, although I confess that I'm not acquainted with the family. It will be something of an adventure for you"—she lifted her voice as she said this—"as the house is actually a large suite in some new apartment building. It is some distance from here, but I'm afraid that is all I've been able to find for you. Mrs. Burnley will give you the information."

At that, the housekeeper stepped forward. She put one hand on my shoulder and with the other reached across and took the paper that Mrs. Palmer lifted from the desk.

Mrs. Palmer got up.

"Thank you, Margaret. We appreciate your service here and wish you the best of luck."

She extended her hand and I, still stunned, took it and thanked her. Her grip was slight, and my palm was damp. She barely gave mine a shake before she pulled hers back. She turned to Mrs. Burnley.

"Thank you, Mrs. Burnley. I believe we are done here."

With that and a nod, Mrs. Palmer sat, and the housekeeper led me out of the study and I turned and I curtseyed and within an hour I was gone from the house after a brief goodbye to the others I had come to know, with my belongings, which fit inside the satchel I'd carried from Backfox. But there was no great sentiment. The Palmers' Sunday dinner had to be made ready and served, even if it was a little late.

14.

"**I** don't know what you have done to deserve your fate, but you must have done something." Miss Bessie Richards said this to me on my first evening with her. She sat on a narrow bench looking across her small table into her small mirror much as Miss Palmer did each night, though she had little hair to brush and slight makeup to remove. The latter quickly done with and the former not bothered with, she turned.

"Sit."

There was a pair of armless chairs on either side of a window that overlooked Central Park with a round table between them. They were covered in a patterned fabric. The idea of sitting in one didn't occur to me until she ordered me to, as Miss Palmer had ordered me to on that strange day when we were first alone together. After I sat, so did she. I remained on the chair's front edge. She sat far back and began.

"How do you like to be called?"

I always had been, was, and expected I would always be known as Margaret. I'd never been asked about it though. I answered, "I like to be called Margaret."

"Margaret it shall be then," Miss Richards said. "Over time I hope you will trust me enough to tell me your secrets." She paused and smiled before adding, "if indeed you have any" and burst into laughter and I couldn't resist joining her. She turned to look at the pitch black in the park, except for some lanterns that marked the carriageway.

Had Mrs. Palmer wished to exile me, she could scarcely have done better than Abigail Richards. She was a widow whose husband died under most suspicious circumstances in a hotel room that was far from the family apartment. He was reputed to have entered said hotel room in the company of a woman who was decidedly younger—the desk clerk testified at the inquest, "likely to be much younger than the age of the wife a gentleman of the decedent's age and lack of attractiveness was likely to have." Which proved to be the case for while the woman who accompanied Mr. Evelyn Richards to the hotel was unlikely to be under thirty—though the clerk testified "she could have been ten years younger or twenty years older, it was hard to tell with what was on her face."

In any case, that Mrs. Abigail Richards was nearing fifty and appeared in the courtroom for the inquest and the witness said she wasn't the woman who accompanied Mr. Richards to his death, little more was formally said about who that companion might have been. She was last seen fleeing the hotel and calling back as she rushed through its lobby that "someone better see 'bout the condition of the gentleman in room 413."

Much was said *informally* about it. This resulted in Mrs. Abigail Richards being shunned by all in society except for one or two families that also came upon their money recently in the oil fields of western Pennsylvania, and several of which also had a troublesome but recently departed master.

It wasn't as though the Richards's house was decrepit. It was not even a "house" at all, but a collection of rooms in a newly built but exotic apartment building where, I learned, the people who lived there were hoping to become but were not as yet fashionable. Mrs. Richards took pains to make things as proper as possible.

In keeping with her style and her money, she spared no expense in the retention of staff, but all was held for one purpose. The development of Miss Bessie Richards. The Christian name predated the surname's wealth and Mrs. Richards resented her new-to-society daughter being stuck with it.

Bessie herself, though, didn't. And this was my first sign that while I was in exile for reasons I didn't and might never know, it might be an adventure for me after all. Bessie seemed so happy to tell me of her family's own adventures in great detail, which is how I learned what I just wrote about them.

Elinor Palmer was plain from the first time I saw her, even in makeup and a hand-made dress. Bessie Richards, though, couldn't be so easily labeled. She was only a few years older than me, I thought, but much older than me otherwise. She wore very short hair. I often saw a woman's hair up, much as Miss Palmer generally wore it, but that was all knots and curls and devices to keep it above the neck. With Miss Palmer, I loved to watch her curls released and falling over her shoulders as I imagined Niagara fell over its cliff.

Miss Richards's hair, though, couldn't be let down because there was nothing to let down. It was short-cropped and from some angles, I suspected it might confuse one into thinking she was a man.

Yet her features were the opposite of masculine. She had a face of porcelain smoothness and color that led down to a pointed chin. It was below a long, straight nose over lips that were small and narrow. Bessie Richards's eyes weren't narrow, though. They had a roundness and were displayed beneath very thin eyebrows that gave her a mysterious look, especially as it was beneath the short bangs of very black hair.

"So now you know our family's great secret. How my papa died. He was a philanderer before we were rich and was a philanderer to the end. How my mother bore it I don't know. Alas, he suffered, and we must suffer, from not the weakness of his character but the weakness of his heart. We were on a low rung given that we came from nothing and won some random prize, but we were at least on a rung. My mother believes we still are and that we might climb up again, but I know she's a fool in this. A lovable fool, but still a fool.

"I, of course, am in the worst position. I had money from when I was young and was sent to the proper schools and academies and tutors. I speak very properly and eat my food and drink my wine in perfect proprietiness. Invited to parties at good though not great houses. I found some friends. Until my papa died. Now none know me. We hire servants not because we need others to take care of us but because we still pretend to be in society though we barely were and were never fashionable. Merely tolerated. And that chapter is long gone."

"What shall you do? Surely you will marry."

I had listened to each word from my new mistress, and she turned to me with a smile.

"Marry? Whom shall I marry? More. Who shall marry me? There have been plenty of suddenly penniless girls in this world. Who shall I marry? Though I don't think I want to marry, it not being consistent with my own proclivities, but I may—"

"I'm sorry. Your what?"

"Proclivities. Natural tendencies or desires. In short, I don't know that I'll ever be attracted to a man, and I promise you that I never have been."

The conversation took a turn that neither of us anticipated, but Miss Richards kept going.

"I'll likely marry if for no other reason than my mother wants me to. But it won't be in America. England most likely. We shall find a penniless lord or duke or whatever penniless sorts they have there who is willing enough to sell a son, by which I mean a title, in return for some cash, of which we have quite a lot. I'll be allowed into society there as simply another of the American buccaneers who have invaded to rescue those entitled to be rescued, by which I mean those who have much land and no money but a title to bargain with.

"I'm not a handsome woman, but that won't matter, and I expect my groom won't be handsome either, if he settles on me."

I didn't think her *not* handsome. She seemed to enjoy making herself odd looking. I didn't dare tell her this. Her peculiar looks were caused by what she did to herself. Her shorn hair. Her not wearing makeup. That so far as I saw, she hadn't worn appropriate clothing. But I thought Miss Richards was a striking woman to look at. There were those who wouldn't consider her pretty, but there were many more who would think she was very pretty in some strange way.

These thoughts shot through me and as we sat we both looked out into the darkness. They didn't keep Miss Richards from saying what she had to say.

"I don't know, Margaret, how long we will even remain here. I cannot say where we will go or whether when we do go, we will take you with us. I believe Mrs. Palmer has played a cruel joke on you for I've my doubts that *anyone* will hire you in service once you are known to have had anything to do with us.

"Given who we are and who we are with, I doubt you'll ever run across Mrs. Palmer or anyone in her family again. I daresay that was what that good lady— who neither my mother nor I have met—intended."

I got up when she seemed done with what she had to say, and I finished my work in preparing my new mistress for bed. It didn't take long. Miss Richards preferred to do as much for herself as she could, and I was more a spectator than a participant as she removed each item of clothing. She was modest enough, though, to turn her back as she removed her robe and dropped her night dress over her head and down her back before turning and assuring me that she was well able to complete the tasks and to bid me a good night.

I had my own room. It was larger than the one in the Palmers' even though it was in an apartment and not a whole house. I think there were more servants once, but several left after the master died. It meant I had the room to myself.

Being alone, though, gave me ample time to think of Elinor and blaming her mother for exiling me from a woman that I was very, very fond of and who I greatly missed. But it couldn't be helped I supposed, and I was left to think of her as I lay in bed often before I drifted off most nights. She, though, was moving into my past, much as the Irish home I had for my first eighteen years already had.

Mrs. and Miss Richards, though, once had bigger plans when they came to town. It was now obvious, though, that the family would never amount to much in New York society. It was all uncertain until one night several months after I started when I was with Miss Richards in her bedroom as she undressed from a small party she went to without her mother. She had me sit on the bed. She turned to me from her vanity.

"It's been decided," she said. "That thing I spoke to you about."

"England?"

"Indeed. Mama and I are tired of being ignored here. She at least thinks our lives will be improved if I acquired a title. So that is what we are to do."

I should have been prepared for this, but I wasn't. I knew nothing of London, but I thought it must be very formal and I hadn't thought Bessie Richards could, well, survive there. Even as she told me their plans, I wasn't sure whether *she* thought she could survive.

"You must come with us," she said. "As with us, there is nothing for you in New York."

Much as I admired Miss Richards and her mother, I couldn't see how going to England would satisfy me, a poor Irish farmgirl at heart. And I told her so. She said I shouldn't be stubborn and that I should think on it before deciding.

I thought long and hard on it, I did. But I hadn't suffered the trip on the *Nevada* to flee to England less than two years later. I liked Miss Richards quite a lot but going to England meant I'd always be her servant. I don't think I was ambitious to be anything dramatic and I did suspect that I couldn't be a servant again in New York after the way I was dismissed by the Palmers and that I was a maid for the Richards but perhaps I could find something I would enjoy.

And perhaps I didn't want to be too far from Mrs. Ballard.

15.

It wasn't long after Bessie told me they were leaving that all the Richardses' things were packed up—the furniture was rented—and I watched their steamship pull from a dock and between a pair of tugs disappear down the Hudson on its way to London. They were very kind, and I was given a testimonial and a significant amount of money to carry me over until I found a new position.

As far as finding a place to live, I headed back to where I first was, not far from Mrs. Bulger's on Henry Street. The money I was given was enough for me to find a well-appointed boarding house on Broome Street. It was run by Sylvia Johnson, a widowed former slave from South Carolina who'd managed to scrape enough together since the war to buy the rundown place and fix it up. She welcomed me on Miss Richards's recommendation, and I had my own, small room on the third floor. It had an iron bed with a thick mattress, a small bureau, a desk and chair, and a wardrobe. Plus I got breakfast and dinner. It wasn't a permanent solution as kind as Mrs. Johnson was. The room and board were more than I could pay for very long so once I had a job I'd seek a room on a permanent basis.

After a few days of doing nothing but walking as far from the tenements as I could, I went to the House of Mercy. There I spoke with Sister Olson. I sat with her in her small office down the hall from the entry foyer and told her what had happened to me.

I promised her that I did nothing improper at the Palmers', and she told me she would write to Mrs. Palmer to confirm the fact. I also told her about being sent to the Richardses' and how they left me (though they did ask me to go with them), and while she said she didn't know the family, she said she'd inquire.

"I'm sorry it has come to this, my dear," she said as she stood, "but I'll see what I can do for you."

She told me to come back in a week. I spent that time again doing my walking. On the Thursday, I was back at the House of Mercy early, and she had one of the younger nuns bring me to her office.

"I'm afraid, Margaret," she said when I sat, "I don't know that I can be of much service to you. Mrs. Palmer replied to my letter." She nodded to a page covered in a dainty script on her desk. "And she said that while you hadn't done anything, as you say, that was improper, she does not feel that it would be appropriate for you to be placed in a house like theirs. She says she hopes you find a position that is satisfactory."

Sister Olson tapped one edge of the letter several times against the desk as she spoke.

"I don't understand it, Margaret. But if Mrs. Palmer won't speak kindly of you to another family, I think it will be very hard for you to find a position in service. I will, however, see if there is something I can possibly do."

I was shocked by this, by being abandoned when I knew I'd done absolutely nothing improper. Why would Mrs. Palmer not speak kindly of me? She admitted I hadn't done anything wrong. The nun said she'd been unable to get information to the Richardses let alone hear back, but that it was Mrs. Palmer's view that was the more important anyway.

Again, Sister Olson led me to the front door, and she apologized for being unable to do more. I left with no idea what was to become of me. It was clear that I should have gone to London with Bessie, but she and her mother were gone, and that prospect was gone with them, sailed away down the Hudson.

I began to get desperate. I still had money from the Richardses but it wouldn't last forever and I needed something to do. On a Sunday about a month after they left for England, without me, I stood outside the Church where the Palmer staff went to Mass. I saw Mrs. Burnley as she left, and I went to her. It was over six months since I'd seen her, on that horrible last day at the Palmers'. She and all the others tried to ignore me, but she was kind enough to finally step from them and wait for me. The others continued walking away.

"I need to find something, Mrs. Burnley. I will do anything. No one will hire me in a house after what happened with Mrs. Palmer and then where she sent me. Sister Olson from the House of Mercy wrote to her, but she refused to say that she thought I should be hired by anyone."

"I'm not supposed to have contact with you. That's what we were told. That's why everyone is so unfriendly like."

"I've been abandoned. I've no one and nothing except what the new family gave me before they left. I don't know what to do. I'll take any work."

"I don't know if you can work as a maid, after working for *that* family."

"I'll do anything within reason."

She looked to the side and then back at me.

"Do you remember Patrick Norman?"

"Of course. He and I spent time in Lenox getting the house ready for the family."

"Aye. He doesn't work at the house anymore. He works at a factory. The factory, last I heard, is over on Grand Street, off the Bowery. They make crinolines. I think they hire girls. If you're willing to work long and hard, I believe a decent wage can be had for you there. And, of course, you'd be freer than you were working in a house. Not at the beck and call of the family all the time. You can even get married, as Patrick has not long ago, so I hear. Go to him.

"He doesn't come to this church anymore. He lives not far from where he works and goes to Mass there with his new missus. A nice lass they say. Was once a nun at the House of Mercy, but they say they knew each other from way back. In any case, I expect he'll be at the factory in the morning. Go early and you might catch him."

I thanked her.

Before she left, she lowered her voice even more. "You should know, Margaret, that if you are truly in difficulty with money, I...I can get you some."

It was a peculiar thing to offer, and I had no intention of ever asking her. When I said nothing, she nodded and turned to go to the others. She stopped and turned back.

"Oh, goodness you, girl. You've been treated terribly bad. That's all I know. Terribly bad, and I hope someday you'll forgive me for what I did, because it was kindly meant." I didn't understand her. Her hand touched my wrist and without another word, she turned and soon caught the others, who'd waited about twenty yards away but too far to hear what we said. She reached them, and the staff headed off to get to the Palmers' so Sunday dinner wouldn't be late.

I had nowhere else to go and nothing and no one waiting for me so I thought I might as well look at the factory where Patrick Norman worked and where, God willing, I might find a job the next day. I walked to the Bowery and turned onto Grand Street.

16.

Walton & Co. was in a five-story brick building some twenty or thirty yards east of the Bowery. It had five rows of windows. "WALTON & CO." was painted below the roof in large black letters. The entrance was to the right side, a large door beneath a rectangular portico. To the property's left was an opening. It was where the loading docks were.

It was eerily quiet. I was never in the city, even on a Sunday, when it was so quiet. I could hear the carriages going up and down the Bowery and their sounds echoed between the factory buildings on Grand Street. The street itself, though, was quiet with not even a cart or wagon passing on it and it made me uncomfortable. I didn't linger but hurried back to the boarding house.

It got very cold overnight, and I found I'd covered myself in a blanket. It was early, but my landlady already had coffee brewing when I got downstairs to the kitchen not long after six-thirty. Mrs. Johnson made me eggs. I'd told her what I was doing when we sat in the parlor after dinner on Sunday night.

Rain had come with the cold, a nasty city rain rarely seen in County Mayo, but I had boots and a raincoat I could wear, and Mrs. Johnson lent me an umbrella.

The factory began working at eight. Twenty minutes before that, I stood next to a gaslight pole under the umbrella and could see workers as they came to the door. Men and women were already streaming in when I got there, and I hoped I hadn't missed Patrick. But then I saw him.

"Patrick," I called. Several men looked at me, so I added, "Patrick Norman," and all but one of the faces turned away. The one who kept staring came over to me slowly but he smiled when I lifted the umbrella so he could see it was me. Then he rushed to me and grabbed my arms, almost causing me to lose my grip on the umbrella.

"Is it you Meg Treacy? Really you?"

"'Tis me, Patrick. But I can't wait to chat. I need work, Patrick. I need work. Mrs. Burnley said you might be able to help me."

Ten minutes later I stood with Patrick in William Walton's office, holding Mrs. Johnson's umbrella to the side hoping he wouldn't notice it dripping on his fine floor. The office overlooked the main factory floor. While it seemed from the outside as if there were five stories inside, there were in fact only two.

On the main, factory floor was the machinery. The floor itself was divided in half. On the western side, the side where the front door was, there were several rows of equipment of varying sizes, the largest to the rear and the smallest to the front. On the other, eastern side of the hall were rows of materials, all stacked high, with ladders leaning against them. There was then a wall and I imagined that the loading docks were on the other side of it.

Soon after we were with Mr. Walton, a whistle sounded, and the factory filled with noise. Material being moved and the machines that fabricated the crinolines clacked. Mr. Walton said this would continue until seven, except for a few short breaks during the day.

I could see, and hear, the work through the window in Mr. Walton's office that overlooked the floor. The men worked throughout, but the women only on the tasks at the smaller machines to the left of where I stood, doing what I imagined was final construction before the product was stacked onto small carts, which were then pulled to the storage area, by the loading docks.

"Why should I hire you, Miss Treacy? I got hundreds begging to work here. Why you?"

"I have experience working on a farm at home."

"Working on a farm? A girl's work on a poor Irish farm? I got hundreds such."

I saw my prospects fading and was already thinking of where else I might go and who else I might see when old William Walton interrupted me.

"Aye," he said, his brogue somewhat softened by his time in New York but its origin in the north of Ireland clear. "Aye, but you have Patrick Norman here in your corner and he is a good man. One of my best. Miss Margaret Treacy, I'll be giving you a chance." He stood from behind his desk and was next to me and we turned to the glass overlooking the floor.

He pointed to the left, to the rows where women worked.

"I'll find someone who'll show you the ropes. I've just the one in mind. Look at what they do." He took me in again, in all my gangliness. "Do you think you can handle it?"

I took a look, trying to understand what it was that they were doing. "Yes, sir. I do believe I can handle whatever 'tis that needs handling."

Even I didn't know whether I believed what I said but I was determined to give it a try.

"Good lass. I give you two weeks. I'll keep an eye on you, and Mrs. Castor, the women I've a mind to watch over you and teach you, will be giving me regular reports. She's done it before, and I trust her as I trust your friend Patrick here."

He returned to his desk, and we sat back down. He told me what the pay would be, and Patrick said it was a fair wage for the work and that he and his Missus were able to live on it. I said I'd be happy to get it.

"You're not looking like you're able to work today, my dear." This was true since I was wearing my best outfit, though it was sopped at least insofar as it could be seen beneath the bottom of my raincoat with Mrs. Johnson's umbrella again across my knees. He smiled.

"I'll introduce you to Mrs. Castor before you go. We start work at eight. You have half an hour for lunch. Everyone brings their food. We have a place to eat upstairs. Mrs. Castor will show you.

"Then from one-thirty to seven, with fifteen minutes for tea at five. Except Saturdays. Then it's eight to noon and you are free for the weekend. Does that suit you, Miss Treacy?"

"It suits me indeed, sir."

The next morning at seven forty-five, I, grasping to remember what Mrs. Castor told me and hoping she would retell all that I forgot since leaving Mr. William Walton's building, arrived for my first day in his factory. The rain was long past and things had warmed up. I climbed the flights of stairs to the "ladies locker room" where I found the locker Mrs. Castor assigned to me. I placed my coat and shoes in the locker and replaced the shoes with a pair that Mrs. Castor told me to buy at a little shop on the Bowery that had ones that were comfortable enough so I could stand for as long as I had to stand for the job.

At my first lunch, I went up to Patrick in the eating room. He rose when he saw me and introduced me to everyone at his table. They were mostly, I thought, from Ireland but there were some dark men I imagined from Italy or thereabouts and some darker men I thought might have been slaves. They all welcomed me as the women had when Mrs. Castor introduced me when we started that morning.

Mrs. Castor seemed to know Mr. William Walton pretty well. She said the work was hard, but he wasn't a cruel boss. She said people worked better when they were treated decent, and his factory produced as much as did some of those run by cruel men and with fewer accidents on the floor.

"He's fair, but don't cross him or make trouble. We're treated well enough and things could be far worse than they are. Do your share, and we'll all be better off."

"My share" was pulling a spool of a pipe through the device and cutting it at the six-foot mark. The pipe was about one inch wide and made of pliable steel. It was a little difficult because the pipe was flexible so that the next person could make it round and connect the ends. It would then be placed in a frame for the crinoline.

Now, it was hard to get it to lie flat and be sure it was exactly six feet. If it was too long, the next girl would have to clip it and if it was too short it couldn't be used since the hoop would be, well, too small.

Several of the others laughed as I tried to get the pipe flat so I could cut it at the right length, though Mrs. Castor glared at them.

"Don't you worry, love," one of the others said, "we all had to wrestle with it afore we learned." She was nice and came to me and showed me just how one was supposed to wrestle it down. And when I had one that Annie, the next girl on the line, said was cut properly, they all clapped and laughed and the one who showed me said I would work out just fine and we all returned to our places. I took a look up at the window in Mr. Walton's office, and there he was, watching me. After the others clapped, though, when I looked up again he was gone.

Mr. Walton's ideas made the difficult work tolerable together with the understanding that Mr. William Walton thought it was best for his business to keep people working. There was the rare accident on the floor, but they weren't as frequent as at some of the other establishments nearby competing with Walton & Co. That competition was fierce, but the demand was great, and Patrick told me that a happy workforce in the end didn't hinder the company's ability to compete as far as he could tell and he didn't think it was worth the bother to move outside the city for cheaper labor, in part because of how much harder it'd be to get his supplies.

"But happy don't mean lax, Miss Margaret," he said, and Mrs. Castor echoed it. "We's all in it together and if one of us slacks off, it's the others that got to do her work. I rely on you and you rely on me and that seems to work out pretty good."

Several days later, as we were leaving, I asked Patrick if he knew where I might find a permanent place to live. He said maybe in his building. He told me to go there with him, and that very night I met with his landlady. The building was a cut above a tenement and was several blocks from the worst of the slums on Water Street. Sanitation facilities had been recently installed and there was a toilet on each of the five floors plus gaslights in the halls and in the apartments. There was a wee room available for me, though it was far, far larger than what I had at the Palmers'. It had a small kitchen with an icebox and a gas stove plus it came with its own set of cookware and plates and utensils. Even a sink to wash things up in or where I could get water to make tea.

The rent was within what I could pay. I was on the fourth floor, with a window to the back. Patrick and his wife, Cath, were on the floor below, though they looked over the front and their apartment was slightly larger, with a separate bedroom and a small sitting area in addition to a kitchen. They could afford it as Mrs. Norman—Cath—worked at a millinery factory several blocks from Walton & Co.

The room had furniture that was plain but sturdy and the mattress was only a few years old. There was even a small rug.

17.

It took several weeks, but I was able to meld with the other women who worked at my stage of the process. At Walton & Co. We did the final assembly of the crinoline used to define the bustle of a fashionable woman's dress, though they were increasingly drifting down to the dresses worn by the wives and daughters of lawyers and doctors and even tradesmen.

It also didn't take long for word to get around of the new unmarried Irish lass on the floor. A bit old, I think some thought, who'd been in service for some years but left for unknown reasons. Most were too polite to ask, and I told the others just that a member of the family took a disliking of me. The prospect of truly moving on and getting married and having a family excited me, I must confess.

Soon, more and more of the unmarried men were paying particular attention to me. I'm only human and I enjoyed the compliments that came my way. Suddenly I was full of thoughts of a husband and a room full of children. My children. I didn't know if it was what I wanted. I thought about it a lot, for sure, but it was also something of a dream of what I'd been told I should dream of.

Now because I *could* marry, I had to think on it harder. I enjoyed spending time with the others, often on a Saturday night at one of the taverns in the area in a group. I was having great difficulty, though, finding someone who I could fall in love with. I was so innocent when I should have been looking for someone who was stable and honest and, I hoped, handsome.

I often sat with Cath. She really couldn't tell me what to do. She was in Patrick's heart from when they were both young and had never left, as he had never left hers, though they spent that time apart when he worked for the Palmers and she was a nun. She told me that she'd been wrong when she thought she had a calling in that direction but that she was always free to leave.

Of those men who paid attention to me, Stephen Moore was the most interesting. He was from New York and, like Patrick Norman, his parents came early in the Hunger. He was a little on the short side and had dark hair that curled on his head. He was very proud of his mustache and beard. This I could see immediately when he was at the lunch table, sitting near Patrick, who assured me that he was a good lad all-in-all and that I could do worse than have him court me and maybe even do more than court me. And Patrick would wink and laugh when he said it.

With that, then, I said yes when Stephen Moore asked me to walk with him after Mass on the next Sunday.

"I don't normally go to Mass," he confessed, "but for you, I'll be happy to sing the praises of the Lord at the top of me lungs."

"You're the devil you are, Stephen Moore, and it'd be a good thing if you are not struck dead when you walk into the church but...I'm willing to brave the threat with you."

"That's kind of you, Margaret."

I leaned in. "Plus, I think the Lord must have a pretty good aim. I'll be safe enough even if I'm next to you."

I thought myself quite clever with this and Stephen Moore enjoyed it, and we entered together, with Patrick and Cath, for the nine o'clock Mass on Sunday. The four of us left together—Stephen Moore not being struck down as he crossed the threshold, coming or going—and it being a bright if nippy November day we strolled together and found a place to get some German pastries we could carry. We walked over to the east to the promenade along the East River and waved at the few boaters who sailed north and south in the current.

It was soon clear at the factory (especially among the women I worked with at my little station) that if anyone caught my fancy it was Stephen Moore. With each day, he seemed to be trying to land me. Bit by bit, walk by walk, Mass by Mass, we were spending much of our little free time together.

* * * *

CATH AND I WERE walking after one of those Masses some weeks later, though I surely don't remember a word of the sermon.

"Padraig says that Stephen Moore is quite fetched by you. He says that Stephen has been known to like to chase after the ladies, as they say, but seems to be thinking about settling down and seems to be thinking of settling down with you. Now, what do you say to that, Margaret Treacy?"

It was an overcast morning but very nice and we walked arm-in-arm in a group with the other women heading the four blocks home from Mass.

The men, at least those who could be convinced into going to Mass—Patrick and Stephen now included—wandered off to some field or other to watch the matches.

Cath and I were alone in the brief period before she had to start dinner. This happened to be a day when Patrick's parents were coming. It was quite stressful for her whenever they visited. Our walk beforehand was, I think, a pleasure for the both of us.

She got me to accept her invitation to dinner, as an ally against the formidable first Mrs. Norman—Patrick's mother. I had little else to do, of course.

To what Cath said, I told her that Stephen Moore seemed to be a fine gentleman but might have had a bit of the wandering eye.

"Ah, Margaret. He is a man. You must get used to it."

"Even Patrick?"

"Oh, he doesn't think I see him, but he cannot help noticing a pretty face. Especially if we happen upon the more fashionable person."

We'd reached our building and with her in-laws coming in less than an hour, we went straight to her apartment.

After spending I don't know how much time in the kitchen, there was a knock, and Cath said quite angrily, "I will kill him, you know. His parents are here, and he's not back."

As luck would have it, though, by the time Cath opened the door, Patrick was just getting to the landing and with a guilty smile and a panting breath, he followed his parents in.

I think I made a good impression with his parents, it being the first time we met. The talk often was on this or that bit of Ireland and what they remembered and missed about the place. Things were difficult back there when I left, but far worse for them in the early harshest days of the Hunger. I thought I might have brought back terrible memories but Mrs. Norman told me that seeing "such a fine young lass, from County Mayo of all places" made them happy about their new one, where Patrick and their other children had such great chances.

After they were gone and I myself recovered from some of the harshness of an Irishwoman's memories, Cath and I did quick work of tidying as Patrick did what he could to make up for being so late. Cath said she forgave him, it being his only day off for the week (which was also true of both of us women, but I kept this to myself) and we sat in their small parlor.

"I've just been telling Margaret how your Mr. Moore intends to court her."

"He isn't 'my Mr. Moore,'" Patrick made clear. "But he is serious, I believe. I've told you, Cath. Always telling tales of the women he has met and his plans for them until he meets another woman and tells the tale of his intending to at last settle down with her."

"Patrick," I said, "this isn't quite the most encouraging news."

"No. That be my point. He always did that till now. He's been with us when we've gone to entertainments. I think he's quite serious about you, Margaret Treacy."

I looked at Cath.

"How well do you know him?"

"Not well, I'm afraid. I've met him only a few times when he's been with Padraig and some of their friends. Several times we've been at taverns on a Saturday night together. And remember those walks the four of us had after Mass? But I always thought him harmless enough. Although that was when he wasn't seriously courting one of my good friends."

I looked at Patrick.

"I must be serious now. Should I doubt his sweet words if he says them to me?"

"He hasn't yet?"

"Well, perhaps, but only in the most indirect way. I need to know what I'm to do if he tells me he loves me."

"You must say you love him too. That is what you must do," Patrick said, and his wife interrupted.

"You can be a fool, Padraig Norman." She turned to me. "Do you think he will?"

"What? Love me? Or say he loves me?"

Cath turned back to her husband. "That is just it, Padraig. A woman won't say it unless she means it, deeply and truly. A man, though, is more inclined I think to say it if he thinks it is what the woman wants to hear."

"'Tis not true."

"Padraig. You won't recall, but I remember when you first said you loved me and surely you didn't *really* love me yet. You liked me, quite a bit. But it was too early to love."

"I'm sure when I said it, I meant it in some way."

His wife turned to me. "Do you see what I mean? To a man, there are degrees of love."

"But," I said, "are you saying one cannot be immediately in love with someone?"

"I suppose. But life isn't some fairytale. I'll tell you that."

"Then how long before you loved Patrick? If you do love him."

"You are an awful woman," she laughed. "Of course I love him. I've loved him for many years now. But as I think on it, 'twas several months after I met him that I *knew* it. Even when I was at the House of Mercy I think I knew it. Though I must confess that I may have loved him without realizing it for some time before that."

"See? So, you admit that I may have loved you that first time I said I did, by your own definition."

Cath reached a hand to her husband's skin. "Yes, Padraig, part of you may have loved me when you said it. I just am not sure what part," and while his triumph was somewhat lessened by what his wife said, he couldn't deny that he too had long loved her.

But that was also a fairytale. He turned to me after his wife's hand left him.

"Seriously, Margaret. I canna promise Stephen Moore is being completely honest in what he says about you, about deciding he wishes to be in love with you. I can say that I've never seen him so...smitten. He is I think in his heart a good man and you would be a...you should give him every chance to fall in love with you and for you to fall in love with him."

That night, as I lay in bed, my thoughts naturally stayed close to Stephen Moore and whether I might fall in love with him.

18.

After my talk with Patrick and Cath about Stephen Moore, Stephen paid more attention to me. I liked it. On a Saturday a few weeks later, Cath told me she was pregnant. She came up to the fourth floor. Before she left, we knelt by the bed and said a rosary. I didn't know for how long Cath waited to become pregnant, but I was overjoyed.

In the morning, I knocked at her door so we could walk to church together. Patrick was in his best. Cath was direct with both of us. We weren't to breathe a word.

"Too much could go wrong, and I couldn't handle the humiliation or sympathy if it did. I'll be showing soon enough but until then no one can know."

This created no difficulty for poor me, of course, seeing as the only person I would be tempted to share this news with was Cath herself. But it took a bit to get Patrick to understand how hurtful it would be for Cath if he revealed the secret and something bad happened. Before the three of us left, she was satisfied that Patrick wouldn't say anything.

In the end, he succeeded. As the three of us walked to the house after Mass, with him between us. It was all wonderfully nice, even with a cold and windy air.

Things quite changed in a different way not long after that. Stephen Moore was with us at the Goat's Head on a Saturday night. This was an Irish pub on the corner of the Bowery and Houston Street. It had a small stage and was known for having players and singers from different parts of the old country who'd nearly always end up leading everyone in a sad, sad song of home or some rebel anthem.

It wasn't too far from where we all lived. The place had a low ceiling and more than one Irishman said it did a good job of feeling like a pub at home. It was popular and loud and stinking on a Saturday night, though not so loud and stinking as to keep women like me and Cath away.

On this Saturday night, we four sat so Patrick and Stephen Moore faced one another and so did Cath and me. I wasn't prepared when Stephen, to my right, reached under the table for my hand. He wasn't looking at me but at Patrick when his fingertips ran across the back of my hand in my lap. I pulled it away without a thought and suddenly both his hands were on the table.

He left me alone as to touching for the rest of our time there, though we enjoyed the conversation with the others. It was like the touching never happened.

Walking home, I was quite beside myself from what he'd done, though whether my thoughts were good ones or bad ones I couldn't honestly say. Cath and Patrick were in front, but they were quiet, and Stephen slowed and I slowed. A gap opened to our friends, and even I finally realized what Stephen was up to and I think our friends must have known it because they kept going and moved away from us. I didn't object. It gave Stephen and me the chance to walk alone and I didn't pull away when he put his arm through mine.

It suddenly felt completely natural. It was the first sign that I might have become very fond of him. I thought he was honest and sweet with me.

That night, we reached the building too soon for my liking. I had never been so close to a man. I found it a comfort, but it didn't last long enough for me as we reached the stoop. The Normans waited for us. Stephen said goodnight all around and shook Patrick's hand before leaving for his place. I followed the others up the stairs, but Cath told Patrick she wanted to speak to me, and she kept going to my apartment.

As soon as we were sitting, Cath asked what I now thought of him.

"I don't rightly know," I said. "I've never been with a man, someone who might be a beau. Do you know he touched my hand below the table?"

"What did you do?"

"I pulled my hand away, of course. Then he kept both his hands on the table for the rest of the night."

Cath couldn't control her laugh. She rolled and then shook her head at me, and I began to get angry at her.

"Oh, Meg, I truly am not laughing at you. You're so innocent. Padraig and I wondered why he kept his hands on the table and didn't move 'em. Didn't you know what Stephen meant?"

"How was I to know what he meant without his telling me?"

"You cannot be so naïve. What do you think courtship is about? It's about the little things. It's about a man wanting to feel a woman's skin, to touch her hand. You had no trouble with him putting his arm through yours as we walked back, did you?"

"No. It seemed natural."

"That's just it. A little touch of the hands that only the two of you would know of. That is courting. Aye, Stephen seems a bit pushier than Padraig was, even though he and I were friends before. He was such a clod and Stephen is a bit too easy with his affections, but from all Padraig tells me he is a good man, ready to find someone. And from looking at him, the way he looks at you, I think he might think that you are that woman."

"I don't know what to say. Worse, I don't know what to do with him."

"I think you must give him a chance. If he does something that makes you uncomfortable, tell him to stop. If he's a good man, like Padraig says and thinks he is, he'll not push things on you till you're ready, much as he might wish it. Were you pleased when he touched your hand under the table?"

"Well, I was surprised more than anything. But I think I *was* very pleased when we walked and his arm was through mine."

"When he does it again, you must tell him that. 'Tis courtship, as I say, and you must let it take its time and you must enjoy it and use it to find if you love him."

"'Love'? I can't imagine that."

She laughed.

"Oh, Meg. You are so naïve, as I say. If it be love, you'll know it. You must give it a chance. You must let him hold your hand."

I did feel the fool. Cath stood and gave me a kiss on the forehead and left me to my thoughts, which quickly moved to Stephen Moore and how, yes, I would like to hold his hand properly.

* * * *

CATH WAS VISITING ME after work on the Saturday afternoon. Patrick and Stephen were watching some sort of game in a field up north off the East River. She and I dressed up and took a trolley over to Broadway to gawk at the displays in the department store windows.

It was too loud to talk as we rocked on the trolley. I'd only been to this fashionable part of town once or twice, when Miss Palmer was on the way to her trying dresses on and buying things.

As I rode with Cath, I thought of those long-ago happy days, and it was hard to get what happened with the Palmers out of my mind. It was a lifetime ago.

And it was shortly after we began our stroll that Cath said she and Patrick couldn't go to the nine o'clock Mass in the morning.

"Padraig's parents want us to go to Mass with them at their church so it'll be just you and Stephen tomorrow."

She paused. "He's quite fond of you, Padraig says. Are you fond of him?"

I was. Since that night at the pub where he tried to touch my hand under the table and on the street when our arms were together. After my little talk with Cath, barely a night passed when I didn't float myself asleep thinking of him.

"Oh, Cath. I believe I'm quite fond of him."

At about eight-forty the next morning, I met him in front of my building. He wore a fresh carnation in his lapel. His suit was freshly ironed. For all his charm, Stephen was lazy about his dress, but it was clear that he could look very handsome indeed if he set his mind to it. He had set his mind to it that morning.

For my part, I also made a particular effort. Cath helped me. She came up an hour earlier "happening to have been out and happening to see some small flowers I thought would go well in my hair" so that when I looked into my mirror shortly before I left, the person who looked back seemed a more handsome version of myself.

Now, leaving Mass and walking east, I leaned towards him and placed my head against his shoulder as I allowed him to ramble on about some or other political event without listening because my thoughts, and I suspected his too, were all about what we'd say to each other when we finally got to the promenade.

The river was five-and-a-half long blocks away. The sky was overcast, but it didn't seem that rain was coming. I had an Irish farmgirl's eye for such things. Since that night when I reacted as I did to Stephen's touch, I often found an excuse to touch his hand and though I didn't feel a jolt as I thought I was supposed to, it was very pleasant.

Tugs were going up and down the river. Mostly they were tending barges. None of the steamships ventured this way. I always found the spot bracing. I couldn't help but look to the south, where on one of those piers I arrived in America. Now I stood there with an American I hoped would make love to me with his words. That he would begin and his words would wash over me. He was no poet. That didn't matter. All that mattered was that *he* said them.

Stephen had quit his political discourse some blocks from the promenade. It wasn't crowded. We turned to the south and I looked down and then we stood side-by-side along the wrought-iron rail and held it as we watched a schooner ride the slight tide north.

I thought he was turning to me, but he stopped. After this happened two or three times, with me waiting until my part was to begin, he finally did turn to face me.

"You must know how I feel about you, Margaret. Surely you must. I'm, you know, not a rich man but I think myself an honest one and I know Patrick and Cath have told you so. I have, sweet Margaret, never been so...well never been so firm in my view that I'll be happy through all eternity if you was to be my wife."

His words tumbled faster as he went. I thought he cut down what he intended to say and likely had practiced again and again to say so he could get it out as quickly as possible.

He looked at me. For all I realized later, I was surprised more than anything but thought that I must accept his proposal. As he said, Patrick and Cath spoke so well of him.

I had no experience with men and doubted I ever would have a better chance at winning a good one. I said, "Yes, Stephen Moore, I will marry you." Stephen grabbed me by the waist and pulled me to him so that he could at last place his lips on mine and we could seal our agreement that I would become Mrs. Stephen Moore.

Though it was a chaste kiss, it was enough for us both, and in a moment, he had turned from the water and was telling me we had to go and tell Patrick and Cath. I said they'd gone to Mass with the Patrick's parents. He said, "well if they aren't at home, we'll just have to wait till they are."

They were at home. They left Patrick's parents as soon as their Mass ended. All talk turned to when the wedding would take place. It would be a small event given the few friends we had.

19.

On the Sunday when the third and final bann was read for my wedding with Stephen Moore, he and I sat together, with the Normans in what had become our usual pew at Immaculate Conception for the nine o'clock Mass. As happened the first two times, we were congratulated by parishioners as we left.

At the sidewalk, though, I saw an older woman off to the side. I told Stephen and my friends to go to the Normans, that there was someone I had to see. She was in her Sunday best. She didn't move as I went towards her. Her head dipped slightly as I got close but she looked up when I got to her. She had a forced smile. I looked back. The others were watching whatever I was doing. I didn't dare introduce her to them, though Patrick surely recognized her.

"Mrs. Burnley, I'm happy to see you. You must've heard my banns in church."

"I did, my dear. I heard about then some days ago. Do you have time to walk?"

"As much as you'd like."

We turned east and quickly reached Fourth Avenue and turned up it.

"I'm afraid I've not been so considerate of you as I might have been, Margaret. But first, let me ask you. Do you love this Stephen Moore?"

This caused me to stop. "Love? Of course I do. I wouldn't be marrying him if I didn't."

She put her hand on my wrist and smiled. "That's all I wanted to know. Good luck to you both."

She removed her fingers and turned. I said, "Mrs. Burnley. It's a strange question. Why do you ask?"

She turned back and again stepped close to me. After a pause and a deep breath, she in a very low voice said, "I need you to be honest with me. More than anything you have ever told *anyone*. You must believe me. Do you *love* him? Does your blood run fast when his fingers touch you?"

I smiled. "Mrs. Burnley. Are you becoming a romantic?"

She didn't return my smile but was all seriousness. "Child. I wasn't always so old, though that may surprise you. I had a husband as a young woman. My dear Mr. Burnley. He was a good man. I enjoyed being with him. But—" She stopped and turned to look at me. "He didn't make my blood run hot. *Ever.* I was glad to have married him and I was sad when he died and that we didn't have any children, and I had to go into service." I realized that she'd grabbed my wrist again.

"I've had a good life. Yet I still think whether there might have been a man somewhere who'd make my blood run had I just waited. I met one or two who might have, but it was too late for me."

"I'm sorry, Mrs. Burnley. I cannot fathom what you are going on about. Does Mr. Moore make my blood run? Well, it hasn't yet but I'm sure once we're married it will be running well fast enough for a household of Moores."

I pulled my hand from her and resumed walking, and Mrs. Burnley waited a moment before catching up to me.

"I said I wasn't kind to you."

We stopped again.

She reached into her pocket and removed an old, yellowed envelope.

"Part of me doesn't regret not giving this to you when I might have. I thought it was for the best. Mrs. Palmer agreed. She and I both suspected what's in it, though neither of us knows for sure. I would never give it to you if I thought you loved this Stephen Moore as a woman must love the person she'll spend the rest of her years with. That's why I asked you my strange questions.

"I give it to you now. Mrs. Palmer knows what I'm doing. Perhaps it's my guilt. But I'm convinced it's the right thing for everyone. Don't open it now. I'll leave you with it."

She paused. "I'm afraid I leave you with a hard choice. You know this letter exists. You can't unknow that. But if you truly love Mr. Moore with all of your heart, you have to destroy it. If you don't, Margaret Treacy, I beg you read it. And I hope to God that I'm doing the right thing."

She handed the sealed envelope so I couldn't see who it was addressed to and, more importantly, who wrote it. I didn't understand what she meant, but I took it and put it in my purse.

"Thank you, Mrs. Burnley. Before you go, though, if I read this letter, may I come to you at the Palmers to talk about it? Will I make things difficult for you if I do?"

"You won't, my dear. You can come. As I said, Mrs. Palmer knows what I'm doing."

She leaned and hugged me tightly.

She whispered, "You deserve your happiness, my dear."

She pushed away and with a last look, in which I saw a tear, which I could never have believed she could have shed, she turned and went south on Fourth Avenue. I did nothing until she was out of sight. I took the envelope from my purse. It was Elinor's handwriting. It was a very long time since I'd seen it, but I knew it at once. *Would opening it betray what I had with Stephen?* I couldn't undo opening it.

I started walking back to my apartment. My fiancé would be waiting for me at the Normans'.

With the letter tightly in my right hand, I walked and soon was on my block and I walked down it and then I was past my building and my apartment and the Normans and my fiancé. I continued and continued east until I could continue no more. I stood on the promenade along the river with its familiar iron rail and groups of friends and lovers waving at the passing boats.

After looking out over to Brooklyn, I found a bench and sat. I looked at the letter. I thought of what it meant if I just opened it. This was a voice from when we were both such different people. I could throw it into the river and go to my Stephen and Cath and Patrick and the rest. A few steps, a simple toss from my hand, and it would be gone. Forever.

I knew that's what I *should* have done. It's not what I did. I didn't. I didn't get up. I stared at the envelope I gripped in my fingers. Before I knew what I was doing, before I could *stop* what I was doing, it was open, and I pulled the letter out.

My Dearest Margaret,

I hope that someday you will forgive me. I cannot imagine fulfilling my new duties while carrying thoughts of you. I cannot help but be burdened by those thoughts, but I am a coward and I at least can remove the sight of you from my life forever.

Please do not blame my dear mama or Mrs. Burnley. I have spoken to them about this, and they have counseled me about doing one's duty.

I know your being cast off in a manner that I hope will assure that we never cross paths again, however accidentally, will impose a hardship on you. I have had my mother make arrangements so that you can find an appropriate position with a family that orbits far from my own dear family's circle. I know of the girl in the family who you will serve and from all reports, though she has her oddness, she will be kind to you and, I hope, will ease you in forgetting me.

I fear that I will have no such diversion. But it is for the best. I cannot do what I wish to do so I do what I must do. I will be Mrs. Francis Ballard and my only hope is that there might come a day when you remember there was a young woman named Elinor Palmer who found your touch the most magical thing she could imagine.

> *Yours in love,*
> *Elinor Palmer*

PS

I realize that I may create an impossible financial burden on you. Although Mrs. Burnley does not know the specific words I write, she knows their tenor. If there comes a time when you have a need for financial support of any kind, you must go to her. I have made arrangements so that she will make any amount available to you for your needs. I make this offer not as compensating you for having abandoned you because I know that no amount of money can do that. I do it because I could not bear knowing that my actions caused you to become financially destitute. And for no other reason.

EP

It was from so long ago, but it all came back. Like everything was yesterday. Elinor. But why did Mrs. Burnley and Mrs. Palmer decide to give it to me *now* and not then?

Looking out over the river wouldn't tell me. Only Mrs. Burnley's story about her own empty marriage could explain it. That wasn't enough, though. Perhaps something she had discovered about Elinor.

I stood and walked to the rail with the letter clutched in my right hand. Perhaps if I threw it in, even after I read it, it would be gone along with what it said. But Mrs. Burnley *had* come and I *had* opened the envelope and I *had* read what was inside. I now knew what Elinor said and why she'd abandoned me.

Elinor confessed to being a coward. But she did her duty and, I realized, I knew *nothing* about what happened to her since I received news of the wedding. I was no longer in service and didn't know people who knew or cared about the likes of Mr. and Mrs. Francis Ballard. I didn't read papers that made any mention of them. She could have a brood of children. Indeed, I understood that love was rarely an element of a marriage among members of society families and yet were all the brides and all the grooms not searching for, as Mrs. Burnley put it, someone whose touch would make their blood run?

I didn't think I needed the money or security or prestige that becoming Mrs. Stephen Moore would provide me. I was valued by Mr. William Walton. My job and my friendships, though there were only a few of those.

I walked from the water and to my building and towards the third floor and then my fist was knocking on the Normans' door and there were cheers nearly all round as I entered. I didn't sit.

"Stephen. You are very kind to me. But I cannot marry you. I'm sorry."

I turned and was going down the steps before the other three could react but hadn't reached the street when I heard footsteps, which I knew were Stephen's, fly down the stairs and I waited at the top of the front stoop for him. I owed him that.

"What do you mean you can't marry me?"

"I don't love you Stephen. I realize that I never will."

"But I—"

"No, Stephen. You like me a great deal. As I like you. But neither of us should settle for that." I ran my hand across his cheek. "I do like you a great deal. But it isn't enough."

With that, I, the great fool that I was, stepped to the sidewalk and began walking to the avenue, not looking back.

20.

Before anything else, I had to see Mrs. Burnley. I was a fool for not doing that before saying what I did to Stephen, but I had *said* it. I said I couldn't marry him and I couldn't take it back.

Mrs. Burnley told me I could go see her. It wasn't far. The walk to Twenty-Eighth Street, through the Sunday strollers helped me calm down. But with each step, I became more and more afraid that I was a great fool for what I threw away with Stephen. It was too late to do anything about that. Yes, I could say I was afraid but had recovered my senses and was ready to move forward with him.

Mrs. Burnley, though, had touched something deep in me. I couldn't change *that*. Or change what those slight but never completely forgotten touches from so long ago did to me. I'd go in the Palmers' service entrance and through the kitchen to Mrs. Burnley's little office. We could talk. Perhaps I could understand why she gave me the letter after all this time.

I was going down Twenty-Eighth Street from the west and had to pass in front of the Palmers' house to get to the door below the stairs. I was afraid I might be seen from inside, so I kept my head down.

Just before turning to go through the gate, however, I ran smack into a woman. She either didn't see me or expected I'd get out of her way. She was very well dressed. As I began to apologize, I saw she was with Elinor. I was sure Elinor recognized me.

Her friend was very fast in mocking me before I could do or say anything, not that I knew what to do or say.

"What have we here? Some sort of illiterate factory or peasant girl in *this* neighborhood. Elinor, what shall we do with her, the idiot?"

There seemed to be, I think, a pause before Elinor said, "Oh, I'm sure she is lost, and we should step aside and leave her to go on her way. Perhaps she'll find where she's supposed to be."

With a laugh, the two went up the steps to the front door. The other, taller woman called to me, "You should learn to watch where you are walking, girl." I can't say that she did, but Mrs. Ballard might have laughed at this. The pair was quickly inside as the door was opened a second before they reached it and closed as quickly. I was left alone on the sidewalk.

I knew Elinor recognized me. Whatever excitement I had about seeing her was replaced by shock at how she reacted when she saw me.

I felt for her letter in my pocket. I was too confused to dare see Mrs. Burnley right then. Instead, I walked the mile or so back to my apartment. Cath was on the stoop. I ignored her. She followed me up and into my apartment.

"Please, Cath. My life's fallen to pieces, and I can't think. You must leave me."

"I won't. What sort of friend would I be if I left you like this? I'll just sit here until you're ready to say something."

"Do whatever you want. I don't care."

She sat in one of my simple wooden chairs, and I found myself sinking down the wall next to it. She put her hand on my head for what seemed like a very long time.

"A chapter of my life opened up," I finally said. If I'd told her of Mrs. Ballard at all, it was simply in telling her the mystery of my dismissal from the Palmers' house.

"So that's what that woman spoke to you about after church?"

"Aye." I turned so I had my back to the side of the chair as I sat on the floor with my legs stretched in front of me. I was speaking not at Cath. I was looking in front of me. My voice was calm and smooth.

"She was the housekeeper in the first house where I was a maid and where I met Patrick."

"Aye, I know about it."

"I became attached to the youngest daughter, a little older than me—I was nearly nineteen—but when she was engaged, I was sent away and I never saw her again. Until today.

"The family wasn't so cruel as to leave me with nothing. They found me a position with a family that was very unlikely to have any contact with them, and I was happy enough there. The girl at the first house was married. She was on her wedding trip when I was dismissed. I was happy enough in the new house, but they had money and no class, and the father was dead, so the mother and her daughter went off to England to find someone with a title and that was that. They'd offered to take me but like a fool I said no.

"I met Patrick at the first house and got his name from the housekeeper when I left the second one."

"Why didn't you get a position at another house, as a servant?"

"I tried, but word went around that I wasn't to be hired, I guess because of a fear that I would run into the girl from the first house. But Patrick gave me the chance to meet with Mr. Walton, who hired me.

"What I found out today was that it was the first girl who got me dismissed, not her mother as I thought. The girl wrote me a letter explaining. At the time, her mother and the housekeeper—she's the one who came to me today—decided that I not get the letter. That it was better that I was ignorant of it. The girl never knew that."

I reached into my pocket and gave her the now crumbled letter.

"Please. Read it."

I watched her do it, though I don't think it was that easy for her. She handed it back, and I said I realized I couldn't truly love Stephen Moore and that I had to try to have something to do with Elinor, in a way I couldn't yet imagine or understand.

"So, I went to the house to see the housekeeper. I was about to go in through the servants' entrance when I ran into her, the girl, on the sidewalk. And…she just ignored me. She was with a friend and she treated me like a stranger. I know she recognized me. Yet she ignored me. Oh, Cath. I'm an idiot for what I did with Stephen."

She ignored my last point. "What are you going to do now?"

"I'll write to Mrs. Burnley, the woman you saw. I'll try to find out why I was treated by Elinor as I was, if she knows."

I wrote a brief note to Mrs. Burnley, asking if we could meet on the next Sunday after Mass. I thought of delivering it to the house myself but decided to get a boy to do so. I found one on the corner as I went to work in the morning and after I gave him a coin he brought it to the Palmers'.

After some miserable days, when I got home from the factory on Thursday, there was a note under my door.

My dear Margaret,

I must beg your forgiveness. I have been advised in no uncertain terms that Mrs. Ballard has no interest in having any interaction with you ever again. I regret that I presumed otherwise when I contacted you. More, I regret if you have broken off your engagement. I hope you can recover with him.

I cannot tell you how sorry I am for what I did. I can only hope that in time you will think that it was done with the best of motives and that you can someday forgive me.

Mrs. Estelle Burnley

I'd been a fool. Again. More than anything, *why did I not be sure about Elinor before breaking with Stephen?* Making things even worse was that much as I regretted having done what I had done with him I might be glad of it. *Glad I wasn't marrying him.*

It all made life difficult for me, and for him, at Walton & Co. Mr. Walton had to be told.

Of course, no other respectable man at the firm would have anything to do with me. People again spent their idle time speculating why I did this strange thing. I did what I could to tell people that Stephen was entirely blameless in the matter. "No," I said more than once, "a question was raised about my past that made it unfair to insist that Stephen carry through on his proposal."

It wasn't much, but it was all I could think of, and if it didn't make me look good, it was what I deserved. Remember, many of them were already suspicious about why I wasn't a maid anymore.

But the tension didn't last. While I think Mr. Walton liked me, he had to dismiss me. Two weeks after Mrs. Burnley turned my world upside down, it was further upset by me leaving a job I enjoyed and that gave me the freedom to live alone and be independent.

All was not lost as to Mr. Walton, though. He spoke to a man who operated a similar factory blocks away and though it was not as welcoming as was Walton & Co., it was good work and I was glad to have it. I did not stay in my apartment long after that. I made Patrick and especially the very pregnant Cath uncomfortable. I found a smaller, darker, and more expensive let well away, and that's where I lived alone and lonely.

21.

It wasn't unusual for a fine carriage to be waiting outside my new church on a Sunday morning, to take a society family home. But I'd never seen one after the early Mass, the one attended mostly by laborers and seamstresses. And now, by me.

But there was the fine, dark green brougham. All the parishioners noticed it and the footman in full livery standing by its door. A white-gloved hand reached out and tapped the footman's shoulder and pointed. It pointed at me, and he followed the glove's direction.

"Excuse me, Miss. My mistress would like a word," he said as if I were somebody. Of course, I followed him. He opened the door and folded down the steps and I climbed in. There I saw and couldn't believe there sat Bessie Richards herself.

"Oh, don't look so shocked, my dear. You aren't an easy woman to get a hold of. But I'll tell you about it as we go."

She looked out. "Desmond. We are ready to leave," and in a single motion the steps were up and the door was shut. Desmond was in place at the rear as the coachman drove us into the street.

"I'm not kidnapping you, my dear. We're going to a little hide-away not far from my old house where neither of us need worry about how people look at us.

"You are anxious. Perhaps wondering what you should call me? Well though I'm in fact Lady Glendale, some chosen few call me Bessie and I wish you to be among them. Is that all right, my dear?"

I burst into a smile and reached for my former mistress's hands.

"Oh, Bessie. You cannot know how glad I am to see you."

"Tsk, tsk Margaret. I was made aware, I'll not say how, that you have run into a string of difficulties lately and it was the least I could do to do whatever it is I can do about it. If that makes sense.

"Because you are undoubtedly curious, I will tell you. After some time in London, my mother was able to find an appropriate, that is poor enough and desperate enough, member of the aristocracy who I could give some of our money to in exchange for a title.

"I was not one of those stupid creatures who surrenders all her family's fortune for one. His father wanted it all, of course, but my mother pointed out to him that there were plenty more sons where his own son came from and not nearly so many more where I came from. So, I had our lawyer here in New York—I didn't trust any of those in London—set up some kind of trust or something to protect me. And my money."

I was again impressed by Bessie's ability to speak without seeming to take a breath. I never knew anyone like her.

"Well, Lord Glendale and his father and duckface of a mother are still in London or out in the country shooting something or other while my mother and I return to the Colonies for a bit of fresh air because, my dear, if there is a trace of truly fresh air in England I have yet to breathe it in. But we will be going back soon enough, so I need to enjoy every moment that

I'm here, and what better way to enjoy a moment in New York than to spend it with you?"

As this last rolled from her tongue, the carriage pulled in front of a building on Sixth Avenue. It was large and took over the entire north-south block. In the center was a series of steps, and a glass awning framed in black iron sheltered it.

Before the wheels stopped, Desmond was opening the door. Before her ladyship and I rose, the steps were down.

"Thank you, dear Desmond," she said as he helped her get out. I thanked him as he did the same to me and though I'd rarely been in such a fine carriage, this time I managed to get out without falling. As we walked up the hotel's front steps, a hotel doorman opened one of the tall doors for us. Bessie turned and said, "Oh my, I hope I've not altered something you planned to do. If I have, you must tell me and we will return you to wherever you would rather be."

"I assure you, Bessie, there is no place in the world I'd rather be than with you." Which was true.

I went to early Mass to avoid seeing people who knew of me and Stephen Moore. Most sadly, this included Cath Norman and her, and Patrick's, little baby. I visited her and the baby sometimes when Patrick was off playing or watching some sport, but Sundays she spent with Patrick and with his or her family after nine o'clock Mass.

Ever since what happened with Stephen Moore, my Sundays began early and extended alone. Including, as I said, going to a different church. In nice weather, like it was the day Bessie Richards appeared, I walked for miles and miles, stopping in taverns for food and drink.

On this Sunday, I followed Bessie through the lobby and then up the marble staircase at its far end and then up two narrower flights until we entered the suite at the southern end of the hall.

Bessie said she'd asked her mother to find something to do while she entertained her friend—me—and the sitting room was empty. It was imposing but comfortable with chairs arrayed in clusters throughout and several pieces of fine furniture. The paper was a dark red with cream trim and fine molding. The room was still bright to the south and the curtains were open, so the sun filled it.

Bessie had on the type of relaxed ensemble she wore when I worked for her. She took her low boots off when she sat and ran her stockinged toes through the thick pile of the rug.

She insisted that I, in a chair opposite her, do the same. Off went my boots. I never felt something so soft below my feet and I laughed at it, though I didn't mean to. She jumped up and pulled a cord. What seemed an instant later, there was a knock on the door and Bessie said, "Please come in."

A hotel servant, a handsome man of perhaps twenty in a short white jacket and black trousers, entered and bowed.

Bessie waved to him.

"Please, please come in."

She turned to me.

"You must order any food and drink that your heart desires, Margaret. Anything at all."

"May I have eggs and sausage?" I asked her.

"Margaret. Anything means anything. You may have the whole chicken if you want. Just tell him."

I looked back and forth between the two.

"I should like some eggs, please."

"How would you like them prepared, Miss?" the servant asked.

"I should like them scrambled, I think. And sausage and bacon and toast, please."

He took down what I wanted. "And to drink?"

I looked at Bessie. "May I have an ale?"

With a laugh, Bessie turned to the servant, "Bring us several ales and I'll have what she is having but also bring us some fruit."

With a bow, he left and the two of us were again alone.

"You must promise never to tell a soul what I'm having," I said, and Bessie laughed again.

There was a sofa against one wall, with a painting of a river and some hills and a bright blue sky with a few clouds. Bessie walked to the sofa, and I followed and we sat at either end.

"I would have searched you out anyway, but I did so as soon as I could when I heard about what has happened to you since we left one another. But you must thank Mrs. Burnley if you are pleased to see me, as I hope you are. Apparently, your Mrs. Palmer saw a notice in the paper that I—'Lady Glendale that was Bessie Richards'—had returned for a visit, and she told Mrs. Burnley and they decided it would do well for me to speak with you."

She got up and went to the small bureau near the window. From a drawer, she pulled out a small envelope and handed it to me before she sat.

Dear Lady Glendale,

You may recall me as the woman who employed Margaret Treacy before she worked in your house and before you sailed to England, where I understand you have fared quite well.

I fear that Miss Treacy has not fared so well and that I am a reason for her misfortune. It is not for me to betray things that are confidential. All I can say is that with Mrs. Burnley, our housekeeper, we told Miss Treacy things that caused her to end an engagement with a man. We believed we were acting in her interest but now think it was the opposite.

I do not know to whom else I can turn. I understand that you treated her kindly when she worked for you. I ask only that if at all possible you speak with her and offer to do whatever you can to be of assistance to her, for which I will be forever in your debt.

Sincerely,
Mrs. Arthur (Natalie) Palmer

I looked up when I was done.

"Tell me what happened," she said in a far more serious tone than she used earlier.

I went from the note to her and back. I took a breath just as there was a knock at the door. To Bessie's "enter," the hotel servant came in with a tray. With practiced smoothness, he set our breakfasts on a dining table that had a view out the window. He stepped to the side and waited for us. He pulled out Bessie's chair and after she was comfortable he hurried around to my side and we repeated the ritual, which was very awkward for me.

"I've brought a pot of coffee and cups and saucers, et cetera," he said, "in case you would like that too. When you are done, simply pull the cord and I'll clear everything away for you."

We thanked him.

"We will hold off the continuation of your telling me of your woes until we have finished this feast." With that, we gossiped about nonsense until we were both full. Bessie rose and pulled the cord, and the young man took everything away but the ales, the coffee, and the fruit and added a plate of cheese to them.

The door closed behind him. She and I went back to the sofa and put our coffees and the fruit and cheese on the coffee table.

"I was about to marry someone named Stephen Moore. He worked at the factory where I found work after you left me."

"I did offer to take you," she said.

"I know. I decided against going, and I still don't know whether that was a mistake. In any case, I had feelings for this Stephen Moore and when we were down by the river and he asked me to marry him, I said yes.

"And I never doubted it. He was a good man. Still is. Then Mrs. Burnley, the housekeeper at the Palmers', showed up one Sunday right before we were to get married. Like you she just appeared. But she asked me strange questions about love. She said if I didn't truly *love* Stephen, I should think of *not* marrying him until I found someone that I did love.

"I didn't know what she was talking about. She gave me a sealed letter. It was so very strange. What she did and how she did it. She said, 'If you truly love him, don't open it. If not, you must read what's inside.'"

Bessie was saying nothing and looking very serious while I was going on.

"And I didn't understand. It was like a riddle. But I walked alone to the river and sat on a bench. *'Did I love Stephen Moore?'* I asked myself. Then I realized that I once had deep feelings like she was talking about for someone else but there was nothing I could do about it."

"Because he was rich? Someone you worked for?" she asked.

"Indeed, someone I worked for, yes. But…And she is now married."

This got Bessie's attention.

"She?"

"It was so unnatural. And wrong."

"What about her? What did she think? Did she have feelings for you?"

I stood and walked to the window and looked out briefly. It was a clear day but there was not much to see other than the similar hotel that was across Sixth Avenue. I turned back, and Bessie was watching me from her chair, waiting

"That's what the letter was about. I opened it. I knew I shouldn't because it would mean I wasn't ready for Stephen Moore. But I did open it. And in the letter this girl…woman said it was she and not her mother who dismissed me and sent me to you."

"Where you'd never be seen again, at least with her types."

"Yes, that's it. The girl said she couldn't live with me being so close so I was sent away."

I returned to my seat, and she reached across for my hand.

"I'm so, so sorry, Margaret. I didn't know. I wondered why you were exiled to us. I'm afraid I thought you must have done something inappropriate. My mother thought that too. We assumed something happened between you and the son or even with Mr. Palmer, but we didn't dare ask about it. You worked quite well with us and as there was no man in our home for you to entice with your charms—"

She paused. "I don't mean to be so glib. You know how happy we were with you."

I smiled. I did know that and I told her how lucky I felt that I worked for her and her mother and how I regretted not going to London with them. That said, I continued.

"I still don't know why I did it, but I immediately told Stephen Moore I couldn't marry him. I wasn't thinking. I was such a fool. I just went there and told him then I went to see Mrs. Burnley to learn more and…"

I paused as the memory hit me.

"And?" Bessie wanted to know.

"I ran into her, my old mistress—"

"Surely she has a name."

"It's Elinor, she was Elinor Palmer but now is Mrs. Francis Ballard. But I saw Elinor on the sidewalk and not only did she ignore me but the woman she was with insulted me and Elinor agreed with the insult and I know that she recognized me. I then received a letter from the housekeeper saying I was never to try to contact her again.

"I lost my job because Mr. Moore and I both worked for Mr. Walton, and everyone hated me for what I'd done. Mr. Walton found me another job. But I was on my own. Completely. And very lonely. And that is where you find me and that is I guess why Mrs. Palmer wrote you that letter.

"Now I spend my free time going for walks or getting books in the library and not doing much in the way of living. No man will consider me even if I were interested after word spread about what I did to Stephen Moore. Did Mrs. Burnley ruin my life? I sometimes think she did and sometimes think she didn't. Maybe I'd have a child now, as my friend Cath does. Of that, I am sure. But I've seen what love is—"

"With Elinor?"

"Yes," my words now becoming difficult, "Yes, with Elinor and I know it is wrong and unnatural, but it was real and now I've nothing and no one."

Bessie said, "I do not know what we shall do with you, but I can tell you that there is nothing 'wrong and unnatural' about having such thoughts for another woman. I have them and I have acted on them."

My head shot up.

"It isn't unnatural for some. I have the money and have managed to be discreet. Plus, I've no reputation to lose."

"What about the Lord? Lord Glendale?"

"Well, our arrangement isn't just financial. We have an 'understanding' about with whom we can enjoy...intimacies. It is actually quite a common thing in England. Though usually the ladies have lords for lovers. But ladies with ladies isn't unheard of. Nor is lords with lords. The key is discretion. Everyone knows and no one knows. That is the rule."

She looked at me.

"Margaret Treacy. If Elinor were a man, would you love him?"

"But she is not."

"You must humor me, girl. If she was."

I looked at Bessie and paused.

"And, of course, we are from different worlds. I cannot say."

"You cannot or you will not?"

My refusal was met by yet another roar of laughter. "You win. I won't ask you again." She leaned closer, and with a lowered voice added, "at least not for now." She pushed back and stood.

"For now, though, I wish to take you to visit some friends with me."

"But I'm not dressed for—"

"I promise you; you are perfectly dressed."

22.

Bessie's friends lived in an apartment on Thirty-Fourth Street east of Second Avenue. It was one of the new buildings. There was a well-dressed man who opened the door for us and another one directed us to the elevator—my first—after Bessie said who we were going to see. He then operated the elevator, and we got out on the fifth floor.

The foyer was decorated with a small table on which vases of fresh flowers were placed and above which was a small painting of the city in the rain, visible in the slight gaslight.

There were four doors, and Bessie knocked on "5D" and simply entered. She called out to a "Carolyn" as we walked down the hall to a large sitting room. Two women sat on a luxurious sofa like the one in Bessie's hotel room.

They stood and the taller said to Bessie, "Who's this, then?"

It was a strong English accent.

"Margaret Treacy, may I introduce Carolyn Fields"—and the taller one nodded—"and Abigail Hudson"—and the other one nodded and reached to shake my hand.

"Pleased to meet you," the shorter one said as she lightly touched my hand before pulling it away and giving her "friend" a slight smirk.

The first, Carolyn Fields, sat back down on the sofa and patted a cushion and told me to sit beside her. "You must tell us how someone like…you came to the attention of someone like our Bessie here."

Before I could speak, the second sat down and said, "Oh, I can imagine how you came to Bessie's attention," and she again smirked till I was rescued by Bessie.

"Margaret was my maid here in New York before we moved to England and—"

"And before you landed yourself your title."

"Yes, before I landed myself my title. She is a sweet girl who's recently had some difficulties and I thought she'd be interested in meeting people like you."

"Like us?" Carolyn Fields said, pretending, I thought, to be offended by what Bessie said. "We are simply independent enough to be free to live and love as we choose to live and love."

"With whom with choose to live and love," the other said. And the other, this Abigail, gave me a smile that made me very uncomfortable. Again, Bessie rescued me, telling me to come to the window to enjoy the view from so high up, which I gladly did.

* * * *

"WHAT'S WRONG?"

"I don't know why you brought me to those horrible women. If your plan was to humiliate me, you succeeded."

I was walking away from the apartment building and away from Bessie's carriage. Bessie spoke to the coachman and said she and I would walk for a bit and return and then she hurried after me.

"I didn't think they would be so bad. Please forgive me. I sometimes forget how horrible I've become, spending my times with the likes of them."

I pulled my arm from Bessie's grasp.

"Don't you see? That is why Elinor could never love someone like me. I'm not a fool. I know that women can love one another."

"I wanted you to see two women who do."

"Yet they are still horrible snobs. With every word, they made it clear that they knew what everyone knows. That I'm just an Irish farmgirl who couldn't even be a servant and has to work five-and-a-half days in a factory putting together parts for dresses and gowns I'll never wear and never see.

"No man will have me. No woman will have me. No one will. Except as a servant. Maybe. Is that what you wanted to prove to me with these women? How worthless and below them I am. Well, you've succeeded."

"Margaret. Come back with me to the hotel."

"So you can make fun of me for being so impressed by riding in an elevator? To display how kind you are to your little peasant girl?"

Bessie, I think, realized that she treated me very badly with that sudden trip to her friends, though I understood that she was trying to show me a world she thought I had no idea existed and that if I felt something for Elinor there was nothing *unnatural* about it. Neither of us spoke more as we walked. I told her to take me to my apartment, but after we were back in the carriage she refused, and we returned to that hotel of hers.

Her mother was napping or at least left us alone in the suite's sitting room.

"There is nothing for you here," Bessie said.

She said she'd take me with her back to London, as a maid or as anything I wanted to be. While I often regretted not going with her in those dark days before I found work at Walton & Co, I was not so sure when she asked me this time. She asked me to think about it. They were going to Pittsburgh about a week later and then returning to London directly from Philadelphia. She said they could come through New York or I could go to Philadelphia if I wished to go with them.

When I was back in my apartment in the dark, I had much to think about. I had some if at times difficult independence and did not want to give it up so easily. Whether I was a maid or not in London, I would be depending on her to live. It'd be luxurious but I didn't know whether it was something I wanted. And part of me, I now think, again still did not want to abandon Elinor, whatever she now thought of me. If she even ever thought of me. It was one thing to be in the same city as she was in and another to be an ocean apart.

With work, I had little time to speak to anyone, even if I had someone to speak to—my letters home were becoming rarer and rarer and my mama would never understand if I said anything—but after work on the next Tuesday, I walked directly from my new factory along Houston Street. The door to the House of Mercy was locked, but I pulled the bell, and a young nun I did not recognize opened the door and let me in. Evening prayers were soon to begin, and I told her that I would wait. I said that I trained there some years earlier and wished to speak with Sister Olson. The young nun insisted that I was welcome to join the others for prayers, and I did.

When we finished, I went to Sister Olson, and she led me to her office. Instead of sitting opposite me across her desk, she sat in a wooden chair that faced the desk and was beside me. I found my hands reaching for hers. We talked. I told her much of what I've written here already and particularly about being ready and trying to decide whether to accept Bessie's—Lady Glendale's—offer to go to London.

"What will you do there, my dear?" she asked. "Yes you trained as a maid and it is certainly a noble calling. But might you consider a calling of a different sort?"

I did not understand. She told me that she thought with my experience I might find myself more fulfilled by helping to train others like me, poor girls from Ireland and elsewhere, to become maids.

"It is something important, God's work in its way."

She smiled. "I must retire shortly, Margaret. All I ask is that you think about what I have said. It may be your calling and if it turns out that it is not what you want, you have the ability to leave us, though I believe we will regret you doing so."

I promised her that I would pray and think on it.

I went to Cath the next night. We rarely saw each other since what happened with Stephen Moore—which was my fault since I couldn't bear to face her after what I'd done—but this was too important. She'd been a nun for some years. Patrick was with us, and we sat together in their small living room for the first time in I don't know how long, with their little Michael on his lap.

After speaking with them and more praying, there and later, I made my decision and had a final dinner with Bessie and her mother in the sitting room of their suite on Sunday night. They left for the train to Pittsburgh the next morning, and two weeks later I moved into a small room on the third floor of the House of Mercy to begin life as a nun who would help Irish girls become American women.

23.

I was among the youngest of the nuns when I moved back to the House of Mercy. At first, I took no vows there. I was not a member of the order. I was free to leave at any time. After a month, though, Sister Olson sat me down to ask whether I wished to commit to the order. It would not be a lifetime commitment, she said. Instead, nuns took simple vows, not the solemn vows taken by a priest.

Each nun took the simple vows of chastity, obedience, and poverty on which the Sisters of Mercy were built. Our allegiance was to the order and the vows were renewed each year. She hoped, she said, I'd renew them annually, as she and the others did, but said she would understand if after spending time in the order I realized that my calling went in a different direction, like it did for Cath.

At the end of my first-plus year, she again sat me down, as she did with all the younger sisters. She and the others were impressed by the work I did with the new girls, mostly but no longer only from Ireland, and who were being trained, as I had been, to become servants.

I did take my initial vows then. I told her I meant to stay. I was happy. Truth be told, though, I didn't have any alternatives. I'd become the chief connection between the new girls and the more senior nuns. I was the nun to whom the homesick came at night. I often sat with one of them to read her a letter from home or to write one to home.

Yet I didn't feel a personal relationship with God though I knew I was doing His work.

I rarely saw men, of course, other than when I was sent on an errand or rarely to an entertainment on a rare afternoon with other nuns. And those who did work in the house and Father O'Donnell, the priest who said Mass each morning and took our confessions—of which I'm sure none of us had much to say—each Saturday afternoon.

As my second anniversary neared, it weighed on me. I'd be speaking to Sister Olson early the next week, but since I had no other opportunities and enjoyed what I did, I expected I'd renew.

In the meanwhile, I had my work. When first in America with my time at the House of Mercy almost over, I sat in the large room when the Palmers and others came. Now, I was in charge of arranging for the girls to be presentable and to identify potential houses where they could work. I was selected for this because I was the first woman in many years who'd joined the order after having gone through the process. Sister Olson thought that my recent experience would help what was such a difficult period for new girls to America.

I had much work to do. The House received many requests for our girls. I reviewed each. Then I sat with Sister Olson, and we decided which girls would be the best fit for which family. This process took place about two weeks before the interviews.

The sixth request I read stopped me.

Mr. and Mrs. Francis Ballard
75 East 35th Street, NYC

We are a family with one daughter, Elinor Margaret, who recently turned three years of age. My husband is twenty-nine years of age and in good health. He is employed as a vice president in his father's financial firm on Broad Street. I am twenty-four. My husband and I are hopeful of having additional children although as yet we are only blessed with our Margaret.

We are Episcopalian but all the members of our staff are Catholic and for the most part attend ~~services~~ *Mass together. There are currently nine servants in our employ: Nurse, Cook, Scullery Girl, Butler, Footmen (2), Housekeeper, Chambermaids (2). I am desirous of employing a third chambermaid to assist, including with our child.*

In addition to our home in town, we maintain a residence in the country house of my father, Mr. Arthur Palmer, in Lenox, Massachusetts. It is expected that most of our servants will accompany us while we are there.

References: Mrs. Roger Ballard (mother of husband), Mrs. Arthur Palmer (wife's mother).

On a personal note, shortly after I came out as an eighteen-year-old and while I was of course living in my family's house, as Miss Elinor Palmer, I had a positive experience with Margaret Treacy, an Irish farmgirl trained at the House of Mercy. I have long regretted that the relationship ended abruptly for reasons for which I bear a large and perhaps the sole responsibility. I have, as I say, long regretted that and am interested in retaining a similar girl from a west Ireland farm for my own house.

I am hopeful about meeting another such as her.

Mrs. Francis Ballard

Elinor's script was unmistakable. Her flourishes, though, weren't as childish as when I first saw them, even in that fateful letter never delivered to me for many years.

With this formal one, I re-read each word, especially each word of those final sentences.

There was one girl who I knew was the one. She was, like me, from County Mayo, though many miles from my own farm. God help her but Nora Duffy was a plain girl with rows of freckles that descended from her eyes and across her cheeks and, of course, rusty hair she couldn't control. More than any other, though, Nora Duffy reminded me of myself. I couldn't imagine anyone more deserving of having a sweet girl like Nora Duffy care for her Meg.

The maid, of course, wouldn't be in regular contact with the girl. There was a nurse for that, and there'd be (as I well knew) more than enough cleaning and mending and polishing and (in the winter) cleaning out fireplaces to keep the newest maid occupied. But over time she'd become important to the child, at least if she were a kind sort, as I knew Nora Duffy was.

Having done that matching, I quickly took care of the other girls and the other applicants. Sister Olson agreed with all my selections (though I didn't dare tell her of my connection with Mrs. Ballard). The interviews would be in a week.

When I was a "trainee," I was told little of what would happen and about the families that would interview me. I thought a better connection would arise should both sides have some basic information about the other, and I got Sister Olson to agree. So, I met with each girl and had a letter with information about each girl delivered to the home of the main applicants I selected.

The family interviews would begin at ten. I spent much of the morning before then trying to keep the girls calm. I went through the questions they would likely be asked and the proper responses. But, I told them, "You must be honest, or you may wind up in a position that's not right for you."

Each girl wore her best maid's frock. At ten before ten, I did a final survey. Each was ready, and I told them so. I led them to the hall and to the wooden chairs lined up against one wall. I knew how nervous each was. I think I felt the anxiety of each of them. As graduates of the House of Mercy, each was deemed suitable to a domestic position, and each would find one. But whether it was the right one is what made my life far more stressful than the girls realized.

The door to the outer hall opened at ten and the sound of chattering ladies floated in. It reminded me of when I had gone through this. Each lady was the mistress of the house and had the housekeeper and sometimes a daughter or a mother, as Elinor came in with Mrs. Palmer and Mrs. Burnley years ago.

There she was again. Elinor. I was in my habit and only my face was exposed, and I kept to the back so she wouldn't recognize me.

She made herself out to be far older than her twenty-four years in a dark brown day dress with a cameo at her neck. Her hair was up in some sort of fashionable weave that barely peaked out under her bonnet. She was with an older, very short woman, who I assumed was her own house's Mrs. Burnley. Her mother was not with her nor was Francis Ballard's.

The maid was to Elinor's left and a little girl was holding her hand on the right. The girl wore a yellow dress with lace fringes and a matching bonnet. Her light brown hair was allowed to roll over her shoulders. I couldn't say how far down it went, but I suspected it had never been cut.

The visitors were soon broken up and directed to small tables that were set up in the center of the hall, as they were when I was one of those nervous girls in a maid's uniform sitting in that row along the wall.

I assigned the Ballards to the table farthest from where I would stand. I told Sister Olson that it would be helpful to me to have another nun assist me, and Sister Raymond was with me.

Instead of moving to the center, in front of the girls, I remained to the side and addressed the visitors briefly.

Sister Olson spoke when the women were seated. "Ladies. Thank you for coming. You know the process. We reviewed each of your requests and selected girls we believe will be best suited to you. Sister Raymond will assist me in bringing the girls to you.

"Because we cannot be sure that any one girl is right for your house, we use this opportunity to have you meet with more than one before you decide."

24.

Particularly in their first months in service, girls returned to the House of Mercy on their evening off and socialized with others they met there and who were perhaps the only people they knew in America. They socialized and prayed and those not quite able to do it themselves would get help in writing letters home. And to have letters they received read to them.

Nora came to me as soon as she was through the door on one such night not long after she moved in with the Ballards. After a curtsey, she handed me a sealed envelope addressed to me in Elinor's hand.

"My mistress asked me to hand this to you, sister. She said God willing you will have something for me to bring back when I leave." She left me alone with a curtsy and reunited with some girls she attended the House with.

Sister Margaret,

I cannot believe that you could imagine I would not recognize you the moment my poor eyes were upon you.

I won't say more. I only beg that you allow me to see you alone. I do not know what freedom you have to come and go from the House of Mercy. But I ask that you tell the wonderful Nora Duffy—with whom my Elinor Margaret has fallen completely in love—if we can meet and, if so, when and where. It will be, perhaps likely be, but a passing moment in your life, but it will be far more in mine.

Margaret. I beg that you give me this opportunity. I know I can never be more than your friend, but it is my most fervent wish that I be so and that you forgive me for what I have done to you.

E

The House of Mercy wasn't a prison. An outsider like Mrs. Ballard wouldn't understand that. I was free on the following Wednesday afternoon. I reached into a desk in a small office off the hall and took out a piece of plain stationery.

Mrs. Ballard,

Thank you for your request. I will be able to meet with you this coming Wednesday at three o'clock in the afternoon at Washington Square Park. I will meet you at the southwest corner of the Square.

> *Yours, etc.,*
> *Sr. Margaret Treacy,*
> *SOM*

It was formal, but she would understand why. I placed it in an envelope, which I sealed before addressing it to "Mrs. Francis Ballard." I returned to the hall. Nora saw me. She came to me quickly. I handed her the note.

"Thank you, Nora. Please give this to your mistress and only to your mistress."

I assured her it had nothing to do with her but related to my having met her mistress some years before. I could not say whether Elinor said anything about me to Nora, but I doubted it. She took the note and began to leave with the curtsey she'd developed at the House.

"And Nora. I'm so grateful for you doing this."

She gave an awkward nod and was soon out the door and on Houston Street. She'd catch a trolley to take her back to the Ballards'.

25.

"If I'm honest, I'll tell you that much as I *didn't* want to see you again, I wanted far more to. You must understand why I did what I did. It was me and me alone."

"I must be honest with you as well, Mrs. Ballard—"

"Please, Margaret. For the love of God, call me Elinor. Only my family calls me Elinor. Not even Francis. Call me nothing if the alternative is 'Mrs. Ballard.' But, Margaret, it would be everything if you call me Elinor."

It was a fine day, with lots of people enjoying it in the Square, and we began to walk on one of its paths.

"Okay, Elinor. I need you to understand something. I can leave the order at any time. But I'll tell you, and only you—I've not even told our priest—that I've doubts about my calling to God. Some of my sisters do have a clear calling. I try to convince myself I do, but I'm very afraid that I don't have *that* calling. At times I think I entered the order because I didn't know of anywhere else to go.

"I won't tell you what has happened to me since I last saw you. I'll only say that...that after I came upon you in front of your parents' house when I was going to Mrs. Burnley to see if I could meet you, if she could tell me what you wanted from me...Well, it all collapsed for me. I didn't understand, but that is what happened."

"Please," she said. "You must forgive me. My intention was then, as it always has been, to avoid hurting you. Yes, I recognized you at once. How I wanted to reach for you and put my arms around you and hold you. I was with my sister-in-law, Francis's sister Scarlett. I realized I could do nothing but treat you as she did. You must believe me.

"Only later did Mrs. Burnley tell me what happened. She and my mother were fools. They gave it to you then, but I couldn't do anything and all I did was ruin you for no reason."

I tried to laugh and forced myself to smile.

"I wasn't completely ruined. And now that I look back on it, I don't think I'd have been happy with the man I was to marry. But it's no use thinking too much about that.

"If you want me to forgive you, I forgive you. I'm sorry about what happened."

"I am sorry too, but that's not the only reason I wanted to speak to you."

She looked down at her hands and then took a deep breath before looking back up at me. Her right hand reached for mine.

"Too often I wish I wasn't married."

This surprised me. "Wasn't it what you always wanted? Mr. Ballard isn't a bad man, is he? I thought you loved him."

She shuddered and her face stiffened.

"God, that name. Its only saving grace is that it is attached to Elinor Margaret."

Speaking her daughter's name seemed to relax her. She shook her head.

"No. Few know where her name came from. I'm often asked." She went from looking at me to looking back over to where children were playing. "I say it belonged to a long-gone, long-missed friend. I expect my mother and Mrs. Burnley suspect or know, but they've never said anything. I'm sure Bridget understands."

We completed one lap of the Square and stopped to sit on a bench that looked in. Girls and boys were running, chasing one another with only nurses to watch them.

"Meg—that is what I call her—is doing much as they are doing in a park near our house." Elinor nodded towards them. "I try to go with her but too often I've other inconsequential engagements that keep me occupied. Charities and shopping and such. All as expected of a woman in my position. I sometimes wish Meg and I could just disappear, maybe simply take the train to the Lenox house for a month. Let Francis toil away at his pretend job at his father's pretend firm."

A ball escaped a group of children and headed our way. She jumped up to grab it. The boy chasing it down stopped until she asked him to come to her for it, and she tossed it to him when he was five or six feet away. He clutched it and with a single syllable "thankyou" turned back in triumph and raced to his friends. She turned towards me as I sat.

"I love you, Margaret." Her voice was flat but there was no doubt that she meant it and that it was hard for her to say it.

"I hope you have some feelings for me, though I don't deserve anything from you but contempt. I wanted to meet with you to ask if you would be my...friend. Nothing more than that. But it would mean the world to me if you said yes. That you would be my friend. If I know you think fondly of me, if only a little, and don't hate me, that'll be enough."

She sat beside me and as I tried to think of an answer, I watched the children and felt her stare at the side of my face. She interrupted. "We could do walks like this. You could meet Meg. It wouldn't be much. But it would be more than I deserve."

At moments like this, hearing what she said, and more and more being so lonely myself I sometimes regretted not marrying Stephen Moore. But my heart was not settled. He was, I heard, now married with a child that could have been mine. And Patrick and Cath now had two children, a boy and a girl. Mrs. Burnley told me that in a letter some months earlier, saying she thought I would be interested and hoping I was well.

I don't know how long I was staring at those children and how long Elinor was staring at me, but it seemed both very long and very brief. Without turning my head but no longer focusing on the children, I said, "I love you. I don't know when it happened, maybe it simply grew and grew, but it is true.

"At the House of Mercy, I devote myself to helping girls like me, like I was. When I received your letter about getting a maid, I thought I was content. Or content enough." I turned. "Then I saw what you wrote. I saw the name you gave to your daughter. Then I saw you. I prayed you wouldn't recognize me, and I thought you had not when you gave no sign that you did." I turned to look out at the children chasing their ball. "Nothing good can come of it."

"You cannot understand how difficult that was. I wanted to knock the table over and rush to you, to hug you as I should have done that last time I saw you. On the sidewalk outside my parents'."

Proper Mrs. Francis Ballard was chortling on the bench, and more than a few passersby looked over at us, the nun and the fashionable lady, in curiosity. I put my arm around her, and she put her head on my shoulder.

It was very wrong. But I liked feeling her. Then, without realizing it, I turned and my right hand, my free hand, reached up to Elinor's cheek. I did it to wipe a tear away, but she held it there as the shock ran through her. Had we been free from observers I might have leaned my mouth in and placed my lips on hers. Perhaps seal something I had thought I had with Stephen Miller so long before. All I could do was let my fingers run across her cheek, feeling tears roll down it, and more than I was entitled to.

I pushed her face back, and she opened her eyes. I pulled my arm from her waist and placed it on the opposite cheek so I could look into her eyes.

"What do we do now?"

26.

"Come with me."

I didn't know the area around Washington Square. But Elinor did. Across from its western edge, halfway between the north and the south side, at One West Fifth Street, there was a large restaurant. It was one of the newer, Italian-style places that were becoming popular.

Pulling me behind her, Elinor went in. She told the man who bowed to her slightly and looked confused by me as we entered that we needed to use the facilities. He sent us to a short hallway near the entrance to the kitchen. Once inside, Elinor locked the door. She stared at me as she undid her dress. I did not know what she was doing as she removed and turned to me.

"Unfasten the buttons," she half-ordered and half-pled, and I did until she could pull the top over her shoulders.

"Look beneath the camisole." She turned so her back faced me. Though the light was weak, the strips of purple flowing roughly down across from her right shoulder were clear.

"No one knows except Bridget. No one. Not my mother. Not my sister. Now, only Bridget and you."

Elinor pulled up the camisole and told me to refasten the buttons and then she put her dress back on. We each used the toilet and left. She left a dollar bill for the person who cleaned the room and another for the man who'd allowed us in, with a thank you as we, the fashionable woman and the nun, left.

I didn't know what to say, and neither of us spoke as we resumed our walk around the Square, going clockwise this time.

"We won't have another child much as I want one because I won't let him touch me. He is a hard, brutish man, even when he isn't drunk. He is more brutish when he is. Which is often. He threatens me, 'I will have a son out of you,' but even he won't violate me as he must if he is to have a son. By me at least. Perhaps he will have one with one of the whores he goes to, and I'm only glad that he brings none of them home with him.

"Perhaps he already has a son, or more, and he will arrange for his bastard to be cared for. But there will be no Francis Ballard, Jr. "

"Why won't you allow him to do what he is entitled to do as your husband?"

Elinor stopped and turned to me.

"He was so different after our wedding day. I promised myself that I would be a good wife. I was afraid I couldn't be if you were near. So, I wrote that letter to you. But I wasn't told until after that incident in front of my parents' house that you only got it that day. After my sister-in-law left, my mother told me. Had I known that I might have been prepared. I didn't know how you must have felt."

"I've forgiven you."

"Which is why I love you."

This was the second time she said it, but it was so natural when she did. We were still walking, but she went to and sat on a bench. I sat by her.

"He was too drunk to perform on our wedding night. Instead, when he was almost sober in the morning, he took his due without regard to me and the physical pain. I didn't know how painful it would be and he put a pillow across my mouth to silence me as he bled me. I felt nothing but pain and was glad that he finished the act quickly. Not then or ever did I feel the slightest pleasure. Only relief when it was over

"He said on our wedding trip how it was my duty to give him a son. I promised him I knew that. He said he wanted nothing more than that from me. He called me his 'fat little cow.' But it would be fine when I gave him his son. He wanted to make his father proud of him.

"He left me alone during the day and I could wander around with Bridget. We were in cities where I knew only the simplest words, thanks to the expensive lessons I had. Oh, I quite enjoyed my Irish companion, as a friend.

"When he was sober or sober enough, he took me, insisting that he had to get a son for his father. I don't know why I didn't become pregnant on the trip. He didn't try as often when we returned to New York. I told him that the chances would be increased if he didn't exhaust his supply.

"He did try to be romantic sometimes. Someone must have told him that it would increase the chances of me getting pregnant, but we both knew it was pretend, the flowers and candies he would give me before…inflicting himself on me.

"I prayed to become pregnant. I wanted a child. I was desperate to have a child. He didn't believe me. He kept saying I would get pregnant if I truly wanted to. And finally, I was and he rushed to tell his parents and he promised them it would be a boy. He was suddenly as he was before we married. We were both so happy again. As were his parents and family and mine, too. And when it wasn't a boy, he was crushed. He said I'd caused him to disappoint his father. It was *my* fault, he said. And his father was very cold to me. His mother too.

"Francis cared nothing for the baby. When I asked what we would name her, he told me to call her whatever I wanted since it didn't matter to him in the least.

"There were no questions about where 'Elinor Margaret' came from. Bridget might have suspected. My mother had long forgotten your name. Or at least I thought so. I'm not sure anymore. Mrs. Burnley, too.

"I extended my maternity period. He kept away for over a year after Meg was born, but he would only wait so long before resuming his efforts. It was all to no avail. He told me it was all down to me, that it was *me* who had some defect that prevented me from giving him a son. As month after month went by and I bled, he became angrier and angrier.

"Then, when Meg was about eighteen months old, I didn't bleed, and he was like he once was. 'A boy, a boy,' he said. 'I knew you would make one for me.' Again, he was a different person when I told him. The old Francis Ballard. *My* Francis Ballard. But soon I felt horrible pain. My doctor came. My baby was gone. It was awful."

She was crying without break. After recovering a little, she continued. "When I told him, he went into a rage. He cared nothing about what I was going through. He blamed me for having done something, again!, to deprive him of his son. He had his mother sit down with me—she was angry with me too—to find out what was wrong with me. 'Wrong with *me*?' I shouted at her, and she never brought it up again and became even more distant than she had been from the beginning.

"He started going to brothels regularly. He said he needed 'satisfaction' and that it was obvious I couldn't give it to him. And then after he started doing it to me again, he still went to his whores. I don't know if he got any satisfaction from them, but he didn't from me. It was always as quick as possible, pulling my gown up and putting himself in from atop me. Sometimes he wouldn't say anything, which was a relief. Still, nothing ever came of it, and he became even worse, which I didn't think was possible."

I insisted that we get up, and we again walked in the warm early summer air. As we began a last circling of the Square, she said, "And then I saw you when I went to get Nora."

She paused in her words, waiting for some response from me. Perhaps she was praying for what I would say. And what I did say, without needing to think, "I don't know what will become of us, but we must agree not to abandon one another again, whatever may happen."

It was the last thing either of us said until we were about to part at the end of that lap, and then all we could say was "goodbye" to each other, near the bench we'd first sat on.

27.

When I returned to the House after my difficult afternoon, I sat with Sister Olson. The time for my vow renewal was getting closer and closer.

"My child," she said after I expressed my doubts without revealing what I had spoken about and, more importantly, seen with Elinor. We were in her office. She was the oldest daughter in a prominent Irish-American family and usually sat at her desk. That day, she sat in front of it for the second time with me.

"The renewal gives each of us the chance to look back on the prior period and decide what is our calling for the following one. You are a wonderful sister, and we couldn't operate as we do without you, especially in getting the girls to understand what will be expected of them when they leave here.

"But that alone cannot make it your *calling*. It is for you to pray and examine yourself. As it is for each of us to decide."

She leaned forward and reached for my hands.

"God will always love you, as will we, no matter what you do. For some of us, the vow of chastity, that we will give all of ourselves only to our Lord, is the most difficult. That is the choice that you must make. We all must."

She released my hands. The interview was over. As I reached the door, she said, "I'll pray for you, sister."

"Thank you, sister. I know."

I was kept busy cleaning the kitchen that night. No one seemed to notice any change in me, if there was a change to notice. I joined the others for evening prayers in the chapel before going into my small room. It had a bed over which a simple wooden crucifix hung, a side table, a small desk with a wooden chair, and a small dresser, on top of which were several books—a woman who was very pleased with a maid she got through us arranged for us to get books for free—though my Bible I took with me from Backfox was kept close to me, on the side table. The walls were painted in dull yellow. There was a single candle and a small window that looked out to the alley at the rear of the building and some sort of warehouse across the way.

It was all intentionally sparse. One of the nuns, though, took to distributing flowers cut from a garden she maintained along the western side of the House's central yard. She cared for a mix of flowers, and we all thought of her as an ambassador of color in our otherwise drab rooms and in the not quite so drab dormitories where the girls slept.

That night, I took my rosary beads from the drawer on my side table and knelt on the hard floor. While some of the older nuns used rug remnants for their knees, we younger ones didn't. The physical discomfort, we knew, made us closer to our Savior.

While I always said a rosary before blowing out my candle, I can't say how many I said that night, countless *Our Fathers* and *Hail Marys* until I couldn't continue and could only offer final prayers for me and especially for Elinor and little Meg. I crawled into the bed with the rosary beads in my hand and was asleep before I could put them back on the side table.

With each day that week, things got no easier. Sister Olson wouldn't let me shirk my duties. I was desperate for news from the outside. When I closed my eyes after saying the rosary each night, seeking guidance for myself and help for her, I *saw* Elinor's scars.

I heard nothing from her. I decided I would got back on Wednesday afternoon to where we'd met. Perhaps she'd be there. On Wednesday morning, after I finished with the kitchen cleaning and was preparing to teach a course on linens to the newest girls, though, Sister Olson asked to see me. I again was in the office, desperately curious, this time sitting across from my superior.

"I'm sorry, Sister Margaret, something has arisen, and you must take care of this afternoon's class. You may have tomorrow off, assuming Sister Annette will be better by then. You may go."

I began to speak but didn't when Sister Olson asked if there was something I had to say. So, I took care of afternoon class and if any of the girls saw how distressed I was, I didn't notice it.

After dinner, before I was to help with clean-up and before evening prayers, Sister Olson took me aside.

"Let us walk."

It was very unusual that nuns left the House this late, but it was July and still light out and so that is where we went. As always happened, everyone on the sidewalk scattered to allow the two nuns to pass unobstructed.

"I'm sorry, my dear, but you need to understand the choice you are to make. The commitment you must undertake. You cannot serve two masters."

Neither of us said anything before we began to circle the block. I told her I understood and neither of us said anything more until we again got near the House's front door.

"I'm here for you, my child," Sister Olson said. "We all are, whether you stay with us or not."

I nodded. She followed me in and we went into the foyer in time to join the others in the chapel for prayers.

28.

The day when I'd have to decide whether to renew my vows was approaching. I knew I had to meet Elinor and sent a note to Mrs. Burnley and could only hope Elinor got it. Would she be at the corner of Washington Square Park at the appointed time?

My note just said, "I would like to see you. I'll be at the spot where we met, at the same time on Wednesday."

I hurried even though I had plenty of time. I wanted to be there before her, but when I could see the bench, she was there, looking back and forth at whoever was entering till she saw me. She didn't move to meet me. She just sat there waiting with her hands in her lap. My stomach had been a mess ever since I sent that letter.

"Please sit," Elinor said. She looked paler than I'd ever seen her. Her gloves were on and when I was beside her and her hands were still in her lap, only her face looked to me. Her eyes were soft.

"I cannot be the cause of your break with God and with the good work you do. I can offer you a position as a maid in my parents' house again. I've spoken to my mother and Mrs. Burnley, and they agreed. It will only be until we can find something more suitable for you, but you can live and be fed and have the necessities you'll be giving up by leaving the order."

I don't know what my expression was in response to this, but she smiled and was suddenly animated, her hands rushing to grab mine.

"Don't you see? Please tell me you won't mind being a maid again. It will only be temporary."

"'Temporary.' What do you have in mind for me?"

She seemed to brighten at my response and became even more excited. "Think about it, Margaret. What have you been doing these last two years?"

"I see to the training of young women to become servants."

"Exactly. I say you can become a teacher."

She said this very confidently, and I looked at her as if she'd lost her mind.

"I've spoken to my mother about it." Her hands were shaking mine, though I don't know that she realized it. "We can approach my father. I didn't know what you would tell me today—please do not reject it out of hand!—so I didn't explore too much, but more and more schools are opening. Not just for girls like me. For girls without the advantages I've had. With my father's support, I'm sure we can find a position."

"But you forget that I know nothing of teaching."

"Of course you do. What is it you do each day at the House of Mercy if it's not teaching? I saw how the girls adore you. I asked Nora. She said how good you were with her and the others."

"But I teach how to fold linen and clean silverware. Things like that. Nothing of any use to someone not in service."

"We will make you educated."

"Make me 'educated'?"

"Surely there are tutors who can prepare you to teach. I'll convince my father to pay for one."

"This is nonsense. And when am I supposed to do this?"

"My mother and Mrs. Burnley agree to allow you several hours each day to meet with your tutor."

"But won't the others resent that?"

"Mother says with me gone there isn't nearly so much work. Indeed, she says she doesn't need to hire another maid at all. They'll come up with some story to explain why you are being hired when there isn't a need and why you will be spending hours each day off learning arithmetic and science or whatever it is that you are going to be teaching."

Her plan was, of course, completely unworkable. Getting special privileges would brand me as an outsider among the staff.

"If you have a better idea, Margaret, you might want to mention it now because my mind worked long and hard to reach this one. Have you given thought to what you would do if you left the order?"

"I hadn't decided whether I *would* leave."

"But surely you thought about the alternative. What would you do?"

"Of course I thought about it but I came up with nothing."

"So, you will concede that however farfetched my scheme is, it is infinitely better than your non-existent one."

I looked at Elinor. Seeing no alternative, I said, "Let's walk."

We once again started along the path that went around the Square.

"I've little time."

"When must you be back?" she asked.

"Oh, I've all afternoon. No. I meant until I must decide."

"But have you decided?"

"I'm not sure. But with what you tell me, I must see your mother and Mrs. Burnley first. Before I decide to do the strange thing you suggest. They've been good to me."

"Better in ways than I have."

I stopped and looked at her. "Elinor. You, all of you, were doing what you thought best. I've forgiven you all and accept that I can only control what happens in the future. That's where we have to start."

There was a tearoom a block to the east of the Square. It was on the corner and had seven or eight tables, each with a white tablecloth. As we got near it, Elinor said her mother was there in case she was needed. I decided I'd be a fool not to meet with Mrs. Palmer and Elinor. We were there quickly. She opened the door and a small bell sounded. We saw her mother. It had been quite a while. She seemed much older.

29

Before I made the final decision, I was in Mr. Palmer's study. I knew it well from all the times I dusted and cleaned it, and it hadn't changed in the slightest as far as I could tell. I'd never actually sat in it before though. Yet there I was, in a burgundy leather chair facing his large walnut desk. My chair was one of a pair of matching ones, and Elinor sat in the other, next to mine.

The library itself looked out over the back of the house. It was large with paneled walls that were lined with bookshelves of rarely opened books. The desk was also large. It had a leather top that matched the chairs and a pair of brass inkwells in the middle and near the front edge.

There was only the one window. It was at Mr. Palmer's back. It was large with eight panes over eight panes with an indentation and a shelf on which he kept a box of fine cigars. A spittoon was to the side, though I never knew that anyone used it. The room had the aroma of a man's refuge, like my father's tiny snug in Backfox.

There was another, smaller chair off to one side, and Mrs. Palmer sat in it. As the three of us waited, Mr. Palmer said nothing. He was leaning back in that chair of his with his chin on his upstretched fingers, as he sought to understand what he was just told by his wife.

"But she is a *servant*," he said finally, making sure to nod at "she" like I was a picture or statue or something.

"Arthur. She *was* a servant. She is now a teacher and all we ask is that she be given the chance to teach if she should leave the good sisters."

"But what can she teach?" He looked at me. "Sister. What is it that you are qualified to teach?"

"Well, Mr. Palmer," I replied as I'd practiced with the others, "I have for the past two years been teaching girls, young women who have no experience how to provide services to families like yours, teaching those with no idea how a great house is run."

"But that isn't proper teaching, surely."

"Let her finish, Arthur," his wife interrupted.

"Thank you," I said. "I realize that the specific things I've taught won't be of great use to most girls, but I believe...*we* believe that the skills I got teaching at the House of Mercy will help me teach more useful, interesting things to others."

"Yes, papa. This is the point," Elinor jumped in, speaking in a rush. "Margaret...Miss Treacy can spend time learning things and then use her experience to *teach* what she learns to others. That is what mother and I have discussed."

Mr. Palmer looked from his wife to his daughter. "And how is she supposed to learn these things? How is she supposed to pay for being tutored in these things? How is she to live while she is being tutored in these things?"

"Why, you are going to pay for them, of course," his wife told him.

"Me?" He looked to Elinor, who nodded. He looked back at his wife.

"Me? Why me?"

Elinor said, "Because I shall be taking them with her."

"You? Now this is getting preposterous. You taking classes to learn to become a...teacher? It is absurd. Why would you want to do that?"

"Because, papa, I'm bored with my life, and I think it would be of use to me to learn more of the world."

"My dear Elinor. You have never given the slightest indication of wishing to 'learn more of the world.' You could have gone to Vassar but never gave a peep that you wanted to. You did what your sister did before you. Got married and had a child. Speaking of which, if I somehow agree to this fantasy of yours, what is to become of Meg? You cannot leave her all day with her nurse."

"I'll bring her to my lessons, papa. It would be good for her to meet Margaret anyway. Margaret says she is very fond of children."

Mr. Palmer looked at me. I thought he might connect my name with his granddaughter, but it passed. I nodded and said, "I'd like to meet her, I surely would."

Mr. Palmer looked at his daughter. "Elinor, I don't understand. She is a servant."

"Papa, she is more than a servant and I grew to like her when she *was* my servant and I miss her and would very much like to have her around when I can."

"But, you have Bridget at your own house. Is she not enough? And should you not be spending time at your house and not at mine? Again, I don't understand."

"Arthur," Mrs. Palmer ended her silence. "I always liked her and since we had to part ways with her—for no fault of her own but because of...circumstances, and *not* the 'circumstances' you may think—she has grown so much and become quite accomplished given the limitations of her world. Elinor suggested that she might do more as a teacher. I met with her, and I believe that Elinor is correct. I think if we can do something to aid her, we should do it. It is something charitable, in its way, for someone not nearly so fortunate as Elinor."

Mr. Palmer pushed back his chair and stood. He reached into his cigar box on the window seat and removed one. He cut it and speared it but only held it between the thumb and index finger of his right hand. He stood behind his chair, leaning slightly on its back. He looked at each of us.

"Mrs. Palmer. Have you made any calculation of what would be involved, financially and otherwise, in this scheme the three of you seem to have concocted?"

In fact, she had. She would retain a recent Columbia graduate to handle the tutoring. I couldn't hope to become a master of the Classics, but if I became a teacher in a school, I'd need a solid footing in several things.

* * * *

ALTHOUGH I OFFICIALLY was no longer a member of the Sisters of Mercy when I didn't renew my vows, I stayed on as a laywoman to finish with the girls I was preparing for service. I remained in my little room till that was over and attended daily Mass and prayers with the nuns and said my rosary before getting into bed each night. I found it all more comforting than before.

I wore clothing I had from before joining and told the girls why I'd left the order. At least some of the "why."

30.

I don't know that I could be ready to meet, actually *meet,* Elinor Margaret Ballard. It was the Saturday, the day I was leaving the House of Mercy for good. A room had been prepared for me in the servants' quarters at the Palmers'. Mrs. Burnley told the servants I was coming with the explanation we'd agreed to about why I was leaving the order. I knew most of the others since they'd been at the house when I was there before. Mary Kavanagh had gotten herself married to a nice bloke and left, they said, but Henry Covings was still the dapper coachman.

The Palmers sent a carriage to take me up after I'd attended my final Mass in the House's chapel. When I carried my few belongings to the foyer where I first entered years ago after staying at Mrs. Bolger's, Elinor was waiting for me and after a somewhat awkward leaving of the House joined me for the ride to her parents' house. I had strange feelings. It was the same trip I'd taken all those years before.

I sat opposite Elinor but she shimmied to one side and patted the seat beside her and insisted I take it. I found it hard to breathe for some reason but managed as our thighs touched and our bodies bounced off against each other when the brougham hit a bumpy stretch. I survived that too and this time I did not fall to the sidewalk in front of the house. I did not enter through the servants' door beneath the stairs. We went in through the front door.

She helped me in my room and before I could get my things put away or ask to see her parents to thank them, we were off to meet Meg herself. We were back on the sidewalk, and Elinor was in front of me, pulling my arm for several blocks until we reached a park on Thirty-Fifth Street which was surrounded by a gate.

The gatekeeper saw her, though. The entrance was open for us as we reached it. She called to her girl. Meg pulled away from her nurse and she flew towards us across the greenest lawn I'd ever seen, and only as she got near did Elinor release my hand so she could squat down and open her arms to her child, who in a blink had her arms around her mama's neck.

After a squeeze, Elinor pushed away and held Meg's left arm. She stood.

"Elinor Margaret," she said. Meg's face turned serious. "I would like you to meet a special friend of mine who I knew before you were born."

Meg looked at me and immediately back at her mama, who gave her a slight shove towards me. Me, all serious, extended my hand to the girl, who took it. She said, "I'm very pleased to meet you..." and she paused till her mother said, "Margaret Treacy," at which point she repeated my name. I shook her hand and said, "It is my pleasure to meet you, Miss Ballard" in the most serious voice I could muster but I couldn't hold back for long and once she let go of my hand, I bent down and opened my arms to her as Elinor had and after a moment and a "go on" from her mother, she threw herself at me, and I was finally able to give her a proper greeting and knew we would always be great friends.

We separated after I don't know how long. She took my hand as her mother had and pulled me towards the bench where the nurse sat watching. The nurse stood, and Meg introduced me to her, an older, matronly woman though Meg needed her mama's help in recalling my name.

Once all this was done, Elinor told the nurse she could have the rest of the afternoon off as she and I would see to the girl, and with a bow to her employer and one to her charge and a smile to me she left. We watched until the gate closed behind her.

And we laughed together, the three of us, till we got some ice cream on the avenue before heading back to the Palmers'. Elinor said Meg's grandparents were waiting, though only Mrs. Palmer was there when we arrived. She and little Meg sat in the corner of the sitting room near the windows looking out onto Twenty-Eighth Street. Elinor and I were in chairs near the mantel. We didn't say much, but here, too, I felt a rush of contentment.

This meeting behind us, we had to begin the first stage of whatever was to become of me. I'd work as a maid in the Palmers' house, starting with the next day's dinner, but that first night I sat in the kitchen feeling right at home helping with some polishing. Both the girls I sat with were new to me. One, Alice Evans, was an American girl but she and her parents also came from a farm in upstate New York before the parents came to town to find better, more steady work at factories. Alice was amazed when I told her that I spent time in a crinoline factory that turned out not to be too far from where her mother worked—and Alice herself was first a maid for another house.

The second girl was Irish, but she'd not gone to the House of Mercy. Instead, she got a position at a house where her older sister was a chambermaid. Her name was Karen Wilson, and she said she was tired of always being under her sister's thumb so that when the chance to work somewhere else came up she took it. She got along better with her sister, she said, now that they weren't working together. She reminded me of many of the girls who went through the House of Mercy and I took a liking to her as we sat with our polishing and them asking about what I had done and why I was there and especially what it was like to be a nun.

I was surprised at how easily I returned to my life as a servant. But I wasn't entirely that though, was I?

Each afternoon during the week, David Schmidt came to the house. He had graduated from Columbia College earlier in the year and was my tutor. He was a tall, slight man of about twenty-one with a very well-trimmed mustache. Over time, but slowly, he spoke to me about himself when I insisted he do so. His parents, he said, had their own hat shop on lower Broadway. One of their customers took a liking to him when he was a teenager working in the shop and helped him in attending Columbia, though he still worked at the store sometimes. He said he stood out because he was neither rich nor Protestant there, but he did well and got along with his classmates. He had his head in the clouds a bit and decided he would teach. While he searched for a permanent position, he took tutoring jobs.

Each weekday morning, he gave lessons to the teenage son of a prominent family. Afternoons were spent with me. We sat in the corner of the drawing room on either side of a round table near the windows.

The lessons went better than either of us expected and especially with my attention on what were to me challenging English novels. He said they were not what a young lady in society was expected to read—Elinor confessed she never had read them—but my students were not necessarily to be society ladies but the perhaps more ambitious daughters of middle-class families. The novels we discussed were far more complicated than the romances I was used to.

Of course, novels alone do not a teacher make. Because the plan was that I be one of several teachers in a school teaching various subjects, it was not necessary that I delve into the sciences, though Schmidt insisted that I have some exposure to them "for you, too, I hope will be a well-rounded woman," as he put it. And we explored history as well. As she told her father she would, Elinor sometimes sat with us but, to be honest, when she did she soon was bored and left us alone or would stare out the window while we spoke of something or other.

In the end, after six months with David Schmidt, I was confident enough to seek and, with the testimonial of Mr. Arthur Palmer, get a position at a girls' school. As happened with my recent period at the House of Mercy, I considered myself at the least adequate as a teacher, this time at Miss Fenton's School for Girls. I was familiar with the schools described in literature, those dark and lonely places in the brutal English countryside that made or broke a boy or girl, but Miss Fenton's was far more mundane. Its students weren't sequestered there but came for the day of lessons. They were the daughters not of the highest families but of those whose enlightened parents had hopes as well as money to spend on a daughter's learning.

Miss Fenton had been from one of the better homes, but the tragedy of her father's death in the war and her mother's resulting insanity had left her and her brothers to the kindness of their grandparents, neither pair of which had the resources to keep the young ones in the luxury they were accustomed to. Her two brothers found real work on Wall Street and she, Barbara Fenton, realized she would never marry well. She decided not to marry at all and with the support of those two brothers obtained a lease on an appropriate space and hired similar women—she called them "damaged goods"—as teachers.

Over the five years since opening the school, it developed a good reputation and was flourishing in its broad Thirty-Seventh Street building between Fifth and Madison Avenues.

I didn't know this when I started. I learned it over several dinners with Miss Fenton and other teachers. I had a small room on the fourth floor of the building, as did several of the others. Most of the rest lived at their parents' homes. But they came to dinner with us on Tuesday and Thursday nights and it was much like the family I'd had when I was a nun. Since we were younger and not, well, nuns, and sometimes shared some wine or ale, however, they were somewhat more lively.

I was careful, though, not to say too much about my past. They were fascinated by my having grown up on an Irish farm and even more by my time at the House of Mercy. But as to Elinor, they only knew that she had been my mistress and that she and her parents helped me train to become a teacher when I found that the House was not *my* calling.

Dear Elinor. Happy as I was as a teacher at Miss Fenton's, my life would have been a misery without my being able to see her. We made sure to spend time together every Sunday when we could. She went to ten o'clock services with Mr. Ballard and Meg and either the Ballards or the Palmers each Sunday and then had dinner in one of the houses. At one o'clock, she and I met at Madison Square at Twenty-Third Street. Sometimes she had Meg with her. Sometimes she didn't.

Rain or shine, we met—except when Meg was sick—and strolled. We had coffee at a small café across Madison Avenue from the Square. We usually sat at a round table in the front and to the side and had a fine view across to the Square. We could sit quietly and watch the promenaders and those lining up to see the torch hand and torch for the Statue of Liberty, in the park as a fundraiser for the base to be built in the harbor, as we had our coffees and sandwiches.

I can't recall a single word we said during those Sunday afternoon outings. I'm sure we spoke of the most mundane things together with the current gossip about the high-born. I know that she was careful about saying anything about Francis beyond the simplest. I at first asked about him, but she wouldn't tell me anything so I stopped.

She did tell me that he sometimes had her followed on Sundays. She said she thought he wouldn't care if she had liaisons with other men but that he wouldn't tolerate shaming him to the world and that he was satisfied when he was told, he confessed to her, that she did nothing more than meet with the same plain woman in dowdy clothing for a walk and some coffee.

"Of course he didn't think it worth his bother to ask anything about my 'dowdy friend,'" she said with a smile tinged, I thought, with anger.

There was an exception to our meetings. Perhaps once a month, Mrs. Palmer organized an outing of her own. A large hamper was prepared by the kitchen staff and loaded onto the family's carriage. After services for them and Mass for me if the weather was pleasant, we met at the Palmers', and Mrs. Palmer, Elinor, Meg, and I would be off for a picnic in Central Park. There were others picnicking in the large field we went to, and footmen were carrying hampers and blankets and if it was sunny large parasols and standing off to the side while their family enjoyed itself.

These events are second only to my more intimate meetings with Elinor in my memory. Meg wasn't a perfect child. She was, I think, a bit spoiled by her mother and grandmother. I don't think her father or Mrs. Ballard (her other grandmother) had much interest in her.

In all this time, I barely saw Francis Ballard. When I met him, I was introduced as "a teacher Elinor had met"—I never knew if he knew I was her frumpy friend.

On days when the Palmers didn't go out, Elinor sometimes asked me to come for "something informal," which amounted to a simple meal with her mother and father and sometimes her brother or sister (and their spouses). None of us dressed particularly for dinner and the atmosphere was relaxed.

Elinor said Francis was usually at some event or other or at one of his clubs (she never mentioned "whores"), but several times he did appear, and I did speak briefly and politely to him even though I knew what he did to Elinor. She'd not spoken about it again, but I think that was because she didn't want to ruin things between us when we were alone together and not because he no longer beat her.

Once he stepped up to me in the corner of the drawing room when Elinor was called to see about something with Meg. Her parents were there but they didn't notice us. I was looking out the window.

"You have been good to my wife," he said in a low voice. "It is good that she has someone like you to speak to."

His voice was sugary and most unlike the tone he used when he was in a larger group.

"She can be quite...emotional, you know. I sometimes think she is too concerned about her little girl. Who is not so little anymore. It can cloud her judgment. I just wish you to understand that."

I didn't say anything and stared out at Twenty-Eighth Street and was afraid I was rude to him. He finished and left me after a slight bow of his head. When Elinor returned, she asked me why I seemed so glum all of a sudden, but I told her I was thinking of my home in Backfox, and she accepted that.

Francis Ballard never spoke to me alone again. When I saw him later, he'd smile. It made me uncomfortable. I never told Elinor about this, at least for a long while, but I never doubted that Elinor spoke and showed me the truth about her husband.

31.

I was tired after a day of discussing *Agnes Grey* in my class at Miss Fenton's. It was a popular choice among the middle-class students in its portrayal of wealthy English families and how they treated (or mistreated) the governess and how the spoiled, selfish children were described. David Schmidt suggested I use it. I was making progress and looked forward to resuming on Friday morning.

I finished my dinner, it being one of the nights when all of us teachers ate (and drank) together, and was in the sitting room with the others when Bridget rushed through the door. She came to me out of breath.

"Bridget? What are you doing here?"

"Margaret, you must come at once."

"What it is?"

"It's Mrs. Ballard and Meg. Just come. We're going to the Palmers'. Mrs. Palmer told me to fetch you."

The others stared at us, and I followed her out. She said nothing on the way as we quickly covered the short trip other than "it's important, it's very important," which she said again and again.

We stepped up to the Palmers' front door. Williams, the butler, opened it after Bridget pulled the bell. We were sent to the second-floor drawing room.

Its door was closed, and Bridget knocked. Mrs. Palmer herself opened it. With her in the room were Mr. Palmer, Mrs. Burnley, Elinor's sister Caroline and brother-in-law, and an older couple who I assumed must be Francis Ballard's parents. Standing off to one side was a butler, though not the Palmers' so I assumed he was the Ballards'.

"Good," Mr. Palmer began. "If you, Margaret, will take a seat."

I found one next to Mrs. Burnley.

"I think we need to start with Bridget. Please."

Bridget bowed to the others in the room.

"It was two days ago, on Tuesday. Mr. Ballard woke me early. He said he had some bad news about his mother. He ordered me to get my mistress and Meg ready because they had to take a short trip. To see his mother, he said.

"I went upstairs and woke my mistress up. I told her what Mr. Ballard said. She put on a robe, and we went to get Meg in her room. While I got her dressed, my mistress left to get herself dressed.

"It wasn't long afore Mr. Ballard came up. He said he didn't want to waste time to get the horses for the carriage, so he sent Mumford, our butler"—I looked over to the unknown servant—"to get a cab and it was waiting downstairs when the three of them went to it. Mr. Ballard said they were going to the hospital."

"Hospital? I can't imagine her going to one. But if she did, which hospital was it, girl?" asked the man I assumed was Mr. Ballard, but Mr. Palmer interrupted.

"Henry, as you will see, that doesn't matter. They never got to *any* hospital. Go on Bridget." He poured her a glass of water from a tall ewer. She swallowed the drink quickly before resuming.

"Well, they didn't come home that day or the next. I thought they had to be at your house, Mr. Ballard, sir, and expected them back any moment. I was a little worried, you know, but I was sure they'd be home this morning. After all, they didn't have clean clothing.

"Then at about three, with me looking out the window expecting them to hop out of a cab at any moment, a cab did stop but it was Mrs. Ballard here who got out and went to the door."

Bridget nodded to the woman I didn't know, now clearly Francis's mother as I knew the other strangers were his father and his butler.

"I stood on the landing watching when Mumford opened the front door. Mrs. Ballard come in. 'My daughter-in-law, Mumford. She was expected for lunch at my house. Can you get her for me?'

"Of course, he couldn't get her since she was gone these two days. To see her, Mrs. Ballard, at the hospital. When he told her that, she insisted it was impossible."

"Yes," Mrs. Ballard interrupted. "It was impossible. I wasn't sick and was quite angry that she was ignoring me. I insisted that I be shown to her room. It was all in order."

"Yes," Bridget said. "I tidied it up after she rushed out."

Elinor's father spoke. "That is all very good. But where did they go if they didn't go to the hospital where Mrs. Ballard wasn't?"

"Arthur," his wife said, "that we don't know. Perhaps they went to Saratoga. Perhaps to Lenox. We don't know. I only found out about this an hour ago when I received a note from Mrs. Ballard telling me she must come here on a matter of some urgency."

Mrs. Burnley spoke up. "When I got home, Mrs. Palmer asked if I knew of someone who might be able to find out what happened. Since it seemed very important, I went to the precinct straight away and spoke to a nice sergeant there. He told me he would send an inspector from police headquarters on Mulberry Street over as soon as he could, and we expect him at any moment."

"I'm not sure you should have gotten the police involved but what's done is done. What are we to do now?" the elder Mr. Ballard wanted to know.

"Well, Henry," Mr. Palmer said calmly. "I don't think there's much we can do. Your son has taken my daughter and my granddaughter. Other than that, I cannot say that we know anything other than that Mrs. Ballard isn't sick."

"Are you suggesting my son…kidnapped his own wife and daughter? I think you are getting well ahead of yourself, sir. I really do and I must say that I resent the accusation. I must say it."

"You can—"

"Arthur. Henry. Please stop." Mrs. Palmer was trying to keep everyone focused. "There will be plenty of time but right now we know almost nothing. Mrs. Burnley, could you ask Cook to make some sandwiches for us? I don't think we can handle the dinner she planned. Sandwiches will do us fine. You can have them brought to the dining room. We'll be down presently."

With that, Mrs. Burnley left with Bridget and me. I think we were all glad to be out of the room. We went to the kitchen and Mrs. Burnley stopped Cook's dinner preparations. After some mumbling about wasted food, Cook and the kitchen girl set out to put a variety of sandwiches and ales together and the footmen brought them to the sitting room.

The others had come down and we three had gone up, and we'd all gotten ourselves sandwiches and drinks in the dining room and brought them to the sitting room across the foyer. I watched and listened to all this somewhat from a distance. I didn't know what to make of it all but knew it was probably very, very bad. I'm sure Mrs. Burnley and Mrs. Palmer had similar thoughts though I doubted they knew all I did about Elinor.

We were in the sitting room and sat and spoke about things only vaguely related to Elinor and Meg when Mrs. Burnley said there were visitors. We looked out. Elinor's brother David and his wife were coming up the steps and Francis Ballard's sister, Scarlet—who I recognized as the one who I ran into that horrible Sunday years before—and her husband were getting out of a cab.

They were all inside, and it was clear that the newcomers didn't understand why I was there and didn't want me to be. But Bridget and I sat on a pair of chairs over by the side and were promptly ignored. Everyone seemed uncomfortable. I saw that the bad blood between the two fathers was bubbling just below the surface and their wives made sure they were as far from one another as possible.

Finally, the front bell rang, and everyone was quiet. Williams opened it. The man we were waiting for, a short somewhat stocky man with a full beard, was at the entrance to the sitting room. Before anyone could speak, he did.

"Ladies and gentlemen. I am Inspector Derrick Washington of the New York Police Department." He handed his coat and hat to Williams and stepped into the room.

"I understand Mr. Arthur Palmer is a man of some importance."

"I'm Palmer," the man himself said as he stood and walked to shake the inspector's hand.

"Thank you, sir. I'll get the identities of the rest of you shortly, but for now, I need information."

An officer in uniform was with him and stepped to the inspector's side. The officer took notes while the situation was explained to the inspector, chiefly by Mr. Palmer but with some details supplied by Mrs. Ballard and Mrs. Palmer and by Mumford, who was asked to remain.

"You," he said, pointing at Bridget. He walked towards her and she stood.

"You were her maid, Miss—"

"Fallon, sir. Bridget Fallon."

"Yes, of course, Miss Fallon. You were the most involved. Is what the others say accurate as far as you know?"

"Yes, sir."

"And would you like to add something?"

Bridget hesitated before saying there wasn't. I think the inspector noticed me slightly shake my head, though if he did, he didn't do anything about it.

"I will have wires sent to the police in Saratoga and Lenox. If that is where they went, they will surely have arrived by now. And if they are there and safe, I think that must be the end of it, at least as far as the police are concerned."

He turned to Mumford. "Is there any way to identify the cab?"

"It was just a cab, sir. I'm not in the habit of recording its number. Just an ordinary cab."

"No, that's fine. I just wondered if there was something particular you recall and apparently there is none."

He looked at the officer, who nodded and made a note in his little pad.

"Officer Clemens here is taking down your information. There is an officer out front who I will instruct on getting those wires sent, if you'll excuse me."

He began to leave the room and turned back.

"I'm sorry, while I step out, may I have a word with you two young women," indicating Bridget and me. We looked at one another before following him out and I believe everyone watched us as we did.

Inspector Washington gave his instructions to the officer outside, who left to take care of the wires.

"Ladies, will you walk with me?" He pulled out a cigar and after we said we didn't object he prepared and lit it, spitting the tip in the gutter, and the three of us began our walk. I looked back at the house, and several faces were staring out.

"You have more to tell me, do you not?"

"Yes, sir," Bridget said.

"Very good. First, tell me who your friend is and how she fits into things."

I did my best to do that. Bridget's position was obvious since she was in a maid's uniform, but it took a bit of explaining for my role to be made clear. The inspector had no difficulty understanding it.

We walked to the corner, some forty or fifty yards from the house. I told him that Elinor showed me the marks from his beatings. I think Bridget was surprised that I knew, but she told the officer that she knew of them but had sworn to Elinor that she would never reveal it. The inspector just nodded at what we told him and at the corner we turned. Before we were in sight of the house, though, Inspector Washington said he didn't doubt that we were correct.

"If he were of a mind to abduct his wife and child, what would be the point of heading to one of the family houses? No, they are on a boat. He must have planned this. Whether it had anything to do with the beatings you mention, that he was concerned that he'd be exposed for them, I cannot say. The point, ladies, is that we do not know or need to know *why* he did it, just *that* he did. He had the tickets ready and the trunks filled and sent ahead. Moved money to a London bank. I can't see them going anywhere else. Yes, I'm confident that in the morning we will find what boat they are on. Then we can consider what is to be done about it. And, indeed, whether there is anything that we *can* do, seeing as he is the husband and father.

"But I ask that you both keep this to yourselves for now. I must think on it and perhaps a wire to Scotland Yard will be in order. They won't arrive for nearly a week and there is nothing for us to do in the meantime."

Before we began to walk again, I said, "Inspector. It has been many years, but I know of a woman, an American who is some sort of lady in England now, who may be able to help. She is quite...sympathetic to

Mrs. Ballard and I'm sure she will be willing to help if that is of any use."

"Miss—"

"Treacy, sir. Margaret Treacy."

"You are from Ireland, yes?"

"Indeed sir, as is Bridget here."

"Yes, I'm not a police inspector for nothing. My skills at deduction are legendary in the department."

It took a moment for us to realize he was joking, our accents making our origins obvious. But his little joke made us like the otherwise dry, somewhat arrogant officer with what I'd learned was a Boston accent himself more than we otherwise would have.

Of course, when we were back in the sitting room, everyone wanted to know what the inspector wanted from us and what we said. Bridget seemed to satisfy them when she said he was just asking about the daily habits of Mrs. Ballard and Meg. He thought it could be helpful.

It was late. Mrs. Palmer suggested that I sleep in Elinor's old room. When I entered it, I could not stop crying. It was sudden. Elinor was...gone. Elinor was gone.

32.

Because Bridget's "family" (the Francis Ballards) was gone and she was no longer part of the Palmers' staff, she was treated as a guest, same as me. On the Friday morning, she went to the Ballards' house for her non-maid clothing. I went to my apartment to do the same. I told Miss Fenton what was happening. She would take my class that day, and we were both back at the Palmers' shortly after half-past-eight. We saw Mr. Palmer in the dining room. He was there, pretending to read *The New-York Times*. Bridget and I sat at the table—another first—with coffee and pastries we picked at.

Mrs. Palmer came in. By nine, Caroline, Elinor's sister, joined us alone—her husband went into his office. Mrs. Ballard and Scarlet arrived after breakfast was cleared and we were all in the sitting room. We were told that Mr. Ballard also went to his office to wait for word. And the others paced more than anything as they waited for Inspector Washington. I was very uncomfortable.

We were nearly out of our wits when he arrived shortly after eleven. I was watching out the window, and there he was, coming up the sidewalk and turning to the steps. He entered the house, the pair of doors to the sitting room opened, and he was with us.

"Any news, Inspector?" Mrs. Palmer asked.

"I have some. I have some."

Before he could sit, he said, "I won't beat around the bush, ladies and gentlemen. They are headed to

England. They are on board the *Erin*. It gets to England in seven days' time."

"Are you sure?" asked Mr. Palmer.

"Yes, sir. Quite sure. England, I think we can safely say, is the place they'll be going. They would be far too out of place on the continent. Our inquiries to Lenox and Saratoga proved fruitless but it didn't take long for us to identify potential ships they could have taken to Europe and as only three sailed on Tuesday, one to Le Havre and two to England, it didn't take long for us to discover the one on which they are aboard.

"This works to our advantage. We know when they arrive, and they can do nothing to prevent our being prepared."

"But Inspector," said Mrs. Palmer, "If they are in England, what can *we* do?"

"It is a good question. We will be in contact with Scotland Yard. We don't know, I'm afraid, what Mr. Ballard's rights are in England as to his wife and his daughter. In particular, I'm afraid, we don't know whether he can be permitted to retain control of them even against their will. I am afraid he likely does but for now at least we can't know. We hope to find out well before they arrive."

This thought, of course, shot right through me like a bolt of lightning.

"But if my brother has the right to control them, why is it any concern of ours?" This was Francis's sister.

"Are you insane, woman?" said Mrs. Palmer. "You want him to be allowed to keep Elinor and Meg against their will."

"But surely he has a greater right to dictate at least what Meg does than anyone. And probably Elinor too."

"Than her *mother*?"

"Of course. More than her mother. He is the father. She is a Ballard. Both of them. That should be enough."

The inspector interrupted. "Ladies. Let us not jump to conclusions until we know English law."

"Well, I think that we have to be united in condemning this abduction, as it surely is," Mr. Palmer said, glad, I think, that Mr. Ballard wasn't there to make clear his view that his son's wishes were all that mattered in the end.

The inspector nodded. The others said nothing.

"Well, ladies and gentlemen. There is nothing I or, frankly, any of us can do at this point. I will return to the station to await word from Scotland Yard. When I have that information, I will return and discuss the matter further with you.

"There is, though, one bit of information I would like to know. I ask you, Mrs. Ballard, to make inquiries."

"Me?" she asked. She'd been quiet all this time.

"Yes, Ma'am. This was planned by your son. We suspect that he has forward a significant amount of money to a bank in London to allow him to live there with his wife and daughter."

"Live there?" Mrs. Ballard asked. "You quite astonish me."

"That may be, Ma'am, but I must consider that that may be his intent. I cannot say. If we know about any financial arrangements he's made, we'll better know his plans. So, I ask that you ask your husband to make inquiries at his bank about any large drafts given to your son. Just for informational purposes at this stage."

With that, he bid everyone goodbye with a bow and was gone.

Mrs. Ballard and her daughter soon followed him out, with Francis's mother promising to speak to her husband about what the inspector wished to know. But as there was nothing more to do and the lines between the families were getting larger, Bridget and I stayed, and Mrs. Palmer I think was glad of it.

The house got very quiet. It was too early for visitors, but Mrs. Palmer wanted to see no one. She instructed Williams to say she was indisposed, and she asked Bridget and me to join Caroline and her in her study. It was strangely comforting since I'd been in it so often, though until then only as the maid who cleaned it each day.

Before we went in, Mrs. Palmer took me aside.

"I've told Caroline in broad terms of the great affection you and Elinor have for one another. She is a clever girl and I think she likely suspected as much, at least since you left the sisters. I cannot say how happy she is about it, and I know she would be horrified were word of it to spread. I'll not try to hide your interest in the matter, and particularly in her sister. But we must be delicate with her. That is what I wish you to know."

I was bothered and surprised by this, although very pleased that Mrs. Palmer seemed to have no reservations about whatever my relationship with her daughter was. For some reason, I reached and without thinking reached for her hand and thanked her.

After we were together again, none of us said much as we sat, other than repeating and repeating what was already said. Mrs. Palmer had sandwiches brought in. But things picked up when I said we should try to contact Lady Glendale. "That horrible woman," Caroline said. "I didn't know that you knew her."

"I went to work for the Richards after I left this house, Mrs. Evans. Before she was a lady—"

"Oh, yes," she interrupted, "The notorious Bessie Richards, now Lady something-or-other."

I ignored this. "Then she and her mother went to England where she did become *Lady Glendale* and I only saw her briefly here in New York before I entered the order. I'm sure she would help if she could."

Caroline interrupted. "I should be very happy not to be in any sort of obligation to that woman."

Her mother gave her a stare. "We may not have that luxury, my dear. Let's hear from Margaret."

"I don't know how we can get word to her. She's in London, I think, and might have connections and information and money."

"Money?" Caroline asked.

"If Elinor and Meg are to get away from Mr. Ballard, they'll need someone's protection. I know Lady Glendale better than any of you and I tell you she's a rough woman but she's also kind and I think she'll help us if she can."

Mrs. Palmer and her daughter looked at one another.

"We'll discuss it if it becomes necessary. But I don't wish to expand the matter too far yet."

Bridget asked about publicity.

"Surely the news will get out. We must be prepared."

Caroline glared at Bridget till her mother said, "Yes, Bridget, we must be prepared." Caroline's glare got worse, and she said, "Elinor always was a stupid, spoiled cow."

Mrs. Palmer I think thought it best not to say anything to this and it wasn't my place to say a word. I was glad, though, that I'd had few dealings before this with Elinor's sister.

And it was becoming clearer and clearer that I was soon to again have dealings with Lady Glendale, who I hoped would remember me.

33

The Inspector's confirmation that Elinor and Meg were taken and were on the way to England was hard for me. They'd both become important, almost crucial, parts of my simple life. I can't say what led Francis Ballard to do what he was doing. I didn't know whether he learned of my relationship with his wife, innocent as it was, and whether that might have been why he did it. But I did know how horrible being so far away from her family—and me—with him would be on Elinor.

Mr. Palmer returned. After Williams took his hat and coat, he asked that everyone be brought together for his "report." Mrs. Palmer, her daughter, Bridget, and I went to his library.

"It is as I feared," he said after making sure the windows were closed. "I spoke to lawyers who put me in touch with a lawyer from England. He confirmed that under English law, Elinor has few rights, as a married woman, independent of her husband, and Meg of course has none.

"He said that there is nothing we can do under the law to get her freed from the monster."

It was jarring to hear him use that word, though I'd seen how uncomfortable he and Francis's father were the night before.

"There must be something we can do," Mrs. Palmer said.

"My dear," he said to her, and to the rest. "I'm told that there is nothing we can do...*under the law*." We were all sitting in chairs, several of which we moved to form a kind of half-circle.

"What we must do is think of something, anything, that will at least bring them home to us."

Before we could do any thinking on this, though, the front bell rang. A moment later, Williams opened the pair of doors to the sitting room to announce the arrival of Mr. and Mrs. Ballard.

"It is as the inspector suggested," Mr. Ballard said before he sat. "He has taken nearly all of his money and he may not intend to return."

"Is there any way to stop him?" Mrs. Palmer asked.

"They are bank drafts. They cannot be stopped." He turned to Elinor's father. "But I'm not sure if we should even if we could."

"He beat her." I said it without thinking.

For a moment, things were silent until Scarlett, Francis's sister, said, "That is a lie. How would you know, anyway?"

"Yes, Miss...Miss whatever-your-name-is," her mother said, "There is no way you would know."

"But 'tis true," said Bridget.

"They're right." Mrs. Palmer said this, and no one dared say anything. "Elinor sometimes confessed she wasn't doing enough to get Francis his son. It's what he wanted beyond all else. For an heir." She looked at Francis's father for this last bit, and he seemed very angry. She ignored him and again was going from face to face.

"She knew her obligations to him and his family. She said she...she...never denied him." Mrs. Palmer looked down and then up again.

"She hoped against hope that a boy would arrive. Then she had the miscarriage, and I think she began to avoid him. She said he was given more than enough chances to sire a son but that it didn't happen. A few months after the miscarriage, when he began to want to resume—she said they never were intimate except for those times—but each month she bled. About a year ago, she told me yet again that she wasn't with child and when I insisted that she must try harder to make it otherwise, she asked me to her room. We were alone. I helped her off with her dress and undid her corset so she was only in her chemise. She turned and lifted it.

"I could see he took a belt to her. Like some type of dog, he whipped her. She said he told her that this would be her punishment. She said he told her 'if you bleed down there, you will bleed elsewhere too,' and he left her.

"She told me not to say anything, that he was in his rights given her failure to do the one thing she was obligated to do. So, I was quiet about it. Each month she told me it happened again. Again and again."

"'Tis true," Bridget interrupted. "But I was sworn to secrecy."

"You stupid people." Scarlett had enough. "I know my brother better than any of you possibly could and he could never have done that. Yes, he wanted a son. It was what he dreamed of. But he would never be such a...villain as you are saying he is." She stood. "And I won't remain here if you insist on slandering him."

"Sit down." She was shocked by her mother's order.

Mrs. Ballard turned to Mrs. Palmer. "My son isn't perfect. But he isn't a monster."

Mr. Ballard stood.

"I think we've all said enough." He looked at his wife and daughter, and they stood.

"We will bid you goodbye and perhaps speak again tomorrow."

We simply watched as he and the women bowed their heads and left us.

34.

Almost as soon as the Ballards were gone, they were replaced by Inspector Washington. He stood in the doorway to the sitting room looking at us all.

He sat, and Elinor's father told him what he and the Ballards were told about the whippings, and he feigned complete surprise, having already been told of it from us when we first met him.

After thanking Mr. Palmer, he asked where there might be a private spot where he could speak to me alone. Mr. Palmer exchanged a glance with his wife and then suggested his study, where we were able to convince him to pay for my tutoring, as the most private.

When we got there, with the door shut, he said, "These disclosures are disturbing, but they also are revealing. I will be plain for you, Miss Treacy. What is your relationship with Mrs. Ballard? The younger. What you tell me won't leave this room, but I must know."

I'd come to like and trust the inspector, which turned out not to be as foolish as it might have, he being a policeman and all.

"We are...close. That is all I can say. We are very close."

He nodded, his fingers running through his beard. "As I thought. I have a proposition for you. It turns on the lady in England you mentioned."

"Lady Glendale."

"The very one. And to be clear, what I am saying I am not saying in my official capacity, is that understood?"

I nodded.

"Now, you mentioned Lady Glendale and I have looked into that lady. I have learned that she isn't among New York's elite. This is I think a good development for what I would like to discuss with you. You must keep quiet about it to *everyone* except Mr. and Mrs. Palmer. You will see why. I don't trust anyone else. The Ballards might be shocked by what you and Mrs. Palmer revealed but in the end, our effort requires the strictest confidence. I know their type and, in the end, they will protect their son. Not a word of this must reach them or it will all be for naught. Or worse."

We spoke for some time before returning to the others in the sitting room. Mr. Palmer was standing at the window, but the others and Bridget were on the sofa or in one of the chairs. Inspector Washington spoke. "Miss Treacy has given me some information that may prove useful. I cannot say whether it will or whether it won't, but that is all I can say now."

I'm sure some understood what the inspector was getting at and that others were completely confused by it, but there was nothing more to be done. And with it done and the inspector gone, a simple dinner was served, after which Bridget and I went to Elinor's room as we prepared for bed, she said, "She made me swear not to speak of it to anyone. Why did she tell you?"

We sat next to each other on the bed, but I didn't look at her. "I was still in the order. I think she wanted me to know how empty her marriage was. And how hard it was for her."

"Is that why you left the order?"

"I don't know." I looked up at her. "I think she needed me. And I might have needed her too."

35.

I couldn't imagine that I'd ever be on a ship again, especially on one sailing to Europe. But I was. Not to Ireland. To England and to London.

Three other people knew. Inspector Washington thought it up. He sat with Mr. and Mrs. Palmer, and they agreed to finance the trip. Others, including Bridget, were told that the Palmers sent me on a matter in Philadelphia that might result in my being away from New York for some time. Bridget, without her mistress, was allowed to remain at the Palmers' house, but boredom led her to rejoin the Palmers' staff, much as I had not so long before.

I told Miss Fenton I was needed outside New York on a matter of some importance, and she kindly allowed me to leave.

As to Elinor, Inspector Washington told everyone that he was in communication with Scotland Yard and that it would be some time before he had enough information to speak of the next step.

"I'm certain Mrs. Ballard—young Mrs. Ballard—and the child will be safe in this period. We must simply wait for more information. They haven't yet arrived in London, after all."

That was two days before I boarded the *Cornwall* and took up in a second-class cabin. Second class was infinitely better than the dregs of steerage on the *Nevada*, I assure you.

After a far, far better passage than my first one—although there were two horrible days when the weather made us keep to our cabins—I arrived in

London. The Palmers arranged for me to stay at a new hotel. I arrived and was shown to my room nine days after I left New York.

On my first night, I ate alone at a small table in the hotel's restaurant enjoying being waited on. Tired from the trip, I was asleep soon after I got back to my room. I breakfasted in the dining room in the morning and when I finished, I went to the concierge in the lobby. He was a very proper man and nodded as I approached him.

"Excuse me. I'm trying to locate Lady Glendale. I knew her in New York some years ago."

The concierge looked me over and heard my west Irish accent and hesitated. But I was a guest, after all, and it wasn't for him to determine who was entitled to know the whereabouts of Lady Glendale and who wasn't. He excused himself and went to a room off the lobby. He returned with a piece of paper.

"Here it is, Miss. Lord Glendale's address is in a directory we maintain."

With thanks, I opened the paper. "22 Dover Street, Mayfair."

"Is it far?"

"Oh, perhaps a mile, Miss. We can arrange for a cab."

"No, thank you. I will walk. I am quite used to walking." I turned to start, but said, "I don't know London customs. Is it too early to visit her."

"Indeed, I'm afraid it is, Miss. No. She won't be up for some time let alone ready to have visitors. You're best to go after lunch, after two or three would be best."

I nodded. "Well, I shall just go for a stroll then."

"Very well, Miss. I suggest you go to the left and it will take you right to Regent's Park. It is lovely at this time of year, particularly when there is no rain, and you must see the rose bushes of course." I nodded a last time and he smiled and I took his suggestion and was soon among the rose gardens in the park, admiring an artist doing a fine watercolor of them, and she smiled and thanked me when I complimented her before I resumed my stroll.

36.

"**H**ave you a card?"

I attributed the butler's haughtiness to the fact that he was the butler in a lord's house.

"I don't have a card. I believe she will see me, however. Tell her that it is Miss Margaret Treacy from New York to see her on a matter of some importance."

"New York, you say," he responded with a smirk, somewhat suspicious of my accent. "Does she know you?"

Losing my temper would not do, so I said, "She knows me, but it has been several years since we have spoken."

The butler—he went by Yeats—looked me over once more and, apparently satisfied by the dress I managed to get thanks to Mr. Palmer's money, he directed me to the sitting room while he went to see if his mistress was in. We thought it best that I not wire ahead about my coming to lessen the chance too many would find out about what I was doing.

The sitting room was a large room with a ceiling higher than I saw in the three or four fine New York houses I'd been in. Two tall, handsome windows faced Dover Street, framed by cream-colored drapes with a dark green trim. The walls were covered in a lighter green paper over off-white wainscoting and the wall space was largely given over to paintings, several portraits (including one of Lady Glendale) but the rest landscapes of both the countryside and the sea.

The portrait of who I assumed was Lord Glendale showed a round man with a thick beard and very thick eyebrows whose eyes were or were made by the artist to be vacant and whose lips showed the slightest smirk insofar as they were visible.

He wasn't a handsome man but my thoughts about him were interrupted when the door flung open and her ladyship herself entered wearing a colorful robe.

"I couldn't be bothered to get dressed when I heard it was you. You have seen me in a robe many times, my dear. Sit. Sit. Why are you here?"

This was said as Lady Glendale seemed to float across to me, and her outstretched arms were quickly around me, Yeats behind her. I barely had the time to stand when she was on me.

37

Nathaniel Johnson, I was told as I sat with him and my dear Lady Glendale in the sitting room in her Mayfair mansion, retired from the Metropolitan Police three years before, after twenty-five years on the force. He was an average-sized man with an average-looking face. His brown hair was the normal length and his beard trimmed in the usual way, with strands of grey lending him *gravitas*. His averageness in looks helped him as a detective, and Bessie said he had a first-rate brain.

He was one of the former policemen that upper-class London placed its trust and thus its secrets ·in. Lady Glendale told me before he arrived that he knew some of her secrets, and those of Lord Glendale, but that she was so far outside society that she did "not care a whit who he might tell."

It was two days after my surprise appearance in this very room. I was still at the hotel, it being thought best not to make my presence too well known. As instructed by Bessie, I told him everything I knew about Mr. and Mrs. Francis Ballard and their daughter. I didn't think it was much, but it was enough for Mr. Johnson to find quite a bit about the Ballards in London. A bit over a week of anxious days after I met him, the three of us were in Bessie's Mayfair study on the first floor. Mr. Johnson was sitting in a chair in the corner but stood and bowed when I went in.

"Margaret, Mr. Johnson has some information."

She nodded at him. Bessie and I sat in a small sofa across from him. He resumed his seat and leaned forward, keeping his voice low.

"I found them. They are in a suite at a hotel on the edges of Piccadilly. A bit of incentive to clerks at several banks led me to the Hibernian Bank, where you told me, Miss Treacy, that Mr. Ballard placed his money"—I'd passed on something Inspector Washington discovered—"I learned that Mr. Ballard comes in every Thursday morning to withdraw cash. After learning this, I made sure to be there on the next Thursday, that is, yesterday, and in the late morning a bank clerk nodded to me, as we had arranged for him to do." Mr. Johnson had a small pad and referred to it several times as he spoke.

"I then followed him from the bank—I had to be on my guard since he was very suspicious of being followed but he didn't see me, I'm sure—to a tavern where he had an ale and"—he looked back at his pad—"and a ham sandwich and then walked back to the hotel I mentioned. It is a good but not a grand hotel."

He leaned back in his chair and pulled a cigar from an inside pocket in his jacket. He held it out, and Bessie nodded which set him on a man's particular routine for lighting the horrible thing. After he was done and took a long draw of it, he continued.

"A further bit of incentive got the concierge at the hotel after he went up to his room to reveal that Mr. Ballard was indeed accompanied by a woman and a girl, presumed to be his wife and daughter, but that they took their meals in their room and that the pair, the wife and daughter, never left on their own."

He took another drag on his cigar and admired it when he was through before turning up to have a smoke ring float to the high ceiling and flicking its ashes in a small ashtray on the table next to him.

"My hotel source said a member of the staff agreed, thanks to Mr. Ballard's own incentive, to ensure that they—the presumed wife and daughter—didn't leave the hotel when he went to get money at his bank or otherwise left the premises. When he does leave, he has a woman from the hotel sit with them so they cannot vanish while he is gone.

"Other than her and whoever brings them food, the wife and daughter ain't been seen by anyone since they arrived."

He took another drag of his cigar while Bessie and I kept watching him. After a last look at his pad, he closed it and spoke to us.

"That, Lady Glendale, Miss, is what I've been able to learn so far. They say Mr. Ballard is always there when someone from the hotel is in the room other than the bodyguard he trusts and he prevents them at least when he's out, that'd be his supposed wife and daughter, from communicating. Some think they might be dumb since they never say anything but at least one person said she thinks she's heard crying late at night and she thought it was a lady."

My stomach churned at this bit, but I tried to hide it.

"Frankly," Mr. Johnson said, "I don't know more can be discovered about them. He rarely goes out and the woman and girl never do."

He stood and rubbed the cigar in the ashtray and after making sure it was out put it back in his inner pocket.

"I assume you ladies need to consider what to do with this information."

He looked from Bessie to me and back.

"Lady Glendale, you know where I can be found if you require any further services from me."

"Thank you, Johnson," my host said. "May I have your bill?"

He reached into his jacket, to the pocket on the other side from where his cigar was, and pulled out a folded piece of paper.

"Thank you. I will see that this is taken care of."

He nodded, this time at both of us, and picked up his hat and began to leave.

"Mr. Johnson."

He turned to Bessie. "Yes, m' lady?"

"I know you will be discreet. But is there anything else you can tell us? Perhaps a bit of speculation."

"Well, now you ask, m' lady, the hotel strikes me as a place where information can be had easily for the right price. Whether one can buy *cooperation*, I cannot say. But my guess is that for a few guineas, you could have certain people look the other way, if you know what I mean."

Bessie smiled the slightest bit.

"Thank you, Mr. Johnson. I think I know what you mean. Good day."

With a final bow to us, the former detective was gone. I went to the window and watched him walk to the sidewalk and turn left.

"What do you think?"

Bessie said this as I watched him go.

"I don't know if it is good news or bad. On the whole, I think it good. We know where they are and so far as we can tell, they are safe."

"Yes," Bessie said. "But for how long? And how much time do we have to do whatever it is we are going to do."

She and I hadn't spoken about what we could or would do, but I think we didn't have to. They must be rescued and so I said.

"You are right," Bessie agreed. "We must decide how we are to use this information to our advantage. But it will take some time."

"And we don't know how much time we have. Do you think they'll leave town?"

"Eventually. But where would they go? Who would they see, with everyone still in town for another month? I think we need formulate our plan to take place in the next two weeks. That's what I think."

She rang, and Yeats entered. She asked that tea be brought up and it soon was, with some sort of English biscuits. He poured the tea and with a nod to his mistress, he left us alone. We said little while we waited but when the door was shut, she went to it. She opened it and looked left and right before coming to me. We sat on either side of the table that Yeats put the tea and biscuits on. After we'd each made our teas as we wanted them and took sips, she placed her cup back in its saucer and leaned closer to me. I did as she did so we were very close.

"You know we must *rescue* them."

I nodded.

"I've an idea," she said, "but I must discuss it with someone. I trust him completely. Do you object to me speaking to him? He's someone who might be quite useful and I believe that we need him and perhaps some very few others."

How could I object? I trusted Bessie so it seemed only right that I trust this man too, and I told her that.

We agreed over the next days. We had to come up with a way to get Ballard to allow Elinor to leave the hotel. They'd already been in London for nearly three weeks and had to be bored sick in their rooms.

38.

"**I**t was a *tour de force*."

Stewart Styles was performing in Bessie's drawing room. She and I were his audience, sitting in comfortable chairs and drinking very fine claret. He, on the other hand, seemed to think he was on a West End stage.

"I walked up to him. 'Excuse me,' says I. 'Excuse me. Did you say Francis Ballard? From New York?'

"'I did, sir, I did.'

"'Henry Ballard's son?'

"'Indeed, sir. Do I—'

"He was quite surprised," Styles said, breaking from the scene. The actor's hands were moving more and more as he told his story. "I said we hadn't met but that I had the greatest pleasure in the too little time I got to spend with his dear father when I was last in New York. *'I'm Lord Glendale. Your father may have mentioned me. How is dear Henry?'*

"Bessie here assured me that this Ballard fellow hadn't met the real Lord Glendale and he is an American and who is he to question someone who says he is a lord? So, we fell into an easy conversation in the lobby of the Hibernian Bank."

Styles assured us that Ballard was completely taken in. He said he had given incentives to several bank employees to display the appropriate obsequiousness to "Lord Glendale."

"We all made it seem that I was in a great hurry, but not in so much of a hurry that I could avoid introducing myself to the son of my great friend Henry

Ballard. And of course Americans have no idea how inappropriate it was for me to just walk up to him and introduce myself to him."

Styles became serious.

"Are you certain the real Lord Glendale will be out on Thursday?"

"Stewart, I told you. His friend's horse is running at Ascot and word is that at least one of the princes or princesses will be in in the royal box and he wouldn't miss it for the world."

"What if it rains?" I asked. We went through this several times already, but I was still anxious.

"The horses will still run, and the men will drown their sorrows at the club and perhaps find some suitable companions if they are sober enough."

"And," Styles reminded me, "if the real lord is here and Ballard is on his way, I'll be prepared to intercept him before he enters the house. I'll tell him that something or other has come up that cannot be postponed, and we will reschedule it for Friday."

It all sounded very chancy to me but I'd agreed that it was our best opportunity.

Bessie and I wrote a letter on behalf of "Lord Glendale" to induce Ballard to visit, which Styles copied. The letter was precise. *Lady Glendale and I would be most pleased to meet with Mr. and Mrs. Ballard on Thursday afternoon next at half-past-two. Lady Glendale is a fellow American and is particularly excited about meeting Mrs. Ballard and their daughter, who Mr. Ballard mentioned.*

It wasn't much, we added, *but it would be a chance for the Ballards to know some people in London and escape the mundaneness of their hotel stay. It might well lead to further invitations, but this, with such an old and good friend of Mr. Ballard, Senior, was a good way to start. It was, in short, quite good bait to attract Mr. Francis Ballard and (more importantly) his family.*

The Thursday broke warm and sunny, and I arrived at Bessie's after Lord Glendale was off to Ascot with several of his friends, and Bessie promised when she joined me that he wouldn't be home until late.

Then she asked, "Are you ready?"

I didn't know that I was but I nodded. How the next hours would pass I didn't know either. By a quarter past two, I was by the drawing room window with Bessie and moments before the tall clock in the mansion's foyer tolled the half-hour, there they were, the Ballards climbing out of a hansom.

Mr. Ballard led his family, looking left and right as his left boot hit the sidewalk, and when Elinor was out of the cab followed closely by Meg, the "gentleman's" arm went tightly around his wife's waist. Meg held her mother's outer hand. The path to the house was too narrow to walk three abreast, so Ballard released his wife and moved ahead and for a moment it seemed that Elinor might stop but she didn't.

As Ballard was about to ring the bell, the door swung open, and I heard Yeats speak to the guests and assumed he showed them into the sitting room as we planned. He said something in the foyer, arranging for refreshments, and then he came up the stairs.

"Lord Glendale"—that is, Styles—entered the drawing room just as Yeats reached the landing.

"Your visitors have arrived, my lord, my lady. They don't have a card, but they said you asked them to visit. They are in the sitting room."

"Very good, Yeats," Styles said. Yeats liked Lady Glendale and had come to like me after our initial, awkward meeting and was happy to go along with our little charade. He said, "I've arranged for refreshments to be served," and he bowed and left the three of us.

"We will see how this transpires," Lady Glendale whispered to me. "You must prepare yourself."

I nodded and watched the others leave.

While they were downstairs, I couldn't help pacing back and forth in the drawing room, thrilled about having seen them and that they seemed fine, sometimes looking out onto Dover Street.

Why is it so long?

What are they doing?

Will I see her? When?

One of the drawing room's doors was open so I could hear what was going on in the foyer, though whatever occurred with them all in the sitting room remained a complete mystery. As the minutes seemed to turn into hours and there was only an eerie silence, I could barely contain my nerves and could not sit. I paced near the door, afraid to step into the hall in case I was discovered, when I heard the sitting room's doors open. Then I could make out Bessie telling someone to "follow me" echoing up towards me followed by a child's voice. Little Meg's voice. I couldn't be discovered by the girl, so I left the door open just a crack as Bessie and I planned.

I didn't know how long I waited, still pacing very near the door, when it opened. And there stood Elinor. She was more shocked, I think, than anyone I'd ever seen. Bessie had taken Meg to the toilet as we planned.

As she did, she'd asked Elinor to look into the "fine drawing room" while she waited.

Elinor and I had little time before Meg would be ready to go back down. We couldn't chance her seeing me.

I only had time to tell her to do her best to collect herself and then to trust Lady Glendale *completely* and to be prepared at a moment's notice to escape with us—for Meg and her to come with us—from their prison. She, Elinor, was shaking and crying but got control of herself as we heard Bessie loudly speaking to Meg and coming down the hall and heading towards the staircase.

Elinor went back to the hallway and as I was about to close the door, she turned. "I love you, Margaret," she said, and I told her I knew and that I loved her and she left to catch up to Bessie and her daughter and I left the door slightly open, not knowing when I would see her again and didn't move until I could hear the three of them laughing as they started down the steps to the foyer.

After a minute or so, I heard male voices and went to the window to watch the Ballards leave. I prayed that Elinor would look up, but she didn't dare until they were at the sidewalk and Mr. Ballard's attention was off to hail a cab. Then she did turn, and I think our eyes met though it was in fact a great distance. And again I could breathe.

39.

Lady Glendale and I met with Johnson on the next Sunday afternoon in Bessie's sitting room. His lordship was out.

"They went to services together, the three of them. I think he must be getting tired of being kept in his small cage. He is stepping out, slowly, to see if he can enter society. I daresay he looked over the celebrants to see if there might be someone he recognized like his father's friend, a lord no less, at the bank."

Now neither of the Glendales were church-going types and I went to Mass so there was no chance of Mr. Ballard seeing Lady Glendale were the Ballards to go to services. Later that day I moved from the hotel to the house in Mayfair, being introduced to Lord Glendale by his wife as "an Irish friend I met in my days in New York," which seemed to strike his lordship as being neither here nor there, which greatly relieved me.

We spoke with Mr. Johnson and told him what had happened days earlier at Bessie's with the Ballards, including what I told Mrs. Ballard in our brief encounter about being prepared. Our thought was that having told her to be ready to flee, we could be ready to rescue her and Meg when Mr. Ballard went to his bank as expected on Thursday. Although he could not endorse the plan, Mr. Johnson told us he "can say nothing against it."

It was agreed that the coming Thursday would be the day. At noontime Monday, though, Lord Glendale saw Lady Glendale and me coming down the steps. He was in the foyer, holding something from the morning's mail. He looked up. "My Lady Glendale, do you know a Mr. Francis Ballard? From America, I believe."

He held a large card.

"He sent me a note asking about meeting me to discuss something he says is of some urgency. Do you know anything about that?"

In the foyer, he handed the card to Lady Glendale. Bessie was not as obviously startled by this as I was and recovered herself quickly.

"This must be someone I knew in New York trying to take advantage of my connection to you."

"But he says he enjoyed meeting with *me*. I have never met the man. Have I?"

"My Lord, it must have been some passing connection. You know we Americans, always trying to boost ourselves with an English lord."

I watched this off to the side, hoping his lordship didn't hear how loudly my heart was beating.

"Yes, I suppose you are right. Some climber no doubt." He put the card on the hall table and left it there as he started to go up to his study. But as quickly, he turned back and retrieved it.

"Though, perhaps he does have an interesting idea. Americans do sometimes, you know. I shall write to him, asking him to visit. What harm can ten minutes with him do, however odious he may prove to be?"

His lordship and Ballard's card went upstairs as we helplessly watched. Bessie pulled me into the sitting room and closed the door. An hour later, we sat in the cramped office of Nathaniel Johnson.

"So, before you left you told your butler not to allow for the sending of any letters from his lordship until you return. That is good."

The office was very dark. One reached it only by climbing a series of staircases with turn after turn in a building not far from Scotland Yard itself. It was warm and Johnson's window was open and the smells from the Thames wafted in.

"You get used to it," he told us when he saw our reaction. He cleared two hard-back chairs for us and apologized for not being able to offer refreshments. Her ladyship assured him that as our visit was so sudden and unplanned, he wasn't expected to have anything and that we were simply happy that he was there when we arrived.

After he mentioned that we may have bought some time with the instruction to Yeats, Bessie's butler, it might require that we improvise and hurry our plan.

"We will have but the one opportunity, my lady. We cannot waste it."

"I understand, Mr. Johnson, as does Miss Treacy. We understand it all too well. We planned on doing what we are to do on Thursday."

"What if we send our own letter?" I suggested.

"Well thought, Miss Treacy, well thought," the investigator said. "Yes, we can have Ballard invited to the house *after* Thursday, when it will all be done. His Lordship must make it for Friday. Or Thursday if it comes to that."

"What about those who watch his wife and daughter, as they do when he is at the bank?"

"That will make it difficult. But I think we can give them incentive enough or at the very least delay officers from interfering."

He stood. "Now, we have much work to do and little time to do it. Your ladyship, you must find when your husband intends to meet with Ballard. If the letter is sealed, you must open it and allow it to go on its way. But it cannot be tomorrow or Wednesday. It must be no sooner than Thursday. We cannot be ready till then. If he suggests tomorrow or Wednesday, you must convince his lordship that there is something else he must do.

"While you and Miss Treacy return to your house, I'll make travel inquiries. You must return as soon as you can to provide me with when Ballard will be visiting."

As we returned to her house in a cab, Bessie cursed herself for not having thought to find out when her husband intended to have Ballard come.

"But Bessie. Mr. Johnson will have a plan. It will be fine as long as his lordship hasn't sent his letter—and Yeats will not have allowed that—and as long as it isn't before Thursday."

At the house, Lady Glendale immediately went to her husband's study. She knocked and she was glad he was there.

"Lord Glendale, have you sent that invitation to that American yet?"

"Well, it is hardly an 'invitation.' It is merely a business meeting. No, I haven't. Why do you ask?"

"I would like to meet a fellow countryman."

"Well, it doesn't matter to me one way or the other. I was thinking about tomorrow."

"Oh, no. That won't do. Thursday or Friday. I'll be around on those days."

"Friday is out of the question. Thursday? Very well. Thursday it shall be."

His lordship pulled out a sheet of stationery and did as he was instructed.

"Shall I ask him to bring his wife and child with him?"

"No," Bessie said. "It will be solely for business and we can go from there. I will just say hello as we Americans like to do. We can meet his family later, do you not think?"

"Of course, my lady. Of course."

He began to write.

Mr. Ballard,

I have received your note. I should be pleased to meet with you at my house this coming Thursday afternoon at two p.m.

Glendale

We preferred not to get his lordship involved at all. Our hope had been to move on Thursday, to get Elinor and Meg while Francis Ballard was at the bank. But things were going quickly and we believed we could do it with him coming to the house instead.

40.

Thursday finally came. It was another fine day. At one, I sat in a hired carriage around the corner from the Dedham Hotel. Stewart Styles stood across from the entrance, positioned so Ballard could not see him and so he could check the clock, which he often did. 1:05. 1:10. 1:15.

Before it reached 1:20, we both saw Francis Ballard and only Francis Ballard bound down the steps carrying some sort of portfolio in his right hand. The doorman signaled a hansom for him and he was soon gone to Mayfair.

Styles waved the umbrella he held, and in no time I was with him. We nodded properly as the doorman held the door for us. Stewart went to the desk and asked to see Mrs. Ballard "on a matter of some urgency."

He was dressed simply but finely in dark blue trousers and matching jacket with a colorful mustard waistcoat over a white shirt and a maroon ascot cravat. Topping it all was a somewhat theatrical black top hat, which he nestled in the crook of his right arm. He said the cravat and hat would draw attention from his face.

As for me, I was my finest day dress, which was not so fashionable as to be noticed in this part of town. Bessie had lent me one of her hats, which complemented my dress, and, Styles said, that would draw attention from *my* face.

Given the room number, we climbed to the third floor, and he ran up the final flight. He banged hard on the door three times. A woman's voice called.

"What yer want?"

"There's been a horrible accident," Stewart said, somewhat out of breath as I reached him. "It is about Mr. Ballard."

There was a slight pause, and the door opened.

Elinor's guard, a short woman of perhaps thirty in a hotel's maid's frock, stared at the pair of us, and Stewart rushed past her with me right behind.

Elinor came from the other room.

"Francis. Is it Francis? What—"

She saw me.

"We've no time," Stewart said loudly and with authority. He turned to the guard. In his hand was a five-pound note.

"For your troubles, my dear."

I turned to Elinor. "Where is Meg?"

Elinor had quickly recovered her wits. She put a finger to her lips and opened the door to the second bedroom, where it was clear the both of them slept.

"Meg, dear. You must come with mama. We are going on a trip." She said it in quite a sing-songy voice.

The girl followed her mother out of the room, looking very confused and holding her mother's hand with both of her own. Stewart ran in to gather what he could. He'd brought a large sack with him. There was little time, but Elinor pulled herself from Meg's grip so she could pick up several items, including two quite nice dresses for herself and a pair for Meg. Within five minutes of our entry, we were gone.

The guard was dumbfounded, sitting in the suite admiring the princely note she'd been given and wondering, I imagined, what she would tell Mr. Ballard and his terrible temper when he returned.

On the landing, Stewart said, "There is a back way out and we must take it."

We followed him down the backstairs and that got us to a kitchen in the basement. It was much like any kitchen in a wealthy house, only bigger and with more cooks and assistants and scullery girls. It had a side entrance for servants and supplies. Without paying attention to the workers who we surprised by our rushing in, we were rushing out through the door and onto a street around the corner to the hotel's entrance. Our closed carriage had turned the corner when I left it and was waiting, and we crowded in, just as Big Ben tolled the half-hour.

Within ten minutes, the carriage pulled up to a house several blocks away from Stewart's. He paid the coachman generously and watched it turn the corner and then we walked—"casually" he said—to his house, with Meg between Elinor and me, holding our hands.

Once inside, we sat in the small sitting room. It was an apartment on the top floor in a five-story building with just one bedroom, but it was enough for Stewart.

Nathaniel Johnson was there with Bessie. After we calmed down, he spoke, with Meg on her mother's lap.

"Now," he began, "We are fugitives. I would expect," he pulled out his pocket watch, "that bedlam has broken out at your house, Lady Glendale, or will within a very few minutes if your husband is prompt."

"Oh, he will be. 'The courtesy of kings' he likes to say."

"In that case," Johnson said with a nod, "Ballard will soon be hurrying his way back to the hotel, having discovered that your husband is not Lord Glendale or, more likely, that 'Lord Glendale'"—he nodded at Styles—"was not Lord Glendale. He will soon be back and learn of what has been done to his wife and daughter, if he is not there already."

"Soon me old mates at Scotland Yard will be called in regarding the kidnapping of the American's wife and child. Oh, that will be exceedingly popular with the gutter press, I can tell you. I'm afraid Lord Glendale will be very much inconvenienced by the reporters who will be hounding him if news of his involvement gets out, though we may hope that Ballard and others at the Yard will have sense enough not to identify to whose house he went on his goose chase. The press will find out, I daresay, eventually and, Lady Glendale, I fear your husband with be very much inconvenienced, indeed."

"That is why I'm going with you, my dears," Lady Glendale said. "He will be even more intolerable than ever for a while and will be particularly upset that they won't believe him when he says that he has no idea what any of them are talking about, that he never met this American or pretty much any other."

Johnson continued. "His discomfort cannot be helped. I'm not overly concerned about the Yard. I will suggest to some of my former colleagues that Mr. Francis Ballard's story is very unlikely to be true and that what happens, though I cannot say I've any involvement in what happens, might more accurately be described as an *escape and rescue* and not a *kidnapping*. I've also arranged for a more accurate story, closer to the truth, to be delivered to *The Times* and other leading papers. That should give some pause in the storyline."

He looked at me with what I thought was a slight smile.

"Fortunately, no one knows you, Miss Treacy, and Styles is an adept actor and I very much doubt he will be recognized."

"I was doing my Pickwick, if you wish to know," the actor said with the slightest of bows.

"And a very good Pickwick, I'm sure," said Johnson.

Bessie rolled her eyes and I smiled. Elinor looked very confused. But she got up when I did after putting Meg on the floor.

Bessie said, "Mrs. Ballard, Elinor, you must continue to trust us. We will get you home to New York. But you must trust us."

Elinor looked at me, and I nodded. "I believe I must," she said.

She quickly changed into one of the better dresses that'd been shoved into the sack, though it was of course quite wrinkled. Meg was put into an appropriate outfit, and in no time we—this included Bessie—followed Johnson out after a last goodbye to Stewart Styles and we dashed across the sidewalk to a waiting coach and four. It was quite like any other, black and inconspicuous.

I got in, followed by Elinor and Meg. On the sidewalk, Lady Glendale thanked Johnson, who tipped his cap with a "m' lady," and when we four were settled, the footman put up the steps and closed the door and he was on the back as the wheels began to roll.

"Don't worry about the coachman," Bessie assured us. "He is a friend of Styles's. He did a great Iago at the

Globe last season. And the footman? They are still talking about his Romeo of last season."

41

Our carriage merged easily into the London midday traffic. Meg kept asking what was happening and who these people were, and Elinor kept telling her that everything was good and we were her friends. She reminded Meg that she saw me many times in New York, and suddenly the girl said, "You're Margaret, ain't you?" I said I was and she smiled.

Other than that, no one spoke until we were well into our trip. We were heading south, to the Channel for a crossing to France and were quickly over the Thames. The thought that we were now fugitives being chased—if not yet, soon—by the police seemed to hit Lady Glendale and me at the same time.

We watched the buildings stretching on the south side of the river, mixing in with all the other carriages and wagons leaving the city, with Meg standing between the seats and with her hands on the coach's window watching everything we passed. Elinor looked at her daughter. I don't think she'd looked at me other than in passing since we were in the carriage, and I was surprised at the tension between us.

It was somewhat broken when Meg climbed back up beside her mother.

"Where are we going, mama? And is papa going to be with us?"

Then Elinor looked at me and then at Bessie, who said, "We are going on a great adventure, Meg."

Her attempt at calming the girl had the opposite effect. Meg glared at her. "Who are you? Why are you taking us?"

"Meg. She is your friend, too." Elinor reached an arm around her daughter and pulled her closer, but the girl didn't take her eyes off us across from her.

"I want to go back," she said. "I don't like you."

"What your mother says is true," Bessie said. "We are your friends."

"We are going home? I don't like being in that place with those people watching us all the time who wouldn't let me play even when I promised to be quiet."

She looked at Lady Glendale. "Were we at your house? It was a nice house."

"Yes, you were. And it is a nice house. But now we must get back to your house in New York."

All of this seemed to calm Meg down.

"Will papa be coming?"

Elinor looked at Bessie and me again and then said, "We will see, my dear. But not just yet. Not just yet."

"Okay," her daughter said, and she got up and returned to looking out the window.

Things outside were less cluttered as we reached pasture and farmland. All of a sudden, the coach rolled to a stop. In a moment, Romeo was at the right door.

"I'm just going up top, ladies. Is everything alright?"

We assured him that it was. Meg asked if she could get on top, and Romeo said, "No, dearie. It's much too windy and dirty up there for a fine lady like yourself." She seemed satisfied by this and smiled and laughed when he left, and we felt the carriage rock as he got up top before we resumed.

With Meg's attention elsewhere, we spoke in low voices, just loud enough to be heard over the noise of the carriage.

I hadn't been a part of several of the conversations Lady Glendale had with Johnson. I was subject to being hanged or whatever the English do with Irish kidnappers of an American woman and her daughter in London, so I was even more anxious than Elinor.

I knew much of the plan, but Bessie filled in details for both Elinor and me. We were hurrying to get to a town on the Channel where we would board a small boat to cross to France. We should arrive shortly after sundown, which would make the crossing a bit more secure. We couldn't know whether word of us and our flight reached Royal Navy patrols off the coast but were assured that the smugglers who would be carrying us were adept at not being caught. We would then take a carriage to Le Havre and then a boat to New York.

"Why do we not simply go from Liverpool?" Elinor naturally wanted to know. "We could just take the train up."

"Johnson says it is a bit of a chess game. They will expect us to go that way and that is where they will focus. Of course, they will know that that is what we will think so as a result we might not go to Liverpool or Bristol and head for the Channel instead."

"Which is what we are doing," I pointed out. "So won't they address that as well?"

"It cannot be helped. We could try a place to hide in England or even Scotland or Ireland, but not only would we have to cross many miles to do so, we would be very obvious, as a bunch of Americans and an

Irishwoman. Eventually, word would get to Scotland Yard, and they will be upon us."

"Assuming Johnson hasn't succeeded in convincing them that we are the victims here and that my husband isn't," Elinor said, immediately understanding the situation. "But why don't we stay on the continent?"

"Johnson thinks our best chance is to get to New York before your husband does. If we get across to France, we can be in New York in ten or twelve days. He won't leave England for days searching for you two. We should be well on our way when he begins his own trip."

We didn't know what would happen when we got to New York, but our goal above everything was to get Elinor away from Francis Ballard, at least free of Francis Ballard in a country an ocean away from home. This made sense, I had to agree. It was the best of a series of bad alternatives. Perhaps I should've given more thought to what would happen if this venture failed, but I didn't. I think because I knew it couldn't fail. It *couldn't*.

We were all quiet. At a small town with the traffic lessened and about two hours after we began, the carriage pulled to the side and stopped. Romeo jumped down.

"We have to change horses, ladies. It won't take long. You can stretch your legs but please don't speak. We can't have people recognizing you as Americans."

It was a relief to be able to move and use the facilities. As Bessie and I got back to the carriage, Elinor and Meg were already inside. Romeo was entertaining the girl with various changes-of-accents.

It seemed that his cockney speech was her favorite, and he again had to deny her request to sit up top with him. As we got underway again, she was wide awake and enthusiastic about the trip.

"Are you a real lady?" she asked the real lady among us. Lady Glendale said, "Indeed I am" and asked if she wanted to sit beside her, and Meg nodded so she and I switched places, and I could at last be next to Elinor.

Meg's attention locked on Bessie, who took on her best Lady Glendale manner, and at last my legs could touch Elinor's and I could discreetly put my hand on hers. She didn't try to move away, either her leg or her hand, and we were both quiet in our thoughts and in our touches, watching Bessie entertain Meg and I was so happy and lifted from the anxiousness at least briefly.

Sometime after, Elinor leaned to me. She was sorry to have caused me so much bother and to risk so much.

"You came here from New York. Just for me and my baby. Perhaps someday I'll understand it."

"Had I given it a moment's thought, I might not have. But I didn't think. It was instinct that brought me. That, and the support of your dear parents."

I didn't truly believe this, or at least wasn't as confident about it as I let on. I had thought long and hard before doing what perhaps was inevitable. But to Elinor it was important that I seem never to have doubted it. She was again quiet and looked out the window on her side at the passing fields and little towns we went through. She held my hand, and I knew she was crying. Slightly so that no one would notice but me.

A small hamper was prepared with food and ale to keep our bodies together. When we next stopped, Bessie had it put between the benches and the four of us nibbled and sipped as we went along. Elinor and I said little worth remembering for the rest of the journey. Meg soon became exhausted by Lady Glendale's antics, and she fell asleep with her head in her ladyship's lap, with Lady Glendale, now "Aunt Bessie," placing a securing hand on the girl's shoulder as she variously looked at me and Elinor and the passing countryside.

Except for brief periods when a cramp caused one or the other of us to release them, Elinor's hands and mine stayed connected throughout. When we weren't eating or drinking, of course.

42.

When the carriage made its next stop, Romeo said we had perhaps twenty miles to go. He took the hamper to give us more room and restored it to the stack of our luggage. Almost as soon as we began to roll again, Elinor placed her head against my shoulder. She wasn't asleep at first, though she was quiet. Then I could hear her rhythmic breathing over the sounds of the coach, and I swore I would never let her escape me again. It was a foolish promise, made without her consent, but I began life in New York minding her, and I would do so again.

That at least had been my final thought as the sun was low enough in the sky so that it burnt directly into the carriage from the west, and I believe I too was asleep as it was dark when I next remember anything. Elinor was shaking me as we were on cobblestones after the dirt road.

"We've reached the coast," she said. Meg jumped up and stood as she had as we left London to watch out the window at the passing houses and then the warehouses and stores. The sea air couldn't be mistaken.

It was soon full dark, and we stopped not far from the water. Romeo jumped down. He peeked in.

"Ladies. We're here. I'm just asking some final directions." He walked away. There was enough light from the street that we could just make out each other in the carriage. I moved to sit beside Bessie, and Meg took my place. Nothing was said and we could pick up bits of conversations of those passing by. The accents were funny to me, but I could make out the mundane talk and salty air of a fishing town.

Romeo soon returned. He poked his head in. "We are nearly there, ladies," and then he was back up with Iago. We were moving again and on the road that ran along the water itself, with small docks running into the Channel. We kept going, though, past the last of the docks and turned onto a side path. While it wasn't much, there was other traffic on the rutted road, so we didn't stand out. Iago pulled the carriage to the side and stopped.

Again, Romeo's face was at the door.

"This is it. No one seems to be paying any attention. We will get your things."

He climbed to get the two trunks that Bessie said Yeats prepared for us. A man walked to us. It was dark and there was no moon, but we could see well enough from the light of the carriage's right lantern.

"Be you the ones Mr. Smith sent? The ones looking for a little 'oliday in France?"

We figured Johnson had not used his true name. Meg took an instant dislike to the man, and she moved closer to her mother, whose arm was tightly around her shoulders. Bessie took the lead.

"Yes, it is us. We understand Paris is lovely at this time of year."

The man laughed. He was in a sailor's outfit of dark trousers and a pea coat over a buttonless shirt with blue and white stripes running across. He didn't wear a hat, and even in the little light we could see he was nearly bald. He opened the door and put down the steps.

"Well, ladies. I shall do what I can to have you enjoy the Froggies' 'ospitality by this time tomorrow."

I stepped out first, followed by Elinor and Meg, who was staying as close as she could to her mother, with Bessie coming last. I glanced around. Carriages were passing in either direction, but no one seemed to be paying us any mind. We were quickly to a quay in a small cove and his small boat. I don't know what kind of boat it was except that it wasn't very long or wide and it had a small hut that seemed to go below the deck. A single mast was empty.

With thanks to Iago and Romeo, who Meg rushed to for a hug, we boarded the little smuggler's boat and went below decks as instructed by our captain, who insisted we call him Captain Cook.

He said we'd need to wait where we were for some time to be ready for the tide and not to arrive too early. "We want it to be a bit after dawn when we arrive, you see. Otherwise we get to France too early. We want to time it so we arrive just at dawn. Everything'll be safer, more normal, that way. So get some rest if you can."

There was little space and less headroom where we were. A lantern was lit against the wall at the front, and the shadows from the wood danced around as the boat moved up and down in the water and those shadows made the up and down far worse. But that was nothing compared to the smell. It wasn't quite the dankness of the *Nevada* but it was still wet and moldy and with the movement, I wasn't sure I could avoid retching but somehow I did and the others were also able to keep their stomachs under control. Even Meg, who said she wouldn't stay in the horrible boat till

Elinor promised her that it wouldn't be for long and that it was something that had to be endured together for us to all get home.

There was a straw hamper to the side and a large bottle, more a jug, of ale beside it. After we'd settled in a bit and were somewhat accustomed to the smell and tightness, Bessie reached in and passed a loaf of bread to Elinor, who broke off a large piece—much of which she gave to Meg—and passed it to me. The same was done with a bit of beef, and it was all followed by the passing around of the bottle.

We didn't dare speak above a whisper, though we heard the crew calling greetings to those who passed on the shore until that finally got quiet.

It was some time, and I'd fallen into a sleep when one of the mates knocked on the doorway and told us we were getting ready to shove off. I cannot say when it was, but the sounds we'd heard when we arrived were gone and all that was there was the waves hitting the shoreline and the hull.

There were three men besides Captain Cook in the crew. The one who looked to be the youngest was the one who came down. He told us that we were in good hands but should keep quiet on the way just in case we ran into any trouble once we got into the Channel itself. We didn't need to be told a second time and tried to be as quiet as church mice.

We did the best we could to prepare for the crossing, with Bessie and me on one side facing the two Ballards. Meg was doing a good job of not crying, but she clung to her mother as the boat began to rock side to side when we reached open water. The young mate came down again. He blew out the candle. "We don't want no one to think anyone's here," he said. "We like to be as dark as we can. It's our ears and not our eyes we use when we cross."

The water lapped against the side, but the boat was no longer going up and down like it did before we started. With the door open, we got the slightest breeze from movement. The smoother motion calmed us as we put some distance between ourselves and England, which calmed us even more, and we could hear the sails beginning to catch the Channel's wind.

Someone came down to us but it was only when he spoke that we knew it was Captain Cook. "We're lucky it is only a slight moon and that won't be up till we'll be well away.

"Don't be worried. Your Mr. Smith has made provisions for providing some incentives, as he calls it"—I heard him pat the side of his chest—"in the unlikely event one of Her Majesty's boats should choose to have a word with us."

He laughed, which relieved me. From what I saw, Mr. Johnson, or Mr. "Smith," was very successful in his doling out of incentives.

The trip wouldn't be long, Captain Cook assured us. We each fell into our own spaces, silent and very fatigued until we heard "Ahoy there" at some distance though I had no idea in what direction it came from. It sounded English. There was no light and Bessie's "Sssh" echoed about.

"Identify yourself," came the first voice, much closer now and very much in the Queen's English.

"We are the *Maestro* from Dover."

"And your business, sir. State your business."

I couldn't imagine what legitimate business could be ours, but Captain Cook said, "We're heading to Calais to collect some fish in the morning to bring back."

There was a bump. It must have been the navy boat hitting us, but it couldn't have been a very large one or we would have felt it more severely. Someone had a torch. We ducked as its light came into the cabin.

"You're free to look, Lieutenant," Captain Cook offered.

There was a bit of silence until we heard boots hitting the deck and I don't know what Elinor was doing except I hoped to God she was keeping her child quiet. For my part, my hand was gripping Bessie's and for the first time since I met her, I felt she was afraid.

Just as suddenly, one side of the boat bobbed up.

"Thank 'ee, Lieutenant. We hope to see you again."

"And you, sir." With that, we could feel the other boat pushing off and we could again breathe.

A moment later, Captain Cook stuck his head in.

"That was indeed close, but we now know they ain't actively looking for you. We should be safe."

"But what—?" Bessie asked.

"Ah, that. Well, if we was smuggling things from here to France, the navy turns a blind eye to it for the most part. I mean, in that case, we be sending the product of a good English farmer or manufacturer to France so there's no real point in stopping us now, is there? No, they're more interested in stuff coming into England that takes sales from a good English fisherman or manufacturer or farmer. But as she rides high in the water, when his boat hit he could tell we weren't really carrying nothing.

"Second, your Mr. Smith's incentives convince an officer like this here lieutenant that it ain't in his interest to look into the hold. The risk is that by offering it to him he would be loyal and suspicious, and we'd be done for. They'd force us back till they found out just who you were and why you were traveling in such a...manner.

"But I've encountered this one before so there was no chance of that tonight. He'll spread the amount to his crew, like a prize, which is more than they'd get if they found contraband which, as I says, the Navy don't care much about. And incentives aren't much good for thems coming the other way, bringing things to England. A Royal Navy crew would put you in chains and tow your boat to the nearest port if you tried to bribe them heading to England. But going the other way? Smith's little incentive won't go to waste. It's like Nelson said, they turn a blind eye to it, they do."

I was still gripping Bessie's hand—and she was still gripping mine—but we both relaxed.

"That was the big test. If they was lookin' for you, they'd have searched and now that we be past 'em, they won't be looking for us no more."

"What about the other side?" I asked.

"Well, Miss. Mr. Smith give us plenty of incentive for them too and even if they looked, what are they going to do with a bunch of Americans as smuggled goods? So even if they find you, they won't do nothin'. Remember for a Froggie, fleeing the English is a sign of honor and they'd probably give us all medals."

He laughed at his little joke before suggesting we try to get some sleep and then he left us. We weren't disturbed again on the crossing, and it wasn't long before dawn when one of Captain Cook's crew called to us to wake up.

Unlike the spot where we started the trip in England, we were in a small fishing village, and Captain Cook thought it safe for us to come on deck. As the sun rose, we could see the finishing touches being made to fishing boats about to head out, with many gulls circling them. The buildings were all different colors like the front doors of the houses on the Palmers' block in New York and quite cheerful. They formed a half-circle around the sheltered harbor.

As we got close to the beach, two crewmen jumped off the bow, and one grabbed a line until we were secured.

"You see"—women and children from the town watched us—"with their boats out, there is room for us on the beach." He pointed to the road along the beach.

"They wonder what cargo we be bringing to them. I hope that they won't be disappointed in seeing you. Do any of you, by chance, speak French?"

Elinor and Bessie said they learned some from governesses, but that it was unlikely to be of much use.

"Nonsense. They'll love you for it." He looked at the rest of us. "And they will love you because you be Americans. Just say '*Vive la France*' whenever you get the chance."

One crewman handed our trunks down to one who jumped off. Captain Cook leapt from the bow and the crewmen helped us off, a half-asleep Meg laughed when she was swung fore-and-aft by the sailor who collected her from the deck before she was placed very, very delicately in the sand. I don't know that she'd ever seen sand before and I knew that I never had, there not being many beaches near Backfox. The captain reached into the pocket of the dark blue jacket he put on before leaving the boat. "I'm to take you here," and he held up the paper, "and then I must bid you '*adieu*,' as the Froggies say."

43.

Once we recovered on the beach in France from the cramped space and rolling on the *Maestro*, we walked across the sand. I think other than a few quick glances, no one paid us any mind. On dry land, I looked again at the boat. It was so small in the daylight. It did what it had to do, though, and we were, I prayed, free from the danger of being imprisoned. In England, at least. What would happen if we made it back to America I couldn't say.

We went several blocks inland, down a narrow street lined with narrow houses of limestone with flowers draped from boxes below most of the windows till we reached one house with a yellow door. Captain Cook knocked, and a man in a nightshirt opened it. He told us to come in and after the crewmen placed the trunks in the small room off the foyer, they saluted us and we thanked them, and the captain shook our hands, including Meg's, who wouldn't let go until her mother said she had to. He bid us *adieu* with a smile and a final nod. We were alone with the man in the nightshirt.

"I wasn't quite prepared for Smith's note, but that little matters. We will get you to where it is you are to go."

He was French, but his English was excellent, although it took me a moment to understand him.

"*S'il vous plait. Attendez...*Wait here. I'll be down shortly."

We were left in a small room off the foyer. Its walls were white and there was a small sofa with a crucifix above and several mismatched chairs across from it. A mirror hung above a small fireplace, and Elinor was the first to look at herself. She was lovely to my eyes, but I knew she wouldn't be in hers. She frowned and made some noise as she ran her fingers through her hair, which dangled unrulily well below her shoulders, and tried to move several strays from her face, which pouted.

She left the glass and plopped next to Meg. I went to it myself. Beyond eyes puffy from a lack of sleep in the trip across and hair nearly as disheveled as Elinor's, I was surprisingly presentable.

Before I could do much, our host was down the stairs, dressed in blue trousers and a ruffled cream-colored shirt that I assumed was the local style.

"We have little time to waste. You can see to your needs in back, but we shall have to be gone within fifteen minutes."

His voice was like that of a man in a train station, simply providing information. We were leaving in fifteen minutes as if we were taking the train to Boston and if we weren't ready it would leave without us.

We took turns in the back, and when we were all together again with one or two minutes to spare, two older boys were waiting with our host. They lifted our trunks down the narrow lane to a broader street where there was an old open barouche in black with gold trim and bright red wheels. They stacked the trunks on a platform at the rear, and the five of us filled the carriage's body. One of the boys restored the steps and closed the door. They'd stay in the town. I sat beside Elinor, who had Meg on her lap. Our backs were to the rear. The Frenchman sat next to Bessie. Our host told the coachman we were ready, and off we went.

Our host identified himself as Monsieur Reynaud and pulled a letter from his jacket.

"I received this from your Monsieur Smith only *hier*, yesterday, telling me of your plan. We must get you to Le Havre tonight so you can get on the boat you *voyagerez*...will travel on in the morning."

He said nothing more. Nor did we once we heard his plan. He pulled a small book with a dark red leather cover from another pocket, leaned back, and began to read. All we could do was watch yet more passing countryside with the occasional view of the Channel to the right till at some point Meg insisted that I entertain her. She sat on my lap facing me, and I tried to make faces, but she was very tired and soon fell asleep. I turned her so her back was against me, and I wrapped my arms around her. Elinor reached over, still looking out, and she held my hand against her daughter's stomach.

As I said, while we were still in the countryside we often were next to the water and we could smell the salt and hear the gulls every once in a while. The sun was to our left, so we were heading south. To Le Havre, I assumed, not quite sure where that was but knowing that many boats arrived in New York from there. After what seemed a very long time, M. Reynaud put his book away loudly and we, except for the still napping Meg, looked at him.

"You must prepare yourselves. You will be traveling with two gentlemen. I believe you have met them. They were with you on the carriage to the coast."

"We knew them as Iago and Romeo," I said.

"Well, I don't know which is which, but one of them will be your husband, Lady Glendale, and the other will be yours, Madame Ballard. And you, Mademoiselle Treacy, will be the Ballards' maid, though they won't of course be the Ballards. They will be the Kastors, and Lady Glendale will be simply Madame Braun. And you are Mary Ryan.

"Your husbands, Herr Braun and Herr Kantor, they are successful German merchants who are going to New York to consider the possibility of settling there. They each met their American wives there."

Bessie spoke. "It is too risky for just us women to travel. We can't know if news won't precede us as we go through the Channel, though we won't be there for long and we'll be far closer to France than to England. But three women and a child traveling alone would be far too suspicious. Mr. Smith suggested, and I agreed, that we pretend to be two couples sailing to New York."

I insisted to Elinor that it was a grand plan and that it would all work out, but I wasn't sure I believed it. I didn't have long to think on it, though, as soon, with us going through more and more villages, the carriage pulled off. It entered the yard for a tavern. It was, M. Reynaud said, *déjeuner* time anyway. Inside, the host spoke to M. Reynaud, in French, and he led us up to the first floor where he knocked on a door and we followed him in.

A large, circular table was in the center of the room, and I was surprised to see that two gentlemen were sitting at the table. As I was about to point this out to M. Reynaud, I recognized Iago and Romeo, who stood when we came in and I can't say how excited I was to see them again. They were dressed like I imagined continental gentlemen would be dressed.

M. Reynaud held out his arm, pointing to the pair.

"I see you have met these gentlemen."

"We have," I said. "They're friends of Bes...Lady Glendale."

"Yes they are, *mademoiselle*. For now, though, the one on the left"—"that is Iago," I said—"then your Iago is Herr Wilhelm Braun and Herr Wilhelm Braun is married to Frau Braun, who you may know as the former Bessie Richards."

Iago bowed. I looked at M. Reynaud.

"As to your 'Romeo,' I assume, he is Herr Herman Kastor and he is the husband of Frau Kastor and the father to Margarite...Margaret Kastor, who are, I assume you now realize, *ton amie* Elinor and her lovely child."

It was all very confusing, and I hoped in time I would understand it. I turned to Romeo. He bowed as well. The pair of them looked like successful businessmen. Traders perhaps.

Romeo came to me and said in quite an accent, which I thought must be German, "*Es ist mir eine Freude* to meet you. I trust we will have a satisfying trip to New York *zusammen*, together."

He laughed and reverted to his normal accent.

"Sit, ladies, sit," M. Reynaud said.

"Lady Glendale, of course, knows this part of the plan, but we were afraid to say too much until we were ready to leave. You, Mademoiselle Treacy, are Mary Ryan and are the maid for the Kastors.

Bessie told Elinor and me, again, that she trusted Iago and Romeo completely.

Before we left, Bessie removed some jewelry from the purse she carried. She handed a ring to Elinor to replace the one she wore. It seemed heavier than what she'd put on when she became Mrs. Ballard she said quietly to me, and I guessed it was more in the "German style" that her own. Bessie did the same with her own ring and placed both the removed rings into the purse and placed it in her bag.

With this done, we left the room and tavern after eating. A second carriage, another barouche, was behind ours, and we divided, with me remaining with the Kastors—and a very confused Meg.

44.

Another restless night was spent, this time in Le Havre near the docks. In the morning, M. Reynaud was all excitement when we met him at a small café not far from our hotel. Of our group, only Iago and Romeo looked like they slept, and Meg was as miserable looking as I ever saw her until, that is, Romeo made faces to her and she giggled. I struggled to drink *le café au lait* and eat *la croissant* that sat before me, and Elinor barely touched her drink or pastry.

"Ladies. You must eat," M. Reynaud said sternly. "You must be strong for the trip."

He signaled to the waiter, who brought eggs and toast, and M. Reynaud insisted we swallow it all.

I did my best, as did the others. Though we were largely alone, our foreign voices were kept low, and Bessie asked M. Reynaud about himself. I listened on and off while he told of returning to his home near Calais—where we met him—after spending years in Paris as a businessman. He never said what business exactly he was in, but no one seemed to care for such details.

Finally, a bell in the town rang.

"That is the sign. *C'est huit heures*, eight o'clock. We must be on board by nine. It is not far, but we must go."

We were soon back in our rooms and since we hadn't unpacked when we arrived, it was easy to be ready. There was a trunk for the Kastor party, and I assume there was one for the Brauns.

Romeo—I had to remind myself that he was now Herman Kastor—said they brought the trunks with them when they crossed the Channel, and they were delivered to the hotel while he and Iago went to meet us at the tavern. We would need, he said, far more than what little we carried with us as we fled London.

He rang for a porter to carry the trunk down and to the ship. We had perhaps thirty minutes to get on board. M. Reynaud came to our room and told us it was time and we followed him and the Brauns to the hotel lobby and out the door, where two carriages waited. It wasn't far, and the air got heavy with the sea air and the sound of gulls when we were almost to the quay. It was chilly, but the early fog had burnt away and it was very bright.

It wasn't long before everything opened to the sight of the boats and sea and the noise of a steamship being prepared for sailing to America. M. Reynaud told us not to speak if we could avoid it as we crossed to the ship itself—it was the *SS Wieland*—and until we were safely in our cabins.

Their cabins, of course, were in first class and there was a small accommodation for me, a servant, across the hall from the "family's." My cabin was dark and very stuffy since there was no window, just some sort of screen above the door to the hallway so I wouldn't suffocate. It had a hard bed and a small dresser. There were several candle sconces attached to one wall and a hard chair opposite the dresser. A row of hooks was on the wall. The bed itself was latched to the wall and a thin mattress was atop it with an old pillow and several blankets. It was, of course, infinitely better than where I slept on my prior voyage to America on the *Nevada*, and I was happy to have it.

I gathered the things of mine that were in the Kastors' trunk and stored them in my little cabin. I then crossed back to their stateroom. It was on the right side of the boat and was quite large with a pair of portholes. Candle sconces were on several walls and there were two beds and a folding cot.

Lest there be any concerns, M. Reynaud immediately said that Romeo and Iago would sleep in the Brauns' room and Bessie would sleep here.

"Alas, *ma cherie*, you must remain in *ta petite chambre*."

With that sorted out, he said we should go on deck, though he again said the ladies should refrain from speaking if possible. Iago and Romeo were freer with what seemed to me to be their passable German and French.

In no time after we got to the deck, a horn sounded and a crewman walked around saying the ship was departing in fifteen minutes and that those who weren't traveling must go ashore or they would wake up in New York. This, at least, is what M. Reynaud said he said as it was in French, and other than the "York," I didn't understand a word.

With that, he bid us *adieu*. He kissed each of us (all except Meg, whose hand he shook very formally), on each cheek before wishing us *bonne chance* and saying he would pray for our safe trip.

"I'm not religious, but it cannot hurt, no?" our *bon ami* said.

With a final nod and wave, we watched him follow some other well-wishers from the boat and he took a place on the quay to watch us go.

Bessie wasn't nearly as calm as the rest of us. She kept watching the gangway. We had shown our tickets and papers as we came aboard, and everything seemed to be in order. The papers weren't really "ours." Instead, they identified us as Kastors or Brauns or a Ryan.

Things were hectic on the dock as final steps were taken and then a man ran from a small building that was between two docks and up the gangway. He handed a paper to the crewman manning the gangway, who took it and ran inside the boat, to the captain I figured. All eyes looked to the bridge and moments later the crewman returned.

We were close enough to hear what was being said, which was of no use to me since it was in French, and Romeo moved closer.

"He says the captain cannot be bothered to search his ship at this final moment, and he will not waste a moment more."

The crewman and the man from the shack were shouting.

"He is being told it isn't the captain's fault that they waited so long and that he'd better get off or he will come to America with us."

The messenger waved at the crewman, angrily I thought, holding the paper in his grip before turning and going back to shore. As soon as he stepped on the quay, the gangway was pulled from the ship and we pushed off and with the help of two tugboats, we were in the English Channel and heading to America, waving to M. Reynaud as we did.

The tugboats pulled away, and we were on our own. I stood close to Elinor. She held Meg's hand. We watched the French shore pass by to the left, reminding me of the approach to New York those years before.

We relaxed when we could no longer see land. We told each other that we should try to enjoy the voyage. We kept largely to ourselves, of course, but found time to stroll. I'm sure there were those who thought I, a servant, was too familiar with my mistress and her child, but that wasn't something I cared about. I simply cared about the time I had with that mistress.

We didn't speak much and most of what we said concerned Meg and much of our time was taken by catering to the girl. Meg remained remarkably calm once we were on the way, thanks especially to Romeo's entertaining her at each opportunity. We all largely kept to the suites beyond dinner and strolls on the deck several times on most days.

There was one horrible day, when we were confined to our cabins—I was allowed to be in the Kastors'—during a hard storm and had only cold food as we fought towards America. To help pass the time, I told the others of the horrors of my first crossing. I think Elinor and Bessie at least were shocked at how brutal things had been for me, and how difficult they were for those poor souls on our own boat, trying to survive the journey in steerage.

45.

When we came down the gangway in New York and went through the federal officials with far more courtesy than I faced when I landed in steerage on the *Nevada*, the six of us walked out to the large plaza that opened to the street. Scores of carriages were lined up for the first-class passengers, and scores of family members were milling about, waiting for loved ones to come out.

We had no idea whether anyone would be there though Bessie instructed Johnson to send a wire to the Palmers of details of our return when the detective received confirmation from M. Reynaud that we got safely on board and were over a day out of France.

Before long, though, "Elinor!" rang out to our right and before I could react Meg was rushing across to her grandpapa and grandmama and we quickly joined her.

I introduced Bessie and "Romeo" and "Iago."

After shaking the men's hands, Mr. Palmer looked to Bessie. "Yes, we've heard much about you in a letter from your Mr. Johnson we received yesterday." He wasn't as hostile to her as I thought he might be. He then turned to the street and waved. A footman jumped down from the family's brougham and hurried to us. He took possession of our trunks from the porter who was pushing them in a small wagon behind us and who was given a coin by Mr. Palmer.

Romeo and Iago had separated their own things before we reached New York and after wishing us all the happiness on our return to New York, with a bow and particular attention paid to Meg by both thespians, they headed on their own carrying their trunk between them to a cab that they got into and we watched it disappear in the hopes that we would sit down with them shortly, once all of us were settled.

We were very tired, though, and since there was not room for us in the Palmers' brougham, Bessie and I hailed a cab which followed the Palmers' carriage to Twenty-Eighth Street, on which our own trunks had been placed with the Ballards'.

* * * *

ELINOR AND MEG WENT upstairs when we reached the Palmers'. Before I could follow them, Williams (the butler) asked Bessie and me to go into the sitting room.

"Mr. Palmer would like a word with you," he said as he opened the doors. I was glad to be in the familiar spot and took a chair by the window so I could watch the passing New York scene. Bessie took the chair beside mine. She hadn't been in the city in a long time and said how things seemed to have somehow gotten faster and more crowded since she had. For me, I didn't realize how much I missed it. I planned on seeing Miss Fenton the next day to explain what happened and see if I could resume my duties.

It wasn't long before the pair of doors opened. We turned, and there was Mr. Palmer. He was alone after Williams closed the doors behind him. He directed us to the couch, which sat in the center of the room. He remained on his feet.

"First of all," he began, "I cannot tell you how much my wife and I appreciate all you have done to return our daughter and our granddaughter back to us. So you know, the police came to us and to the Ballards two days ago with information that you were on the ship you were on. The Ballards also received a wire from Francis saying he was coming home. The families agreed to wait until you all arrived and asked the police to stay clear in case it turned out to be some sort of misunderstanding."

He coughed and reached into an inside pocket of his jacket and removed a bank draft. He handed it to Bessie.

"I do hope that this covers your expenses. If it doesn't, please tell me and I'll see that you are fully compensated."

He handed her his card and turned to me. "And I...I cannot tell you how thankful Mrs. Palmer and I, and Elinor and Meg, are for what you have done." He reached into his other pocket and pulled out a second bank draft. He handed it to me.

"I hope this is satisfactory to compensate you for your services and that it will aid in your obtaining a place to live and a new position."

I looked at the draft—it was a year's salary at Miss Fenton's—and back to him.

"I don't understand."

"Of course, we can have no further dealings with you. Either of you. It will be all the talk of the town when word gets out, this interference with my son-in-law and my granddaughter. It will be the ruination of us and, more importantly, of Elinor and Meg. They will be outcasts. Surely you see that."

I was stunned, and Bessie reached over to my wrist. Before she could speak, I did.

"I didn't do it for money. I did it for her. And Meg."

"I'm sure you did, my dear. It is just that whatever might have been before she was taken from us cannot be again." He repeated, "Surely you see that."

"What does she say to it?" asked Bessie.

"Oh, she is in no state to say anything about it. But in time I know she will see reason. Surely you both can understand that."

I, of course, could not understand that. Whatever we had before had grown and grown as we returned to New York. Her father walked to the doors, turning before reaching them.

"Williams will help you with your things, to send them to wherever you will be staying."

He waited when his hand was on the right doorknob.

"I must say that should you, *either of you*"—he looked hard at me as he said this—"attempt to contact my daughter or granddaughter again, you will give us no choice but to contact the authorities. You have, after all, kidnapped them."

"But," I said, "they came willingly. We rescued them."

He let go of the knob.

"My dear, even if Elinor agreed—I won't say she does or if she ever will—Meg was in no position to do so. Much as I might otherwise be sympathetic and much as you would try to implicate Mrs. Palmer and me in your scheme, the Ballards are clear that they will never be and our joint adventure is to rehabilitate our families insofar as they can be rehabilitated and your continued connection to us cannot *and will not* be allowed.

"Good day."

With that, he pulled open both doors, and we heard his steps going up the grand marble staircase. A moment later, Williams entered. He stood silently, with his hands behind his back as Bessie and I tried to think where we could go after we left the house with her telling the butler that she would send a note advising just where our trunks should be sent, and when she did, she included Elinor's own, despised wedding band.

* * * *

BESSIE AND I HOLED UP in the hotel with the fine view and efficient servant where she stayed when I visited her some years before. We kept to ourselves, particularly after initial reports arrived from London that repeated either the kidnapping or the rescuing stories, although without naming the Ballards, let alone us. Our only relief was from the regular visits by Iago and Romeo, who were thrilled with New York and tried several times to have us join them at an entertainment, but we were afraid to leave the hotel and limited our dinners with them to the fine meals we got in Bessie's suite.

About two weeks later, things changed when the *New York Herald* had a long "exclusive" story on its front page with a picture of the three: Francis, Elinor, and Meg. It was all, the paper said, a simple "misunderstanding." Francis had, the story had it, gone to London to explore some business prospects at his father's request and was concerned about his wife and child being harmed were they to wander around the streets and avenues of the unfamiliar city.

Elinor misunderstood the situation and felt trapped and homesick. When she happened to meet an acquaintance from New York, the story went, she arranged to take a ship home with her daughter and because of a miscommunication she neglected to tell her dear husband. He in a panic naturally assumed some harm had befallen his family and got Scotland Yard involved. He heard that they were returning to New York and, of course, took the first possible ship to be with them.

They apologized to those who thought there was a kidnapping of his family and to those who thought there was a rescue of his family.

"We are happily back in our house, my wife, my daughter, and I. We hope that we can return to the quiet lives we led before this unfortunate disruption," Mr. Francis Ballard was quoted as saying.

46.

Aletter came from Mr. Johnson. Bessie showed it to me.

Your Ladyship,

Your matter is one that I admit was as peculiar in the end as any I have been involved with. After I returned to London with you and the others safely aboard a ship heading to New York, a battle royale raged among London papers, of the kidnapped-rescued variety. It seemed that papers took their position based not on the facts but on their readings of their audiences. Which is no surprise.

Apparently, Mr. B early on accused his lordship of being complicit in the scheme to recover his wife, but his lordship denied it and threatened to bring a legal action against the American if he continued to make the claim and the claim was quickly dropped. For his part, thankfully, Lord G insisted he had nothing to do with whatever happened and said that would be an end to it, at which point he decamped to the estate in Derbyshire and has not been heard from since. I trust that you will be able to communicate with him there should you wish to.

Mr. B apparently quickly realized that a man's worth would be seriously reduced should it be known that his wife abandoned him, so he insisted that she was taken involuntarily. That is until he was discreetly shown a letter written anonymously to a chief superintendent at the Yard specifying in great detail the abuse his wife suffered at his hands.

Fearing the letter would be disseminated and, as the poet said, discretion sometimes being the better part of valor, he elected to take the position that there was some sort of misunderstanding with his wife and that he would be going to New York to make things right again.

This, I am told, was communicated to the Yard and a wire was sent to the New York police asking that they "stand down" from taking any action until the true state of affairs could be determined.

This is all I know and all I can tell you. Although there has been speculation that you played a personal role in these events, the threat of your husband against Mr. B has been of benefit to you as there is now scarcely the suggestion of your involvement. I believe that you can return to London with your reputation burnished as a woman of intrigue and excitement.

I appreciate having had the opportunity to provide a service to you, for which I hope you are satisfied.

> *I am, etc., etc., etc.,*
> *Nathanial Johnson*

"Come with me," Bessie said two or three days later. "There is nothing for you here. She won't see you. Palmer's threat will hang over you. You can be my friend in London."

Since I had few options in New York, or at least any better ones, it made no sense for me to stay now that I had the financial support of Bessie. I spoke with Miss Fenton, and she was glad to see me and would be happy for me to return, but the thought of being in New York was now far too much for me. Being so near yet so far from Elinor would make things intolerable. What I would do was left unsaid, but Bessie and I were smart women.

By the way. I wasn't a fool. I quickly opened a bank account and deposited the money that Mr. Palmer threw at me (and that he could easily afford).

Perhaps the most difficult thing for me was to go to my old apartment building and knock at the door of the Normans. I doubted they would welcome me even if they were willing to speak to me at all. Things had changed so much. In the end, though, it was far more enjoyable than I dared hope it would be, and I was heartbroken when I left, knowing I'd never see Patrick and Cath and especially their two little, or not so little, children again.

Enjoyable, but fall less emotional, was Bessie's and my final evening with Romeo and Iago who only left us when we ran out of things to drink and stories to tell about them having begun to capture the attention of several New York theatrical impresarios.

I had to leave New York, though. And first, Bessie insisted that we visit her mother in Pittsburgh. She tried unsuccessfully to have Mrs. Richards stay with her in London when she landed Lord Glendale, but her mother preferred the simple life. It wasn't, to be sure, nearly as simple as it had been before the enormous wealth, but she could use her money to entertain her old friends and help here or there and contribute to several worthy charities.

Leaving New York would also help me clear my mind of the unpleasantness that came upon us so suddenly. Some weeks after Mr. Palmer threatened us, then, weeks when we thought it best to minimize our going out into the city, though I did once walk past the Ballard House, on the other side of the street, we took a ferry across the Hudson and found ourselves aboard the Pennsylvania Railroad bound for western Pennsylvania.

While I took a train in County Mayo to begin my trip to America, it was nothing compared to the luxury of the one I shared with Bessie and that in the end began my journey *back* to Ireland, though it would take much time and more journeying till that happened.

47.

We—mostly Bessie—had quite a lot of luggage, chiefly things she bought in New York when she had little to do but shop, including insisting more than once over my objection that I buy several dresses that were far too formal for me. She wired ahead, and as we reached the main Pittsburgh station, two men rushed to us, nodded at Bessie, and hurried to take our trunks from the railroad man pushing them on a trolley. She led me through and to the street where a well-appointed and very shiny dark green brougham carriage was waiting. A footman held the door open for us.

"Good evening, Jenson," she said to the footman, who returned the greeting. I said "thank you" as I passed him, and we waited for several minutes for the trunks to be put on the rear before going to Bessie's mother's house.

It was a large house, somewhat halfway between the Palmers' house in Manhattan and the one in Lenox. It sat on a hill overlooking the city, with a string of factories belching smoke over by a river. Much less congested than Manhattan.

The Richards' house had a porch. As the carriage pulled up, Mrs. Richards came down the four or five steps to the path. She was sitting in an Adirondack chair waiting, and she and her daughter collided in front of me.

Bessie had written to her about me, but she said she of course remembered me from my days in service for them. When I knew her then, she was meek compared to Bessie but seemed far more comfortable in her native region and away from New York.

She was very nice, and the house was very big, and I was given one of the largest bedrooms I ever saw. Pittsburgh was bustling and the view of it was great, even with the smoke. Bessie took me into town several times, introducing me as her secretary or her companion, as circumstances dictated, and more and more as the latter.

In certain places in some of the less fashionable but (I think) more alive parts of the city, she was welcomed as a conquering hero. Her friends from long ago insisted on referring to her as "Lady Bessie" and as it was meant in good fun, Bessie said she tolerated it even if sometimes she hated it. "They all aspire, or at least aspired before they settled down to their own lives, to what I have, and I won't begrudge them their little joke."

There were times when Bessie went off with one of her friends or sometimes an attractive stranger. At first, I found this disorienting as I was left with people I didn't know or barely knew, but those strangers found me so enticing—an Irish girl who was once a nun in New York!—that they kept me entertained for the hour or so while Bessie was gone.

She never told me where she went or what she had done but I was no longer so naïve not to know and as she was so kind to me, and tried to be so kind to Elinor, I didn't care about that and was actually glad she was able to enjoy her passing liaisons.

But after three or four weeks of partying and frolicking in the two worlds she inhabited, she began to speak of resuming her journey to London. She could not say precisely how Lord Glendale would look upon her reappearance after what she had done. She'd wired him that she was well, but he had not responded.

"It is no matter," she said when she again talked of it, "I have money enough and friends, true friends, enough and my title will come in handy."

Though I had neither money, friends (other than her, of course), or a title (and I was a Catholic from the west of Ireland to boot), I was happy enough to sail with her. She assured me that we wouldn't be arrested for our daring plot with Elinor. I tried and so much wanted to believe her.

"I wrote to Mr. Johnson. He's confirmed to me that Scotland Yard has no interest given the differences in opinion of whether your Mrs. Ballard was a victim of us or of her husband. His family have no interest in bringing it up again. The farther they stay from London the better, so I don't think we need worry about running into them when we arrive. Plus, I can show you his lordship's house in the country and we can be enchanted by the numerous flowers that grow there."

She said this to me well after one of our fine dinners in Pittsburgh and after her mother went up to bed. We sat with cognacs in the sitting room, looking out across the city and hearing the thumping of a few mills that were producing whatever it was that they made. She dismissed the servants for the night. We were alone as we had so often been over the last month or so.

"You must tell me, my dear," she began as we sat on armchairs turned to face the window, a small table between us, "what *you* wish to do. I'm always telling you and you follow."

She put her glass down. I did too.

"We talk and talk but never really about you. I want to understand you," she said.

She was right. We talked all the time, but only in the most general terms. Her manner of speaking, with the propriety drummed into her by her governesses so she would pass in society, was rubbing off on me more and more since she was nearly the only person I spoke to regularly.

I was between servant and friend. I was doing for Bessie what I always did, without giving a thought to what *I* wanted to do. But the truth was that I had no idea. I reacted to things, and I didn't know if anyone ever bothered to ask me what I wanted. I don't know if I ever asked myself.

She was anxious that particular night. She couldn't sit still, and she reached for my hand. She was with the possible exceptions of Cath and, maybe, Elinor, who were forever in my past, my first true friend since I left Backfox, and it was only as we sat there that I finally realized it. Not even when she risked so much to rescue Elinor did I appreciate her. I knew I loved her as the greatest of friends and that for all she had she would never abandon me. I knew she loved me and as I look back, I wonder whether she hoped for something more from me than I was able to give. If she did, though, she never treated me differently for not having won me.

Then, though, with the cognacs in a meeting like that first one at her apartment overlooking the dark of Central Park, I didn't know what I wanted to do beyond one thing, or at least one thing that was possible.

"I'd like to go to London with you. I don't know what else will become of me." I looked at her and tightened my grip on her hand, "but I would like to be with you."

The plan had always been for me to go to England with her, but that night was like I was setting my future in stone. She seemed puzzled by my response, that I was making love to her, so I quickly said, "as no more than your dear friend."

She smiled after a moment but said nothing. I hoped I hadn't disappointed her.

"I think you are my only friend," I said.

Frankly, I didn't know if Bessie had any other real friends herself. She had walls of acquaintances. In New York, she was nothing but a carnival act. Certain circles in London, too, she said, were very cold to her. In part, it was because she was an American. But more it was that she was so disrespectful of tradition. I don't know if she did this on purpose. It was who she was.

To my admission, she smiled. "Then my dear friend you shall be," she said. "How do you wish to carry yourself?"

Even with her disregard for convention, I had to think of how I was presented.

"I shall be your secretary."

"Yes, you cannot be a maid. I won't allow it."

"I think I can be a good personal secretary to you."

This cleared the air between us, and we were both grateful for it. What I would do as her "secretary" I couldn't say, but I was sure it would allow me to make good use of my time and my abilities.

So, with a last party at her mother's house the night before our departure where a number of long-time acquaintances enjoyed themselves, Bessie said goodbye to Pittsburgh and her dear mother and in the morning we were on a train heading east to Philadelphia for a steamer to England.

48

It wasn't a surprise that his lordship wasn't overjoyed, to put it mildly, when Bessie and I pulled up to the mansion on Dover Street. Things weren't as hectic about the brief *L'Affaire Ballard* as they apparently had been. London, Bessie said, had long been a place where scandals were like Irish weather, always changing. Lord Glendale was generally considered to have had nothing to do with the messy business, and it wasn't long before he was pointed to as another reminder of the perils of marrying an American, however rich (or especially if you were rich). His lordship, though, resented the inconvenience and notoriety and had he a choice, I doubt he would have allowed Bessie to return to the London house.

Bessie and her (New York) lawyers, though, had structured the ownership of the couple's assets—almost entirely from Bessie's side—so that she didn't need his lordship's permission to occupy whichever of their houses she wished to occupy whenever she wished to occupy it. She cared not a whit if he went back down to Derbyshire. We were staying in Mayfair.

Notwithstanding her rights, she was careful not to push too hard and a sort of truce was kept once we were through the door. He could maintain whatever he maintained with the women who sympathized with his plight as he sympathized with theirs—loveless marriages being the norm in certain parts of Mayfair and Piccadilly—and Bessie could do as she wished with what women she wished (and it happened that his "woman" and her "woman" were in several cases the same).

Me? I was in some respects a "kept" woman to Bessie and I think many people who knew *of* me believed I often shared her bed though I never did. She was quite open about the possibility on the trip back notwithstanding what I'd said to her before we left Pennsylvania, and I admit I *was* tempted. As I sat in my bed in the small, lightly rocking first-class cabin next to hers on the ship, the *SS Lord Gough*. I could not help that my thoughts turned to Elinor each night and I couldn't see myself being anyone's but hers and thus I couldn't see myself being anyone's. Yet I was next to Bessie. I resisted whatever temptations leaked into my cabin from hers.

* * * *

IT WAS NAÏVE OF BESSIE to think she wouldn't be the subject of intense interest when she returned. Word traveled quickly, and on our first morning on Dover Street, several reporters stood across the way, lined up and looking towards the house. I noticed it when I glanced out the window in the sitting room shortly before eight to see what the day looked like. Unlike her, I preferred to go down for breakfast as I had done in my first stay at the house.

On that first morning, there they were, five or six men who I took to be reporters milling about, and I quickly moved to the side before, I hoped, they would see me. I ended up peeking around the corner at the gang of them in their suits and hats and sucking on their cigars and holding pads in their hands.

I went to Bessie's room, which faced the back of the house, and told her. She went with me to the sitting room, she in a robe over her gown, and we both peeked, on either side of the window at the group of men.

"This will complicate things," she said.

She decided to accept her fate. "We must show them that we're not afraid of them and that we're strong enough to ignore them," she told me.

Precisely at one p.m., she led me from the house and down the steps to a waiting closed carriage and two. We didn't have any particular place to go but dressed as if we did. She said we had to get this over with.

As Yeats opened the front door and she walked through, I was a step behind her. She had outfitted me in a fine day dress she bought for me in Pittsburgh, and she was in an even finer one that was made for her when she was last in London. The men ran across when they saw us, cutting off a very unhappy Hansom cabbie as they did. Though the footman who held the carriage door open tried to block them on one side and another footman who'd come with us from the house tried to block them on the other, the reporters shouted and shouted.

"Are you happy to be back, m' Lady?"

"Have you seen his Lordship, m' Lady?"

"Is this your latest conquest with you, m' Lady?"

"Are you going to be arrested, m' Lady?"

The questions were ignored, as Bessie told me they would be, and we both looked straight ahead, as she instructed me.

"We will keep silent," she said as the carriage drove us round and round Hyde Park till we had gone long enough so people would think we had places to go and people to see—or people who would see us. The reporters repeated their shouting on our return. And Bessie repeated her ignoring them and their questions.

Each day, the number of reporters seemed to decrease until there were none. That's when Bessie said we could do as we pleased since we no longer had to do what reporters expected us to do.

It turned out, though, that there wasn't much that I wanted to do. Lord Glendale largely ignored me, though I was never snubbed, as I followed her ladyship around and when we ate. After an uncomfortable breakfast with just the two of us, I took breakfast in my room.

The three of us didn't dine often together as he went to one of his clubs most nights. When we did eat together, as I say, it was uncomfortable for me. Since there wasn't much any of us did during the day, his asking what we had done or Bessie's asking him what he had done took little time and the only sound was often the noise of our utensils on our plates and the occasional belch and at times a sneeze that a footman couldn't stifle.

49.

Much as I loved Bessie as an unwavering friend, I couldn't stay with her. It wasn't as though she had any objection to my presence. She seemed to very much enjoy having me around and, in some respects, I was, as I say, her dearest friend. But neither of us wanted to be anything more than that. I know it was selfish of me, but I began to resent being kept by her. There was no ill will to it, but I knew I *was* being "kept."

Plus, I was bored. She did very little, and it didn't seem to bother her. Yes, I enjoyed the leisure at first and I spent hours reading either in the mansion or in a park. But vicarious reading was just that. Vicarious.

Plus, I knew it would get worse. Bessie told me to prepare for a trip to Derbyshire. I'd find even less to do there. I might not speak to people in Mayfair or Hyde Park but at least I *saw* them. *What was there to see in Derbyshire?* I lived on a farm for my first eighteen years. Even if it was a desperately poor farm, it too had fields and trees. Stone walls and drafty nights. Eating dinner with the same people.

I could understand why Bessie's mother tossed it all away to move in luxury back to Pittsburgh where she could be with...friends. I had no friends but Bessie.

She wasn't surprised when I brought it up. She didn't go out often in the evening and I never did. It was more likely that her friends would appear for dinner at the house, and Lord Glendale tolerated the disregard of the social requisites, though just to a point, and Bessie tried to be considerate of his feelings and applied subtlety to her exploits.

After a month, I finally brought this up with her. That is a lie. I tried to do it several times, but before I could say anything I feared she would think me an ingrate and so the words were caught in my throat. It was her who said something. As she had in Pittsburgh.

We were strolling in Hyde Park, which we were able to do since there were no reporters and we could ignore the whispers of the other walkers.

"I think we are both unsettled, Margaret."

We were arm-in-arm beneath our parasols on a stretch of the park just north of Speaker's Corner and she said it matter of factly. I replied in the same way.

"I didn't want to say anything. You've been so kind to me."

"How kind is it for me to keep you in the prison where I must live out my days?"

Since Bessie was barely over thirty, this seemed a horrible and very sad thought for her to have, let alone a thing to say. I felt very sorry for her and the role that I played in making it so. I hoped not for the first time that she might find some fulfillment if she did the expected, old as she was, and provided his lordship an heir. I thought she'd be a very fine mother, though I doubt many would agree with me. That, however, would be some time in the future, if ever.

"I won't abandon you."

We walked several steps before she responded.

"Posh. Dublin. What about Dublin?"

It was something I hadn't thought of.

"What can I do in Dublin?"

'You can have a job."

It was my home island, that there was nothing for me in New York, and it was just a ferry and train trip to London.

50.

I stepped from the cab, carrying a satchel over my right shoulder. It was chilly but the sun was out, and it wasn't raining as it had been when I left Liverpool on the ferry that morning. The building in front of me was a bit on the small size compared to what I saw in the City of London and in New York but was still impressive. A doorman in a red coat and a black top hat stared at me until I started to walk towards him. He doffed his hat and said, "You be wishing to come in?"

I nodded. It had been quite a while since I'd heard a deep Dubliner's accent.

"And who might yer be wishing to see?"

A travel-weary woman carrying a satchel wasn't, I daresay, what he was used to seeing, but he smiled when I said, "Dodson & Kenney."

"'Course," and he stepped back and opened the door. It was a fine door, gilded in gold with large windows and shiny brass fixtures. The doorman rushed in when I was through and announced to a similarly dressed man, though without a top hat, and said "She be going to the Dodson firm." He looked a last time at me before turning and heading back to his post.

His twin (in spirit though not in flesh), sitting on a stool at a tall desk, looked down.

"So, you're here for Dodson & Kenney, that right?"

"I am, yeah."

"And who might yer be seeing at Dodson & Kenney."

I reached into my satchel and pulled out Bessie's note—it was at the top so I would have no trouble finding it.

"A Mrs. Richard Dodson," I read, and he seemed satisfied.

"Fourth floor. We have a lift, you see," and his head nodded to his left. "I'll take you up to see Mrs. Dodson. A fine lady, she is."

And he did that and when he re-opened the gate, I was on the fourth floor, and he told me it was the last door to the right and I thanked him.

The hallway was quite bright, lit by several gaslights on either side, and the door at the end had a large, frosted glass on which

Dodson

&

Kenney

was stenciled in black with gold trim.

Inside, a clerk sitting on a high stool at a large, angled desk with a stack of papers and a quill pen in his right hand looked at me.

"Can I help you, Miss?"

It was another Dubliner's voice. He seemed a tall man, and he made me think of Bob Cratchit with a vest and white shirt and strap on the upper arm of his right sleeve. He barely moved and stayed on his stool.

"I'm here to see Mrs. Dodson."

"Ah. Mrs. Dodson, is it? I should've known. Let me get her for you. Wait here. You can put your coat on the hook," and he nodded to a rack by the door.

The large, open room itself was very paneled and dark with several chandeliers evenly spread around the ceiling. Two offices were on the far and right sides, each with a closed door that had writing on its glass portion.

I watched "Cratchit" as he ambled down the aisle after placing his pen in its holder. At its end, he turned left and passed several doors before he came to one next to the corner office, which he knocked on. He opened it and was gone for a moment. He reappeared and came back the way he went until he was close enough for me to hear him. He said, "follow me, Miss" with a tight, insistent wave, and I did just that and soon I was in Mrs. Dodson's office. The door didn't say "Mrs. Dodson." It said "Clerk" and I was disappointed, seeing as Bessie led me to think I was visiting someone of importance and not a clerk. But needs must, I reminded myself.

She was at a desk but stood to greet me, and when I was through the door she thanked "Ellis"—I was disappointed it wasn't "Cratchit"—and walked around to close the door.

"Have a seat, Miss Treacy."

The office was small. It had one window, which was behind the desk. The desk was so large that it almost filled the room, and papers were stacked on top of it in no order apparent to me. More papers were stacked on a table to the left of the desk and several stacks were on the floor. My first impression of my hostess, though, was that *she* knew what each piece of paper was and where it was.

The desk chair was well-worn burgundy leather, and there were two chairs for visitors. They were wooden. They didn't look comfortable.

I sat, and she went around the desk to her old chair. She was plainly dressed. She had no bustle. The dress was a dull blue and looked to have been bought some time earlier.

As she passed, I noted she wore a sweet perfume of the type I recalled from my days at the Palmer house. I thought it the one affectation that she had.

"So, how is Lady Glendale?"

She smiled, and I assured her that Bessie was quite well, thank you. I reached to hand her the letter, but she waved it off.

"If she sent you, that's all I need. I'll finish shortly. Where are you staying?"

I said I hadn't decided but wanted her suggestion for a hotel for me until I found "something more permanent."

"Oh, surely not. No. For now, you will stay with me. We will figure out where you will live later, but for now, I could use your company and the chance to get to know you."

I liked her. She was well dressed, though casual and not up to fashionable London's standards. A little shorter than me but not by much. Her hair didn't quite reach her shoulders but was well coifed. It was auburn, and not so different in color from my own. It looked far more glamorous, though that may have been because I'd smelled her perfume. Her eyes were as blue as I'd ever seen in a pair of eyes.

"I'll be just a moment and we shall have an early dinner and return to my house and then you can tell me about yourself. From what Bessie says, you have had quite the adventurous life so far."

She smiled again. Not in any way false seeming. She finished reading something and she pulled out a pen and placed her initials in the lower right corner, to the side of the signature line, and blotted it. She placed the paper on top of a number of similar looking ones in a wooden box on the left front of the desk.

"You will learn that there are certain...conventions we must follow here. This office is one of them."

She placed her pen at the front of a brass piece with a pair of inkwells and then with a wave of her hand around the small room, she stood and so I did too. "I'll explain while we eat."

There was a hook on her door, and she removed her coat and put it on. Her bag hung from the hook, and she took that and placed it over her shoulder. I moved my satchel to my shoulder too and followed her, and after I got my coat from the rack by the door, Ellis opened the door.

"'Tis an early day, Ellis," Mrs. Dodson said. "I'll see you tomorrow."

He nodded, and she stopped.

"This is Miss Treacy. I hope she will be joining us to help me."

He adjusted his hands on the doorknob so he could extend his right to me, which I shook.

"Welcome, Miss," he said, and I was truly glad to meet him.

Though it was still light out, we said good evening to the elevator operator and the doorman as we left the building. After about a block and a half, we turned down a short alley and soon were at a plain red door. There was a doorman in a top hat here too, who opened the door and greeted Mrs. Dodson by name.

The moment we were through, we were set upon by a lady in a very fashionable dress.

"You are early tonight, Mrs. Dodson."

"Thank you, Agnes. Aye. A new girl has just come to town, and I need to get to know her."

Agnes smiled and glanced at me and asked whether we wanted Mrs. Dodson's "usual table," and that's where she led us. It was a small round table in a somewhat dark part of the room. The chairs were armless and covered in a cream-patterned fabric that draped nearly to the floor. A long linen tablecloth covered the table, and it dropped well over the sides. Plates painted in a floral pattern were at each place setting and elegant silverware and a pair of crystal glasses, one larger than the other, framed them.

We weren't there for a minute before a young and very pretty waitress brought a candle, which she used to light the one in the center of the table, surrounded by a bulb. That done, she left us but was quickly back with a carafe of dark red wine. She poured some into the smaller of the glasses that was in front of Mrs. Dodson.

A sip from my host and a nod and my glass was filled as was hers. Before the waitress was gone with the carafe, Mrs. Dodson said we would both have the salad and lamb stew.

Alone, she said, "I don't know how long you've been away, but I thought a bit of Irish stew would sit well with you."

She sipped her wine.

I didn't know what Bessie said about me, but I'm sure she made me sound far more competent, and adventurous, than was true and I hoped I wouldn't disappoint Mrs. Dodson.

Strangely, I felt more comfortable with her than I ever did with anyone who was above my station. I felt comfortable enough with Miss Fenton. And Bessie, of course. (Elinor was another thing entirely.) Maybe it was her being Irish. Maybe it was the wine. The waitress made sure that neither of our glasses came close to being empty. For sure it was Mrs. Dodson's treatment of me. Respectful.

51.

I knew about fashionable houses in New York and London. Mrs. Dodson's didn't come close to them. It was small and on York Street, just a few blocks from Stephen's Green. Its four stories were tucked in between two identical houses. This part of Dublin, then, seemed much like the Palmers' neighborhood in Manhattan, with identical houses distinguished on the outside only by the colors of their doors and of the flowers flooding over the sides of their window boxes. It had a stoop of ten or twelve steps lined on either side by black, wrought iron bannisters that led, in her house, to a blue door. I tell you about it as it was to be my home in Dublin. It was where I had Bessie ship my slight belongings from London.

She had a manservant, a cook, and a maid, with the latter also acting as a scullery maid. The dining room was to the left of the foyer, and it wasn't large. Its table was set much as the one at the restaurant was, with a crystal chandelier hanging above, though without a linen tablecloth, and it was trimmed all around in a beautiful striped inlaid wood. The chairs were like those at Agnes's, covered in fabric with high backs and no arms so they were easy for a fashionable woman in a bustle to sit on. The walls were a dark red above cream-colored wainscoting. A large Persian carpet covered most of the floor and to the rear was a swinging door that I assumed led to the kitchen.

To the right of the foyer was the sitting room. It was larger and dominated by a mantel. A large Persian rug covered nearly the entire floor here too, but it was chiefly in blue while the one in the dining room was the color of a claret wine. In addition to the sofa that was perpendicular to the mantel and that was separated from two chairs by a coffee table, there was a small seating area near the large window that looked out onto York Street. It had two chairs, in a fabric that matched the sofa and were also armless, and a small, low round table between them.

The gaslights were on when we entered after her manservant—a short man called Seamus—greeted us. Mrs. Dodson said we would take care of ourselves, and with a bow, he left and went to the kitchen, which was in the northwest corner of the ground floor.

The walls were covered in a middle blue paper with slim yellow vertical stripes and had several fine paintings. Most were of landscapes of what I expected was the Irish countryside. A portrait of Mrs. Dodson was to the left of the mantel with a simple, wide gilded frame and eyes that could not help but draw one in. On the right, in an identical frame, was one of a handsome gentleman, who I expected was—and Mrs. Dodson confirmed—the late Mr. Richard Dodson.

An oval table in mahogany was to the right of the mantel, and several etched crystal decanters with liquids of various reds and browns sat on a silver tray to its rear. Mrs. Dodson looked up at her husband as she lifted the top from one of the decanters. "Gone too soon, my dear Richard."

My hostess and, I hoped, new employer and perhaps even friend poured cognac into two crystal snifters with similar etchings before restoring the stopper. As she cradled the two glasses, one in each hand, and approached me in one of those chairs by the window, she said, "It is rather lifelike, and I miss him every day."

She handed me the snifter and sat beside me. "I wouldn't be where I am without him."

She took another, longer sip, and I did too.

"So you know," she said with the glass's short stem between her right middle and ring fingers and its bowl in her palm, "he was killed in a train accident on a business trip to Belfast. He didn't suffer, they told me, though that may not have been true."

She took another sip, and I did the same.

"That was four years ago. I was already assisting him at the office. It was his firm. You'll meet Thomas Kenney tomorrow, but he was Richard's assistant." She placed her glass down. "Now he is mine."

She leaned back in the chair. I leaned forward.

"As I say. I was helping him, but we kept it a secret. No one would entrust their money with a *woman's* firm. I was able to extract information from the women I knew that proved invaluable in considering investment opportunities, and Richard would take my recommendations and massage them so they were thought to have come from him and we, the pair of us, proved rather successful.

"He knew many people from Trinity College, and we made a point of mingling with them and their wives as they began to have money. That's how we got them to give us their money to invest. And he used his Trinity friends to get recommendations, as I did with their wives."

She reached to the table and again drank from her snifter.

"Then he died." She got up again and looked at the doors, which were still closed. She paced in the area by the three chairs. She said they'd never had children, that she now regretted it, regretted thinking there'd be time enough for that.

"It was a big funeral, of course. His parents and brothers and sisters. My parents and my brothers and sisters. Clients. Investors. And they started coming to me and to Kenney, even when we returned from the cemetery. 'What's to become of the firm?' they asked. 'What's to become of our money?' is what they wanted to know.

"Kenney said *he* would be reviewing all the records and would speak to each of them within the week. Though, of course, it was chiefly me. In any case, we had seven days to figure it out. Richard's death was so sudden, he and I'd never given a thought to it.

"A few bankers approached Kenney, and some approached me about taking us over. 'Helping us through the difficult period,' they said."

She was back at her chair and sitting.

"Flock of vultures. Even a few came over from London. But I knew the records. Knew them better than Richard. I sat with Kenney at his house. No one else was there and I explained that we could and would continue largely as before. That my Richard's death wouldn't change anything. Yes, Kenney would have to take his place at coddling the clients and getting new ones. He wasn't very good at it at first, but it wouldn't matter if we got results.

"That was my job. I got results when Richard was alive, and I saw no reason I couldn't with him dead."

She sat back, the glass again on the table and her hands interlocked in her lap.

"That's what we did. We act as if Richard is still with us. 'He' still has his office. It's like a shrine. I have his clerk's office, and it suits me. I meet every morning with Kenney, and we plan out the day. And we have done very well since my poor Richard died."

She stopped. She looked over at me. I hadn't moved since she first stood.

"You aren't here as a matter of pity, Miss Treacy. You are here because Bessie Richards wrote to me. I was introduced to her by a mutual friend when I was in London and I found her quite...likeable and we've written to one another occasionally. About you, she said you have a good head on your shoulders and that you are loyal. Maybe to a fault. She said she thought I could make something of you, and you could do something far more interesting than any of the alternatives a 'spinster'—I use the term without derogation—from County Mayo could hope to enjoy."

Her frown switched to the smile I would come to love in her, and I was solidly in her little conspiracy of deception. And we toasted on it.

The next morning, she introduced me to Kenney. He was a man of medium size and medium build and I'm afraid the best I could say about him at the time— though my opinion is far more approving since—was that he was a friendly sort who likely got along well with those whose money was entrusted with Dodson & Kenney.

After introductions were made, including to several clerks who looked much like Ellis, an office next to hers was allotted to me. It, too, was small, but as with hers, it was enough and it had "CLERK" on its door window.

52

I was Dodson & Kenney's newest employee but had little idea what to do. Mrs. Dodson was a good (and patient) teacher, though, and it was as much common sense as anything.

At the house, I had a room down the hall from hers. It was medium in size and looked out over the back, across the garden of the similar house one block to the east. It had a four-poster bed, well big enough for me, and I daresay for the Queen herself (though she looks to be a wee woman as far as that goes). The wallcovering was a yellow with maroon stripes. She offered to have it changed, but I found it comforting in how calm it seemed.

She insisted that we have breakfast together at eight each morning (but Sunday, though we went to Mass together). A cab came by at nine, and it took us to our office, though if the weather was at all pleasant, she would wave the cab off and we walked the less than a mile, including crossing the Liffey on the Ha'penny Bridge.

The regularity of our conferencing at the office meant it wasn't long before we ended the formality and usually spent the day in the late Mr. Dodson's corner office.

Some month and a half after arriving in Dublin, I felt established enough that I asked Mrs. Dodson if I could go home for a visit. Since I left so many years before, I wrote to my parents but not as frequently as I should have. I got some news from home when I visited with my brothers in Liverpool on the way to

Dublin, and I wrote a letter to my mama and papa when I got to the capital.

Mrs. Dodson thought it a grand idea and within the week I was aboard a train for the day-long trip due west to Atherny and after a night at an inn there it was several hours more on a series of stagecoaches north to Backfox itself. It was late though not yet dark when I got there. The farm was some miles to the west of the village and a farmer I knew from when I was a lass and who lived out our way took me in his wagon, which I think he quite enjoyed as it gave him the chance to tell me all about what happened in the place since I'd left so long before, as had so many others.

Now after stints in New York and London and Dublin, I saw the farm as a horrible...shack. I'm ashamed to say how glad I was to be on my way back to Dublin much as I enjoyed the time with my parents and visiting those who remained in neighboring farms since I left.

I hated myself for how I reacted when I reached the house. It was where I and my siblings were raised, lovingly. We had very little and sometimes not even that, but we made it through.

It was in some ways, though, a nice break in the routine I returned to in Dublin, which was becoming more and more my home. I wasn't bored by it. Mrs. Dodson was increasing my responsibilities and we both often worked late. I engaged with her. To an extent, that had been true of Bessie. But I was much more of an equal to Kathleen Dodson.

At worst, it put my lack of a social life into contrast. Other than either going to her club or to a restaurant with her or entertaining at the house or to plays and once or twice to a light opera, I met few people and none of them made my heart skip a beat. It was foolish, but old Mrs. Burnley had planted a seed within me.

53

"Margaret. Something has arisen and I can't make it to a meeting at the club. It's important. Will you do it?"

Mrs. Dodson sometimes took me to meetings with clients at Agnes's. She liked the more informal spot to reassure those who were nervous that their money was safe. It was also a good way to solicit new clients. And since she was a woman, she couldn't join let alone do business at one of the clubs that male bankers could, much as "openly conducting business" was frowned upon in those places. Thomas Kenney was a member of one of the less prestigious clubs but because even it wouldn't allow women in its dining room, clients and potential clients were never taken there, at Mrs. Dobson's insistence.

Most clients learned fairly soon after placing their money with the firm that Kathleen Dodson was the one making the investment decisions. Those who didn't know it found out after she took them, as I say with me sometimes in tow, to lunch at Agnes's.

But I'd never gone to meet one by myself.

"Is Mrs. Dodson coming, Miss Treacy?" Agnes asked when I was through the door. I told her I was alone, and she led me to our usual table.

"I'm meeting a client. He'll ask for Mrs. Dodson. Please bring him to me."

She nodded and left. For a change, I sat in my boss's seat, with my back to the wall. I could look over the dining room. It wasn't much into the lunch period so only a few other tables were taken.

I watched everyone who came in, now and then sipping from the water in my Waterford crystal goblet. I recognized some and I exchanged nods with them. Others were led by Agnes to other people waiting.

I paid little attention when a woman entered wearing what I recognized as being in the New York style. Which I noticed because few women wore such in Dublin as we were somewhat behind in terms of fashion. Mrs. Dodson wasn't one of those, though. She even had several direct from the House of Worth in Paris, which she wore when aiming to attract a portion of a sizeable account of someone who'd appreciate such excess.

But this woman with Agnes was not that. Her head was down and her face was largely obscured by a hat some seasons old. She was a plump thing, and the voluminous fabric and awful hat didn't serve her well.

I paid her little mind until Agnes led her close enough to me that I could see her clearly. She saw me stare. She stopped between two tables. Elinor stood not ten feet from me.

I was up and rushing to her in a flash, with the eyes of those at several other tables following. Before I did anything else with her, I said we had to walk, and she followed me past a confused Agnes and out to Abbey Street. We reached the Liffey before long, and that's where we stopped. I looked over the water.

"I'm free of him. Forever."

I didn't understand and kept looking out over the water.

"Do you not wish to know?"

"You'll tell me what you want to tell me." I didn't mean to sound so harsh with her. My mind and my world were in turmoil.

"He is dead. I couldn't stay there. Meg and I and Bridget—you remember Bridget?"

I said that of course I did.

"My parents gave me money for the trip, and I left soon after the funeral. We went to London and to Lady Glendale's. She told me where I could find you. She was quite surprised to see me again."

Neither of us moved much, but I led her to a bench that looked over the river, where we sat.

"And so, we are here. Bridget is with Meg—who isn't so little anymore—in the hotel."

Her hands were in fists in her lap.

"I don't expect you to say it yet. But can you tell me that someday you will forgive me? Again?"

I still hadn't recovered from my first sight of her at the club and I'd long since placed my anger and disappointment at what happened when she and I and Bessie returned to New York somewhere deep within myself. If I saw a reference to New York or even just America, it would churn up again, but I learned to tolerate it. Otherwise, I couldn't have survived.

Could I forgive her? As we sat, I didn't care. She'd put me through hell, and as I sat on that bench looking across the Liffey, I Did Not Care.

"They wouldn't listen. They knew. They all knew. After the hubbub from London, I was made a true prisoner. Again and again, they made me promise that I was content. That I was insane when I did what I did with you. That you and Bessie forced me. That I was sorry. So sorry.

"Not only did they threaten to take Meg away, they said they would have you and Lady Glendale arrested by the police, or Scotland Yard if you went to London, for kidnapping us. Especially for taking Meg, who they said couldn't have decided for herself to go with you.

"They didn't trust me. I don't know that I was ever alone again. When Francis was out, they made Bridget sit with me but then they didn't trust her. They hired someone else to take her place. She was a horrible woman. All fawning with me. 'Yes, Mrs. Ballard.' And 'No, Mrs. Ballard.' She made me sick, but I couldn't get away from her or from his family. My parents couldn't do anything about it. If they made noise they'd be stricken from society, and it wouldn't do any good anyhow."

I don't know whether she took a breath while she spoke. I'm sure *I* didn't. My poor Elinor. And she wondering whether I could forgive *her*. There wasn't a thing I could have done when I was there. I would've been arrested were I to be seen within blocks of the Ballards' house. Or the Palmers'.

"Now I'm free."

We got up and began to walk, but she was spent and told me to take her back to her hotel. It wasn't one of the better ones. It was a small, narrow place not far from the docks. She said Bessie wrote a letter to Mrs. Dodson that got there a day or two before she did, and Bessie told her that Mrs. Dodson approved of our meeting and did what she did to allow it to happen.

"I must tell you. They all in New York believe I'm responsible for his death. My parents helped me leave under a false name so they could not track us as they did when *he* took Meg and me before they could take me. I may be hanged, but I needed to see you."

Whatever else was in my mind vanished.

"Hanged?"

"He is dead. They think I did it. That I fled will prove it to them. I didn't, Margaret. I promise you I didn't, but I doubt I can prove that and if I cannot prove it, I'll be hanged."

She put up her hand.

"There is nothing to be done. I cannot run forever. I cannot take Meg forever."

Elinor's hotel was a dreary place. Her room was on the third floor, and it looked out over an alleyway that stank of discarded trash. It was a small room, and Meg looked like a homeless waif and Bridget looked lost and confused when we came in. They both brightened when they recognized me.

I cursed that Mrs. Dodson would allow such a thing, for them to be in such squalor, but Elinor said it was she who insisted. She wouldn't, she said, endanger those who helped her, including Bessie and Mrs. Dodson, by being in too public a place.

We had no food, but I couldn't eat even if we did. Bridget took Meg to get something, and they brought some back and Elinor and I nibbled on it. It was dark, and I wouldn't leave. I lay in her bed with her with Bridget and Meg in the other bed and I fell asleep.

She wouldn't allow me to accompany her to the constabulary in the morning, insisting that I stay with Meg and Bridget. We waited some time before we couldn't wait any more. The three of us went there, Meg between us and each of us holding one of her hands. We stood on the street outside the squat building by the river in a chill air. We stood there for some hours.

They let us see her the next day, but only briefly. We visited her each day after that. I don't know which was harder, the seeing her or the being forced to leave her.

Elinor was moved to a room in the courts along the Liffey where office furniture was replaced by a bed for her and where they were waiting for word from New York about what was to be done with her.

Bridget and Meg stayed with me at Mrs. Dobson's. They each had a small bedroom, and the three of us spent our days with Elinor. Mrs. Dobson visited as well and promised to do what she could, but we all knew it was not much.

Less than a week later, we were told Elinor would be leaving in the morning. She'd be taken across to Liverpool where she'd get a steamer to New York in the custody of a Dublin policeman who volunteered for the service since he could meet his sister in New York. I had told myself again and again that this would happen yet the reality that it was about to happen shook me more than maybe anything ever had.

Our parting that morning was difficult for us all. As we all knew, though, it could not be avoided. The three of us took a carriage to the Dublin quays and watched as she was manacled and taken to the ferry to cross to England and stayed until the ferry, and she, were gone.

54.

The headquarters of the New York Police Department was at 300 Mulberry Street. It stood on the west side of the block between Houston and Bleecker Streets, an imposing building of four stories, not counting the basement where I understood there were holding cells. One entered it via a row of marble steps.

I arrived there alone. The front door was green, very big and heavy but it was open. I walked into a large hall with a tall ceiling and four chandeliers dropping from it. To the right was a high desk, at which several uniformed officers with chevrons sat. Chatting or filling out one form or another. Other uniformed officers came and went, some leading in men whose hands were cuffed, as I stood waiting for the eye of the sergeant who sat in the middle.

"Aye, Miss?" he finally said, looking up from his ledger. He had a slight brogue, much less strong than my own, and I gathered his parents were from the Irish west and he was from New York. I wore the finest dress I brought with me back from Dublin, clutching my small purse. I'd taken a ship from Liverpool this time, and our final stop before crossing the Atlantic was Queenstown, where I first left Ireland in that horrible boat years before. This time, though, I had a second-class cabin. Bessie and Mrs. Dodson insisted, and they paid for it. They paid for Bridget and Meg to go back several days before I did, and before I decided I could stay away no longer.

I was consumed about Elinor nearly every moment, even after arriving in New York on a rainy Wednesday. There, I took a trolley north and to the west side of Manhattan. The hotel on Eighth Avenue and Thirty-Seventh Street seemed far enough away and as it was on the edge of the tenements, I wouldn't stick out in my Irishness and within a day of arriving I bought some clothes far better than those I had in my early days in New York City years before but not so good that anyone would particularly notice me.

The maroon day dress with minimal embroidery and a high collar I wore to the police was dated, but it would have to do. It was a sunny day.

"Yes, sergeant. I understand there is an Inspector Washington here."

He looked me over before nodding and saying, "Do you have business with the inspector?"

"I'd like to see him. It's important. I met him some years ago."

He glanced to the officer to his left, who was also looking me over, and then turned back to me.

"I'll send someone for him. What's your name?"

"I'm Margaret Treacy."

"From Ireland?"

"Aye. County Mayo, but it seems like forever ago. The inspector helped me in a matter some time back."

"Very good, Miss." He called to a boy who was sitting on a bench.

"You. Go fetch Washington." Back at me, "If you'll have yourself a seat, Miss Treacy, he'll be here shortly."

There were several wooden benches across from the desk, on the other side of the aisle through which people were coming and going in a stream. I set my eyes on the staircase and saw the boy followed by a dapper gentleman. That was the only way to describe him. So different from all the others in his suit and multicolored waistcoat—a watchchain dangling from one side to the other—blindingly polished shoes, hair and a beard that looked to have been trimmed just moments before he was summoned, and he held a fine hat in his right hand.

By the time he reached the floor, I was on my feet. He was as I remembered him from our dealings when Elinor and Meg had been taken to London by Mr. Ballard. Not a tall man but one with a thick beard. The boy pointed to me, and the inspector approached.

"How might I be of service, Miss? My God. Is it the former nun I met in relation to Mrs. Ballard?"

"'Tis, Inspector. I'm Margaret Treacy. Just Miss now. And it is about poor Mrs. Ballard I'm afraid. A matter of some delicacy."

He nodded. He pulled out his gold pocket watch and checked the time. "I've nowhere I must be just now. We should take a walk."

He called to the sergeant, "I'm seeing what is on this sweet lass's mind," and held his arm out towards the door and I preceded him to Mulberry Street.

We turned to the south, towards Houston Street. It was only a few blocks east of the House of Mercy, and I looked towards what had been a pleasant and peaceful home for so long and it affected me more than I expected. But I had other business now, and by the time the inspector and I reached Houston, he knew what it was.

"I, of course, know of the case of Mrs. Ballard. I'm not working on it. I do not know what you wish from me. I'm thought too close to the matter after my earlier dealings to be officially involved."

Neither of us thought it wise to discuss that episode and we walked silently for several steps. He smiled and ran his fingers through his beard. "Miss Treacy. I can guess why you are here."

We were by then walking east on Houston Street, cutting through the many pedestrians who we shared the sidewalk with.

"You must prove she didn't kill her husband."

"I see. And how do you suggest that I, a New York police inspector not assigned to the case, do that? And why I should?"

I stopped and we moved to the side, next to a building.

"I *know* she didn't do it. And isn't it your job to seek out the truth?"

He was looking at me and gave the slight smile he sometimes displayed. It wasn't meanly meant. "My job, Miss Treacy, is to do what I'm told and investigate what I'm told to investigate. That doesn't include the killer of Mr. Francis Ballard. I'm sorry. I truly am. But I cannot help you."

With that, he turned to head back to police headquarters. I watched him go. He stopped after some steps and returned to me.

"Tell me, Miss Treacy. Where are you staying? I may wish to contact you again. I cannot promise that I *will*. Do you understand?"

I told him I did.

"Good." His hands were behind him and he nodded. "Good," he repeated.

I gave him the name of the small hotel where I had gotten lodgings. It was, as I said, off to the west side, near the Irish tenements that stretched to the Hudson but not of them. He doffed his hat and turned again to leave. I watched him go until he turned right on Mulberry Street to get back to his office.

My hotel room was very small and on the fourth and top floor. I couldn't have anyone know I was in New York. Bessie made me promise that Inspector Washington was the only person I would identify myself to. "From what you've told me about your earlier dealings with him, he can be trusted," she said. "No one else can." She repeated this last bit.

How this would affect my seeing Elinor I couldn't say.

After my visit with the inspector, I was beyond distraught. My stomach was knotted and my head was pounding. He was my only prospect for doing something. *It was not his case. He could do nothing.* Plus, I told him, a policeman, where I could be found.

I couldn't tolerate the small, stinky room a moment longer than necessary, and went to the street. I would walk up to Central Park and lose myself, figuratively, there. But only a day after I met him, I saw the inspector—or the inspector's back—in the lobby of the hotel, at the manager's little desk.

"'Thar she is," the taller man said, and the inspector turned, impeccably dressed as always. He removed his hat.

"Shall we walk yet again, Miss Treacy?" he said with a smile and slight bow.

He pushed his left elbow out so I could run my arm through his, and together we went to the street.

"That was a foolish thing you did. Coming to me."

"I had no alternative, sir. But I couldn't think of who else to see and I thought you of all people would understand after what you learned when she was taken to London."

"I know what happened when you all returned to New York, and I was sorry for how it was handled by the families. His parents asked me to meet with them, and when I did, I convinced them, and that sister of his, that it would a disaster for everyone were they to pursue the matter through the police. I feared when I heard about their treatment of you and the lady you knew in London and when I saw the stories in the newspapers that it had all been for naught. I'm sorry for that. I'm sorry that it came to what it came to."

He placed his right hand on mine. He wasn't a tall man, nearly my height, and my arm fit easily through his.

"Frankly, I'm not entirely surprised by your approach yesterday, though I confess to having no idea of what became of you since you came back with her."

"I was happy and settled in Dublin when Mrs. Ballard appeared there. I had no idea what had happened about Mr. Ballard."

"Well, that explains why she surrendered herself in Dublin. That was a mystery, though I shall reveal this to no one."

"Thank you, Inspector. She came all that way to see me and then voluntarily surrendered to the Irish police to be sent back. Surely that must count for something?"

"I think it will, but you must know if she is found guilty, she will hang."

Seeing my reaction, he continued as if he hadn't used that awful word.

"Still. I've given thought to this...case. I sat briefly with the inspector responsible for it. An Inspector Michael Norris. A good, capable man. He says it is a clear case of premeditated murder. Mrs. Ballard, everyone believes, tired of the abuse she suffered at her husband's hands. Or, more likely, fists. Statements about the marks certain people saw on her back did not help her.

"It was an easy matter to obtain some white arsenic and put a little bit in the hot drink he never failed to take with him to their bedroom before they retired.

"Norris says the only people other than the wife who could have done it were the staff. He interviewed them all and found none had the slightest motive. If an abusive master were enough, our morgues and our cells would be overwhelmed."

I strangely found comfort in his wit. He continued:

"Some members of staff would talk only after a bit of prodding and, well, threats. In the end, they all said that Mrs. Ballard must've done it. They all said they wished it wasn't true, but they were convinced it had to be. They all knew how he treated her. They were the ones who told Norris about his nightly draught."

I was becoming nauseous, and he directed me into a small café. It wasn't crowded, and we sat at a small table towards its rear. Those nearby were empty.

Inspector Washington insisted I have some tea and biscuits to settle my stomach while he took coffee.

"Did you know he beat her?"

"So, she claims and so you and some others claimed when I first met you."

"I saw the marks. Years ago. Before he took her to London. She showed me. She has more recent ones, too, as I understand it."

"I understand that and believe it to be true. But don't you see, my dear? It wouldn't matter. He could do to her what he wanted. It wouldn't excuse murder. I'm sorry, that he beat her is more evidence that she *did* kill him. It provides her with a great motive to do it. As I say, it isn't a defense to the charge. If all the world knew, it wouldn't matter. I'm sorry. But I fear she will hang."

He drank some of his coffee, but I hadn't touched my tea, or the biscuits.

"We weren't at first suspicious, but his parents insisted that a postmortem be performed. We dug him up. Before it was done, she took their daughter and fled to Europe. London then, as you know, Dublin."

"But she surrendered to the police there."

"I know she did. That could simply be that she couldn't face life as a fugitive with her daughter. Now she has the prospect of the poor girl getting some stability in her life."

I didn't doubt why she ran, and I was sure it hadn't a thing to do with trying to flee justice. But no one else could understand that.

"The postmortem showed the arsenic."

He took another, deeper sip of his coffee.

"Tell me, Miss Treacy, where Inspector Norris is mistaken."

I had no idea. I *knew* she didn't do it but that was far different from being able to *prove* it.

"You see, Miss. You have no answer."

"What about the...the other women he saw. Mrs. Ballard said he turned to them."

"Prostitutes, Miss Treacy? Yes, we were alerted to their existence, and we satisfied ourselves that none had an interest in shortening his life. Quite the contrary, I'm afraid."

He was right. I had nothing for him. I looked into my cooling tea.

"What happens next?" I asked.

"Her case will be presented shortly to a grand jury. The prosecutor will present evidence to try to establish that there is enough for her to be tried for murder. It is a preliminary step and from what I've seen I don't think there is any doubt that she will be indicted and required to stand trial."

"Where is she now?"

"She is at the Halls of Justice. It's a jail on Centre Street not far from Police Headquarters. She is allowed visitors, but you admit that you don't want anyone to know that you are in New York, and they will take down your name if you visit and your presence will become known."

"There must be something I can do."

He finished his coffee as I had finally finished my tea sip by sip.

"My dear. I truly wish there was. But I don't see it. The evidence is clear that she killed her husband and even if it were to free herself from his beatings the law won't care and I'm afraid it is more likely than not that she will be hanged."

That word—"hanged"—he kept using struck me like a stick each time. It was always a possibility but for someone like Inspector Washington to use it so easily and so often made it worse.

"What of the Palmers?"

"They too see the inevitability of what is to happen to their daughter. I don't know that they can, or will, do anything. Perhaps they will seek clemency from the governor, so Mrs. Ballard finishes out her days in prison. I don't know. I think his parents would have to agree to that, and from what I see and hear, they are not inclined to show the least sympathy to their daughter-in-law. They'll almost certainly get, or their daughter will get, custody of the girl so it's not as if the Palmers could exchange that for their daughter's life.

"In any case, the Palmers and the Ballards both are surely forever banished from society and at best will get visits of sympathy from those who were their closest friends, but it will be only a single visit and they will never be seen by them again. If they have a house elsewhere, it will be best if they go there and watch the grass grow until they die.

"This will not, as I say, incline his parents to support a clemency plea."

I was shocked.

"I'm sorry to be so blunt, Miss Treacy. That is the reality we must all deal with. You, perhaps, most of all. Now I'll walk you back to your hotel. I regret not being more useful to you."

55.

I spent most of my days on Centre Street, across from the jail. It was a large, imposing building with classical columns that I understood gave it its nickname, the Tombs. She was there, in that building. I couldn't be with her. All I could do was stand outside. Even in the rain.

There was news about her every day in the newspapers. Some called her a "Black Widow," and fantastic drawings of her were splashed in each day's editions. I thought of trying to see her, but Inspector Washington was right. I didn't want people to know I was there. Surely there were reporters inside waiting for anyone who visited, and other than her parents and Bridget—who I recognized when they went in or out—I don't know any who visited her. Not even her brother or sister.

* * * *

IT COULDN'T BE HELPED that my standing there every day was finally noticed. More and more of the men who stood outside the jail's door as reporters of their type had outside Bessie's when we first went to London crossed the street to question me. I declined to answer and left. I was silent since my accent might give me away. They gave no sign that they'd leave me alone, as those reporters eventually did in London.

After this started, I kept away for several days but I read every development in the stories that appeared in the city's daily papers. Even if there was nothing new, and there almost never was, there would be a story. Sometimes different papers had different stories. But they all agreed.

MRS. BALLARD MURDERED MR. BALLARD

Whether it was to break away from the abuse or to clear the way for a lover was one point of disagreement. That she did it was never in doubt.

A search went on for this supposed lover. Some papers offered a reward to anyone who could name him. Then it was discovered that she never was allowed to leave the house alone since returning from London. If she left, it was with her husband or with her mother or her mother-in-law. (Never, it was said, with her sister-in-law.)

No friends, *if she had any*, visited the house. Speculation bubbled that a servant or a deliveryman or even a pretend deliveryman could be the man, the lover.

A sympathetic New York paper had a series of "A Lady Locked in her Tower" stories with an illustration of Elinor in a tower and the hair of Rapunzel dangling to the ground. There followed a daily exchange in the papers of whether if this were the case she was justified in murder. Experts were called in to opine. Lawyers. Doctors. Even a judge from Boston.

There was never the least doubt, though, that it *was* murder and that Mrs. Ballard poisoned Mr. Ballard.

Servants of the Ballard house and of both sets of parents were waylaid as they went for chores or even to or from church by reporters wanting to know "the truth of what went on inside." I gathered they were told to say nothing although at times "Chambermaid A" or "Footman B" was quoted as hearing from someone who heard from someone that Mr. Ballard drank too much and lusted after young women or that Mrs. Ballard was often in a laudanum haze and had a hankering for older men.

There was eventually an item about a "mystery woman" who appeared regularly across the street who must be holding a vigil for Mrs. Ballard, though, as I said, I wasn't recognized and ignored the reporters who asked me to say who I was and why I was standing there day after day. The papers were either in sympathy for her or in sympathy for her martyred husband.

I couldn't stop "visiting," but now I only did so irregularly and briefly, usually not daring to stop for a moment and never daring to be on the side of the street where the Tombs was and always wearing a large plain hat I bought on Orchard Street just for this purpose. I would walk by with my head covered and hurry past and then walk around the block before heading, on foot or by trolley, to my hotel, where I sat and fell deeper and deeper in love with her.

In good weather in the afternoons, I walked, mostly in Central Park. I didn't know for how much longer I could last on the funds from Lady Glendale and Mrs. Dodson. I expected it was several months, and my return trip to Dublin, should I decide to take it, was paid for. I sent them both letters upon my arrival and at least once a week after that. They were the only people in my world. Other than the most important. Though she was only a few miles from me and my hotel, Elinor could not know how close I was to her and always, *always*, she was so much farther from me than Mrs. Dobson in Dublin and Lady Glendale in London.

I was surprised on one of my walks past the Tombs when I saw Bridget leave alone. Before then, she was always with Mrs. Palmer, and I never dared approach them, mindful of what Bessie said about trust.

I stopped to look, and reporters were upon her in a flash as she left, tightening the shawl around her shoulders. I watched as she ignored them and pushed her way through. She turned and walked north, and the reporters soon gave up and returned to their positions outside the door waiting for the next person who might have information of interest to their readers.

I walked up Centre Street, on the opposite, western side, for several blocks. Her walk was fast, a determined walk. She bent forward slightly and knifed through the slower pedestrians she overtook.

She looked to be walking the several miles back to the Palmers' house and was either too poor or too aggravated to take a cab or even a trolley. I imagined she was no longer at the Ballards' or wherever it was that Meg was being kept but was with the Palmers as an act of kindness until...it was over.

Four blocks or so north of the jail, I was sure no reporter was behind her. Having in my days in New York acquired the ability to get from one side to the other of its avenues without the need of a constable, I hurried across Centre Street to catch her. She was startled when I put my hand on her left shoulder and turned rapidly with as fierce a glare as I ever saw on anyone in my life. It was a woman's and not a reporter's hand, she realized. I quickly put my arms around her, fearing she would fall as she fell to sobbing.

"I don't know what to do." I don't know if she then knew who I was, but she understood I was a friend. She gained some control over herself when she saw that it was me and she smiled.

"She is very bad. Thank God she ain't in a normal cell but in an office with a window and bed. She wouldn't survive elsewhere in that horrible place. Her parents visit but no one else but me. They won't let her see Meg. It is very bad."

"Where is Meg?"

"She is with Scarlet, Mr. Ballard's sister."

"More with a nurse most likely."

"I don't know. I ain't been allowed to see her and every time I come here with Mrs. Palmer pretty much all Mrs. Ballard wants to know about is Meg and all her mother can do is say she's fine. The Ballards let Mrs. Palmer see Meg once a week, on Sunday afternoons, but she's never alone with her, and I don't know that Mr. Palmer has seen her.

"Elinor sits and reads all day. She is learning how to sew, if you can believe it, and does repairs for some of the women in the real cells. If she eats anything, 'tis not much, and her clothes are falling off her."

"Has she given up hope?"

"She says her lawyers have little hope. I don't know how, but she knows what's said in the papers. She says she didn't do it. I believe her."

"So do I. I spoke with Inspector Washington."

"The police officer we met when Elinor and Meg were taken?"

"Aye. But this isn't his case. He's the only soul in New York who knows I'm here. Excepting you, now. I think I can trust him, but I don't have a choice. Who else could I go to? He says there's little he can do since it's not his case. He knows much of the evidence, he says, and says it's all against Elinor."

"Is there nothing that could prove she's innocent? I *know* she didn't do it. He was horrible cruel to her. But she wouldn't leave. She tolerated it for Meg. I don't think she could do such a thing. Much as she might've wanted to, she'd never take the chance of losing Meg to that mother or sister of his."

"She'd know she would surely be caught and...hanged. That's what she's told me and her mother again and again."

I didn't know what else to say, so I asked about the wallpaper.

"Wallpaper?"

"Bessie sent me a letter after I told her he died of arsenic poisoning. She said it's known that certain wall coverings have arsenic and people were dying of it before they realized it. But the inspector said they knew all about that and they tested the covering in the bedroom and there was no arsenic and Miss Elinor showed no signs of being poisoned and she would have if it was in the paper."

"They tested the wallcovering where?"

"In the bedroom I assume."

"But he didn't sleep there."

I didn't understand.

"He slept in an old secret room off the master bedroom for years."

"Did you tell the police this?"

"They didn't ask, and I didn't think it could matter."

"Bridget. It may be everything."

It was like the sun burst through, however briefly. I grabbed her wrist and pulled her with me to police headquarters on nearby Mulberry Street.

An exasperated Inspector Washington appeared after a boy was sent to fetch him, and I rushed at him in the foyer. Some policemen started towards me to protect him till he said it was alright. I stepped back and said I had most important information for him. He looked over at Bridget, though I don't know if he recalled her from when they met earlier, and back at me.

"Let us walk," he said. Soon we were again on either side of him, heading south on Mulberry Street. I had Bridget repeat what she told me. About how only she and the butler knew it, but Mr. Ballard slept in a secret room that was carved out of the master bedroom. He insisted that appearances be maintained even for the staff. For all the world they were a happy couple that shared a bed. While most couples had separate rooms, for some reason he wanted people think his marriage was something special and particularly intimate and admirable. It was absurd, of course. Everyone in the house knew they were unhappy, but only Bridget and the butler knew the truth about where he slept.

A secret panel was installed, and it led to a small room with a comfortable bed. It was where he slept. He was only in "their" bed when he took her, and according to what Elinor told Bridget he'd not done that for some time.

The inspector was far calmer than either of us. He stopped, and we stood in front of him and turned.

"This is very interesting," he said. His hands were in his pockets, and he rocked slightly back and forth. "Very interesting. I shall mention it to Inspector Norris."

He asked that we return to headquarters the next morning and he would tell us what Inspector Norris had to say about it. He asked that we not tell anyone of this and of coming to see him.

He nodded and with a "ladies" and a touch of his hat, he turned back to headquarters leaving us to watch him. I found my hand clutching Bridget's.

"Do you think it could be something?" she asked.

"I don't know but I will pray."

And pray we did. As we headed north, now going very slowly, we came upon St. Ann's on Twelfth Street. We sat together in a pew off to the side silently and holding hands until we knew we had to leave and Bridget went to the Palmers' on Twenty-Eighth Street and I went to my hotel on Eighth Avenue.

56.

I couldn't go with the two officers—one who knew it was a wild goose chase and the other who I hoped thought it was not—with Bridget to the house. I didn't know how long they'd be. Inspector Washington told me it might take some time and that it would take far longer if they found suspicious wallpaper in the secret room. He promised he would visit me at my hotel as soon as he left the Ballards' with whatever was found in the initial visit.

I couldn't bring myself to resume my vigil across from the Tombs but was in far too much turmoil to sit in my hotel room. Instead, I walked and walked and walked near and around the hotel countless times before I was hungry and exhausted and stopped at a small café across from it. I sat at a small table on the sidewalk, which allowed me to see who came to the hotel. I had a cheese sandwich and an ale. I never took my eyes off the building and after my sandwich and ale were gone, I ordered a coffee so I could maintain my senses and paid my bill so I could leave in a flash.

As time passed, though, I became more and more anxious until suddenly a hansom pulled up in front. I saw both Inspectors—I recognized Inspector Washington and assumed the other man was Mr. Norris—leap out one after the other and stride into the hotel. Bridget wasn't with them. I knocked over the chair and ran across Eighth Avenue. In the lobby, the two officers stood at the front desk, and I only just caught them before they turned to head to my room.

"Inspectors?"

I was out of breath, but the two turned to me. Neither gave the slightest indication from their expressions of what they did, or didn't, find at the house, but Inspector Washington was the first to approach me.

"Miss Treacy. This is Inspector Norris. He has, well, tolerated my interference with his case with quite an open mind when I told him that it was an Irish lass who was being so persistent."

Inspector Norris removed his hat, nodded, and extended his hand, which I shook. Inspector Washington said, "It will be some time before we *know*." My hope was nearly dashed but he recovered it by quickly adding that they'd discovered Mr. Ballard's "secret lair"—"I cannot say how we failed to find it earlier"—and that it did appear to have a peculiarly heavy and old wall covering and that they would be bringing someone up in the morning to examine it.

"Miss Treacy. Inspector Norris and I agree that there may—I emphasize '*may*'—be something in this theory of yours. We will have the paper examined. That is all we can tell you now."

Inspector Norris said it would be "foolish, very foolish" of me to be optimistic, but that they'd tell me as soon as they got the results. They said that Bridget knew what they found but said it would also be foolish of me to go see her as she would know nothing more. At least not until they had those results.

With that, the two nodded, and I watched them leave.

I breathed again and was famished so it wasn't long after my sandwich and ale that I went to a nearby restaurant and ate something simple but filling, meat with potatoes and beans, which I washed down with yet another ale. I'd become a familiar face there, and the staff and regulars nodded to me when I entered.

I slept but not well and was awake very early the next morning.

57.

Word quickly got out about the "development" in the Ballard Murder Case and was just as quickly made known to all of New York.

INNOCENT:
SHE DIDN'T DO IT

That was from the *New York Sun*. On the other hand, the *New York Herald* took the opposite approach:

GETTING AWAY WITH MURDER
VICTIM'S PARENTS SHOCKED!
DISMAYED! LIVID!

The other papers were similar, depending on which side of the issue they took before.

Inspector Washington gave me the happy news in the afternoon several days after he, Bridget, and Inspector Norris went to the Ballards'. I couldn't breathe. He was waiting for me outside my hotel, and I saw him when I finished a walk that must have taken me hours though I couldn't under oath say where I went.

He warned me about being too "boisterous"—that's the word he used—about it since it might be best for me to continue to keep my presence in town a secret, at least until we could know how the news would be received. He told me he would advise Bridget and the Palmers and that he wouldn't mention me. That, he said, was for me to do.

58.

On Monday and Thursday afternoons, Elinor Ballard left her parents' house, where the young widow had been living since being released from the Tombs jail. She and Meg had long since abandoned the house her parents bought for her and Francis when they married. It was on the market and it was expected that there would be an epic battle between the families as to where exactly the proceeds would land. Eventually, though, the bulk was placed in a trust for the benefit of Meg, with her two grandfathers acting as joint trustees.

On each Monday and each Thursday, Elinor Ballard walked west to the corner of Madison Avenue and Twenty-Eighth Street. There she lifted her right arm and hailed a cab, which took her west to Eighth Avenue and my horrible hotel. I'd yet to decide what was to become of me, so remained there, bolstered by funds happily advanced by Mr. Arthur Palmer.

Depending on the weather, we stayed inside or went for a stroll, sometimes reaching Central Park. Several newspapers published that I was the strange woman who often stood across from the Tombs jail while Elinor was a prisoner and several reporters tried to question us about it as we walked but they tired after we applied Bessie's approach and refused to say *anything* four or five times.

Some very pleasant hours after she arrived for each of her visits, I stood with her on Eighth Avenue, where she hailed a cab to return to her parents' house, and I went back to my hotel.

It was a pleasant routine. We added other visits with each other now and then, but the Monday and Thursday ones were consistent. I spent my other time doing my wandering. Sundays I sometimes headed to Immaculate Conception Church, where I joined Patrick and Cath Norman and their two boys and one girl for Mass and then to the larger apartment the Normans rented in the same building for Sunday dinner. Again, weather permitting, we went for a stroll.

One Thursday, though, *Elinor* didn't leave the house and get a cab at Madison and Twenty-Eighth. She didn't come to my flat. Nora Duffy did. She'd become part of the Palmers' household. She wore one of Elinor's dresses. My hotel room was empty when she got there but she stayed for several hours.

While Nora waited, keeping away from the window, I stood near a Hudson River dock at the end of Twenty-Third Street, wearing a simple dress and coat I bought on Orchard Street. Elinor arrived not long after I did. She wore a very plain dress with fraying— not unlike the one I tore so many years before. We boarded a ferry. We would take that across the river and embark on a train trip to Philadelphia. From Philadelphia the next morning, we would be aboard the *Wisconsin*, and it would take us to Queenstown, where I'd left Ireland, also so many years before. Our trunks had been sent to Philadelphia days before and would be on the ship when we reached it.

Bridget left the Palmers' separately in the early hours with Meg and they were already in Philadelphia. This was the plan. Elinor and I, both dressed as middle-class women heading on the Hudson River ferry for an extended trip, were approached by a man who was breathing heavily and who I saw had just made the ferry before it was untied from the dock.

"Mrs. Ballard," he said when our backs were to him and, too quickly, Elinor turned.

"I would like to have a word," he smiled when he knew he had us.

"And Miss Treacy, is it?"

I couldn't do anything but nod that it was true.

He tipped his hat to me. "I'm not such a fool as the others, with your little ploy, clever as it is. They are not so foolish, though, that they won't figure it out pretty quickly and they shall decide that you are either getting a ship in New York or, as seems to be the case, getting one in Philadelphia. Sailing where?"

I spoke. "Queenstown."

"To Ireland, as I suspected. Not to England again?"

Elinor looked at him. "I doubt I shall ever be there again."

We remained silent after that. The New Jersey quay couldn't come soon enough, but I knew it wouldn't matter. We were caught and would have to rely on...something from this man, who I took to be a reporter, an assumption he quickly proved true.

He was Michael Stewarts for *The New-York Times*. It was not quite the sensational press as were some of the others that were covering the Ballard case and its aftermath, whose reporters were presumably wondering why Elinor and I hadn't gone for a stroll as we usually did on nice Thursday afternoons, as it was that day. We would have preferred rain to further shield our escape, but that was out of our control.

As we approached the dock in Jersey City, Mr. Stewarts accompanied us to the railway terminal.

"I have a proposition for you ladies," he said as he joined us to buy tickets to Philadelphia.

We had no choice.

"Your story. That is the price you pay. I'll forget where you are going, I promise. You will be departing from an unknown port on a vessel to parts unknown as far as I'm concerned. No. I want your story until you step aboard whatever ship you step aboard. I cannot say you won't be found sooner or later, but I expect if it is later, few will particularly care."

He led us to an empty first-class compartment on the train waiting on track no. 6. It had room for four, but we hoped not to be disturbed.

He was a reporter, but we had no choice to do as he asked or word might get to Philadelphia of our plans, and everything would be ruined. Of course, in our favor was that Mr. Stewarts would lose his scoop and his story so Elinor and I could only pray that we wouldn't be treated unkindly by the man from *The New-York Times*.

As the train began to move, the fourth seat remained empty. He said he knew quite a lot about us. He insisted that the story was about "the two of you." He explained that there was something he was unsure about given the long-term relationship I had with Elinor and that he wanted to understand it. A lady and her maid. To know the effect it had, if any, on Elinor's relationship with her husband.

He told us straight off that he favored the view that Francis's death was an accident but that if he changed his mind based upon our conversation, he wouldn't refrain from saying so in print.

As the train cars rocked heading south in the early afternoon, we told our stories. For my part, it was largely what I have written here, though far less detailed, and Elinor heard many, many things she didn't know.

There were things that she said to him that I didn't know, especially the feelings about me she couldn't explain and couldn't control. How quickly her hopes of becoming a good wife vanished with the reality of sharing a bed with a man who became a brute. How both she and Francis felt the pain of not having a son. Then the horror when she was told he was dead and even worse the happiness she felt when she heard it. Her initial hesitancy was overcome by her wish to tell someone about certain of these things and foolish or not that it was a reporter seemed not to bother her, perhaps because she was also telling me.

We were rolling along the river into Philadelphia as we were finishing, and Mr. Stewarts insisted that he accompany us in a cab to the dock itself. We were in no position to refuse.

And he was as good as his word, so far, and he accompanied us to the base of the *Wisconsin*'s gangway in the morning. We came to enjoy his company, to tell our stories, and I may be a fool for saying so, but I think we were sufficiently guarded when we ate dinner together with Bridget staying with Meg at the hotel, that we didn't disclose things we didn't wish to disclose. He was a reporter and was likely good at getting people to do just that.

He tipped his hat and wished us a *Bon Voyage* as we walked onto the ship.

"Can we trust him?" Elinor asked when we looked back at him and waved before finding our stateroom.

"I don't think we have a choice" was the best I could do.

We were directed by a crew member down a flight of steps to a long corridor. Doors for cabins were to the right and a plain wall interrupted now and then by a door ran along the left side. Our cabin was about halfway down and on the right, or starboard I was told, side. It wasn't large and was appropriate to two young middle-class widows heading to Ireland to see the Irish one's family with the daughter of an American. It wasn't steerage and it wasn't first class but it was what a pair of middle-class widows could afford.

Next door was a similar cabin, in which an Irishwoman was bringing her daughter to Dublin after the girl's poor father, an American and himself an orphan, died of consumption. The girl, Meg, hoped to renew her life with the only family she still had. In Ireland.

The boat wasn't full belowdecks since it was going to and not coming from Queenstown. The cabins themselves were very plain. Each had a small window. Two metal beds painted in grey with small mattresses were hung on the right walls, one atop the other. They were barely wide enough for one person and each has a blanket folded atop its sheets and a pillow at its head.

And the four of us, Elinor, Meg, Bridget, and me, ate and walked the deck together and if anyone knew who any of us was, they didn't say anything and by the time we were two days out of Philadelphia we didn't care.

59

I knew my papa wouldn't accept anything from me, so I never offered. The best I could do was buy him things that would make his life on the farm a little easier and present them to him as a birthday or Christmas gift, and my mama told him it would be rude not to accept them. She sent me lists of what might prove useful, and I did what I could to get them to the farm.

For my first Easter back in Ireland, Elinor, Bridget, and, of course, Meg took the crowded boat across to Liverpool, and the four of us spent several days with my two brothers and their wives and several children (some older, some younger than Meg). It was grand, and they in their turns came across to see us in Dublin.

Elinor had no head for figures, but she could talk the ear off a stalk of corn. Several days a week, she came into my office at Dodson & Kenney with me—she soon had her own desk in my new, larger office next to the corner one that was Mrs. Dobson's and no longer a shrine to Mr. Dodson—and especially if we had a client or prospective client come in, she was the one who put them at ease while I ran through this number or that.

My position was established by Lady Glendale's decision to place some of her money with Dodson & Kenney. She sat for some time with Kathleen—as Mrs. Dodson had long since become known to me—and me several months after Elinor and I moved to Dublin with Meg and Bridget sharing rooms at the Dodson house and the lot of us taking strolls in Stephen's

Green. Lady Glendale satisfied herself that putting money with us—it was *her* money protected from his lordship via a trust—wasn't a favor, but a wise business decision and I worked very hard to prove her right.

THE END

Acknowledgements

As always, I must thank a number of people who have read and commented on drafts of this book. Several are among the Writers Community on Twitter and I received particularly helpful comments on certain historical elements from GL Robinson (@gl_robinson). More general comments came from Renée Gendron (@ReneeGendron), Louise Sorensen (@louise3anne), and Mackenzie Littledale (@MackenzieLitt13). Plus my sister Clio Garland.

As always, any mistakes are on me.

Other Books

This book is set largely when *Róisín Campbell: An Irishwoman in New York* and *A Studio on Bleecker Street* are.

I have two contemporary novels, also set chiefly in New York. *I Am Alex Locus* is a tale of a young woman's search for the truth about her family, including the mother who died when she was fourteen. *Coming to Terms* is the story about a family and two generations of that family and the romances and loves they (most of them) enjoy.

All my books are available at Amazon and elsewhere. They are described at DermodyHouse.com/books.